Also by J. Robert Lennon

The Light of Falling Stars

The Funnies

ON THE
NIGHT
PLAIN

J. ROBERT LENNON

ON THE

NIGHT

PLAIN

A Novel

A JOHN MACRAE BOOK

HENRY HOLT AND COMPANY   •   NEW YORK

Henry Holt and Company, LLC / *Publishers since 1866*
115 West 18th Street / New York, New York 10011
Henry Holt® is a registered trademark of
Henry Holt and Company, LLC.

NOV 0 8 2001
A portion of this book appeared in a different form in
Harper's Magazine and in *Prize Stories 2000: The O. Henry Awards.*

Distributed in Canada by H. B. Fenn and Company Ltd.

Library of Congress Cataloging-in-Publication Data
Lennon, J. Robert, date.
   On the night plain: a novel / J. Robert Lennon.—1st ed.
      p. cm.
"A John Macrae book."
ISBN 0-8050-6722-1
   1. Sheep ranchers—Fiction. 2. Rural families—Fiction. 3. Ranch life—Fiction.
4. Brothers—Fiction. 5. Montana—Fiction. I. Title.

PS3562.E489 O5 2001
813'.54—dc21
                                                                    00-068252

Henry Holt books are available for special promotions
and premiums. For details contact: Director, Special Markets.
First Edition 2001
Designed by Victoria Hartman

Printed in the United States of America

1 3 5 7 9 10 8 6 4 2

To my grandparents,

Robert and Mary Stein

PART ONE

ASEA

1

When the war was over, Grant clipped his hair close and made the long ride out to the flats where the railway ran east-west. He left in the night with the moon near full, taking a horse nobody would much miss if it failed to come back. There was no hurry. The sun and train were hours away, the packed dirt full of hoarded August heat. Stars jumped where the heat met a night breeze. Hoppers beat themselves against his legs and the horse's flank. He had an early apple in the pannier and ate it all but the seeds and stem, which he spit into the weeds. Once he'd spotted the tracks he followed them west to the empty station house and dismounted. He freed up his bag and shouldered it and turned to the old horse.

Hi! Go on home!

The horse was still. Grant made to lunge at him and he backed off a few steps and turned to browsing in the grass.

Go on! Grant said. He took off his hat and swatted at the horse and kicked him gently in the ribs. The horse shied and let out a disgruntled squeal. He rolled his head and let out a snort and turned around north. After an interval he walked off without looking back.

This had been a town called Grissom, but nobody lived in it now. When Grant was a boy two Mexicans had been hanged here for stealing horses. This was long after such things were decreed by courts, but the men had no local family and not much English, and no one who knew of their crimes objected to the punishment. That they were guilty was beyond doubt. They were found on the range asleep near the stolen horses, with their Winchesters lashed to the riggings. Grant was not sure where they'd been hanged, he'd been told the low rung on the water tower, but he did remember that for some time nobody bothered to cut down their bodies. Not long after this the last inhabitants of Grissom quit the town for good.

There was some doubt that the train would stop at all. Grant had sent a letter saying he would be here to meet it, but he had not requested a reply. If the train came, he planned to get on it and ride it as far as it took him, and if it didn't he would go back to the ranch and resume work as if nothing had happened. His parents and brother would know what he had tried to do but wouldn't be inclined to mention it.

As it happened somebody was already waiting, an old man wearing a crisp new suit and clutching a shabby carpetbag. His jaw worked with an involuntary motion, but he regarded Grant with clear eyes that followed him as he walked to the only other bench on the tiny platform. The bench shifted under him then steadied. Above hung a sign with GRISSOM painted clearly on it. The windows of the station house behind him were covered by bare boards. Across the tracks stood a silo with its elevator in ruins at its foot, and behind it in the indeterminate distance rose a solitary table of earth, disfigured by an irregular rocky outcrop the wind had spared, that could have served as a stage where giants performed for travelers of the ancient past.

Grant took off his hat and looked over at the old man. The old man had been watching. Now he looked away.

Since the victory over Japan Grant had given this journey a great deal of thought. He had pictured himself much as he was right now, seated and calmly awaiting his train. He had imagined the rocking motion the train would make, and the swaying of his fellow passengers with it and the soundless slosh of his breakfast coffee in the dining car. Less clear in his mind was what he might do when he got off. He supposed there would be work wherever he went and people who could tell him how to get it. His only certain intent was to reach the Atlantic Ocean and walk barefoot into it, his shoes and socks behind him on the beach. Beyond that imagination failed him.

Something moved in his peripheral vision and he looked up to find the old man coming toward him, holding his bag close as if somebody might take it.

Time? the man said.

Grant had no watch. He said he didn't know. This didn't seem to satisfy the old man, but he asked nothing further and remained standing between the benches, as if to return was more than he could manage. A strong wind passed like a ghost train through the station and both men touched their hands to their hats. Light began to gather as if pulled by the wind. Grant offered the man a seat on his bench.

'Bliged, said the man.

He was on his way to Chicago, he said, to visit with a son and the son's wife and children. But the visit filled him with dread. He could not remember the name of his son's wife, nor the names of his grandchildren or even how many of them there were. He feared that he wouldn't recognize them at the station and that they would turn him away. And the ride in his son's car to their home outside the city: he'd seen pictures of the thousands of cars that raced along the highways and worried about an accident. Grant didn't know what to tell him. These seemed like valid fears. He asked the man where he lived.

Oh, right 'round here.

Grissom?

The old man frowned without meeting Grant's eyes. Not no more, he said.

Some time later the train came into view in the distance. It came slowly and didn't seem to get any larger as it approached, so that when it stopped before them it appeared a small thing to Grant, powerless to bring them any significant distance. Its doors fell open but no one emerged to usher them inside. Grant stood up and asked the old man if he'd like a hand with his bag, but the man ignored Grant's question and made his own way onto the train and disappeared.

Grant followed with neither reluctance nor eagerness, mounting the three steps because it was what he had anticipated doing. Though the day was now bright, the car was dark. A few passengers sat in grimy pools of light cast through soiled windows, while unoccupied seats remained shadowed by heavy opaque curtains. The passengers were asleep. Grant walked to the center of the car, raised his bag to the overhead rack, then thought better and set it down on a nearby seat. He slid in after it. No pull was visible for the curtain so he grabbed two handfuls of fabric and pushed them aside. Already the train had begun to move. He watched the strange butte roll out of view, then brought his bag onto his lap as if he might open it. But there was nothing inside that he needed and he put it back.

He fell asleep. He sensed the braking of the train and the passage of people in the aisle. Around him more curtains were opening and whispered conversations grew louder. He felt a hand touch his shoulder and opened his eyes to find the conductor standing over him, one hand holding his tickets and punch and the other in his change pocket. He asked how far Grant was going.

Where's it headed to?

Chicago.

Okay, Grant told him, and paid. Then he fell back to sleep.

When he next woke the sun was high over a miniature range of hills with cattle walking on them, and a heavy man of about sixty sat beside him. The man had one hand in Grant's bag, which Grant had left open when he paid the conductor. Now the hand withdrew.

Where're you headed, soldier?

Grant met his eyes, which were small and hard like plum stones. Chicago, he said.

You ought to know better than to leave your belongings unguarded beside you like that. You may find them made off with.

Grant zipped the bag shut and pushed it under the seat with his calves resting against it. The older man settled himself, stretching his body out, shoving both feet beneath the seat in front and nudging each shoe off using the toe of the opposite foot. With his creased wool trousers and starched shirt mussed by travel, he carried the air of a modest businessman, of monotonous work reluctantly done. An occasional tic wrinkled his nose and mouth. He was ewe-necked, with a large head that nodded like a daisy when he talked. He had not taken his eyes off Grant.

Been on the Pacific coast, have you? Back from where?

Grant glanced out the window. A motte of tall leaning cottonwoods passed, cupping a cluster of what could have been broken tombstones. Though he'd just woke up, he felt played out. He would have been riding line right now, seeking fence to fix. Instead his brother Max was likely doing it. About now they would all be acting like Grant had never been.

Okinawa, he said as the graveyard hove out of sight. Peleliu.

The man nodded. Not Iwo, huh?

No.

Ever eat dog?

No, Grant said.

The man was laughing. Damn good thing, he said. These boys come back saying they ate dog as if it's a admirable thing. God damn. He stuck out a bent hand, the knuckles tough and enlarged like knots in a branch. Sam Kroch, he said, high at the end like a question, so that Grant did not immediately know it was his name the man was speaking.

Grant Person, Grant said presently and shook the hand.

You a farm boy, son? You have got a sunpecked look to you.

Yessir.

You going home? Indiana? Illinois?

Indiana.

So you're a hero back home, are you. Look at you, all in one piece. Some of these boys come back all tied up together like a pot roast. You get yourself shot?

The wound grew hot at the question, the one thing Grant had as evidence if he needed it. He had suffered it when a neighbor's cow wandered onto their land and mired herself in mud. Grant pulled her out and she bolted, jerking the rope from his hands. The rope whipped around his calf and cut a channel through his trousers and into the flesh. This was four years ago. Scarred white and without hair, it could pass for a bullet wound if it had to.

I took one in the leg at Peleliu, he said. Healed up good. He cleared his throat. I still favor it some, he said.

Kroch laughed as if at a clever joke. I don't doubt that, he said, not a bit. And he tipped his head back still smiling and went to sleep.

·

For a short time there were six of them, all boys. The oldest was called Edwin. He was eight the winter Grant was seven, naturally broader in the shoulders and face and taller due to his age. This was at the onset of the Depression, and of all the children only Edwin seemed to understand the gravity of the situation. Under it he grew serious and sure, like a person expected to take control of the outfit at any moment if necessary, which in fact he was. At seven Grant was still thought of as a child, his horsemanship a form of play, not work, his assigned tasks around the place chores as opposed to duties. The others truly were children: Thornton was slow even for a four-year-old; Robert, at two and a half, was his playmate and protector. Max could barely walk yet and Wesley, a newborn, was already sick. In which way he was sick was initially unclear. He was declared to be colicky and cried evenings for many hours before sleep. He refused the breast. When Grant thought about this time, which was not often, he remembered Max sucking greedily, his shod feet dangling off their mother's chair, while Wesley lay silent and watchful nearby in the bassinet. Wesley was born too small and never grew significantly.

Their mother's name was Asta. Their father was called John. He was raised in the north of England and collected her from her home in Iceland during the first war. She had kept house with her mother there while her father raised sheep, and now in America she kept house and bore sons while her husband raised sheep. Growing up Grant never heard a single word of Icelandic from her and few of anything else. Nevertheless her English was good. Although she would not have been called beautiful, she stood apart from other women in the clarity and fullness of her features and by her great height, nearly six feet. She was feared and respected by the ranch men, most of whom were not as tall. Among those who feared her was John, who was short and talkative and boastful and whose strange skills, such as carving toys out of pinewood and playing the fiddle, distracted him from ranch work, at which he was mediocre at best. Away from Asta he seemed to blame her for his ineptitude. He could often be heard wondering what good she had done him, with all of her supposed sheep smarts. In her presence he would blame the shiftlessness and disobedience of the boys, once they were old enough to blame. Asta ignored him and continued to provide him with sons. She knew as well as he did the worth, on a ranch, of six boys.

On Christmas night 1929 they ate dinner together alone, without the hands. This uncharacteristic family privacy made them all uncomfortable and they struggled for things to say. Wesley nursed weakly for a short time, then once laid down began to cry, and the sound seemed to unhinge Asta, who held her knife and fork tightly but didn't touch them to her food. When John told her to go quiet him, Edwin got up from the table, went to the bassinet and whispered in the baby's ear. In minutes he was asleep.

The following morning Wesley woke congested in the nose and throat and spent the day facedown on their mother's lap, expelling mucus. Two days later he began to turn gray, then dull purple in blotches, and his fingers went cold and stiff. The following afternoon his head began to bulge at the fontanel. He stopped crying. That night he fell into a coma and he died under the doctor's care in the late morning of January 1.

Grant dreamed that a gentle horse, a blood bay, had entered the house and knelt before the bassinet, and tiny Wesley had climbed onto its red back and ridden away into the night. That afternoon he went to his mother where she lay next to the baby's still body and told her what he had dreamed, and without turning over to face him she reached back and slapped him hard enough to knock him down. In the morning they buried the baby in a wind-scraped corner of the starveout. John enclosed the grave with fence, leaving ample room around it as if he knew what was to come.

◆

While Kroch was sleeping, Grant tried to imagine what life in Indiana might have been like had he actually lived there. He expected it was gentler, with more time for sleep. The animals were healthy and tractable and crops always brought a good price. The train was nearly to Minnesota now and night was falling. Passengers filled the compartment. The look of them made Grant glad Kroch had chosen him. It was not uncommon during the war to see women alone or alone with children, but the women in this car were accompanied and all the solitary travelers were men. The men varied in age and appearance but all had the eyes of outlaws, or so it seemed to Grant. They carried bought bags with few signs of use, as if they were only props for some private performance. Activity in towns they passed looked staged, and of course with his first lie Grant had become an actor. This was not a simple matter of making up a story and telling it to whomever he encountered. It was himself he was inventing, a version of him who had spent years in the company of other young men and had known the drudge and racket of war.

But he hadn't. He had lived in increasing solitude without reference to anyone. He had gone among the men back home without making an impression and he had never paid his own looks or talk any mind. He could vanish in the creases of land and not be thought of at all. Now suddenly he was traveling in a landscape of eyes, and he wondered for the first time what he had done to himself, wondered if the part of him he had hidden from the world could ever be found.

He was able to sleep with his heels clinched tight against his bag for safekeeping. When he woke it was to a scene of straight flat paved roads and cars that waited at intersections for the train to go by. Towns flashed past until they ran together, and this was the city. Passengers woke as if by a sixth sense. Kroch was among them, his clear eyes on Grant.

There she is, son, he said.

Grant looked out to make sure he meant Chicago and not some specific structure. A sign read UNION STATION. I reckon my daddy's here to meet me, he said.

Maybe I ought to wait around and see that. A hero's welcome.

Grant reached out and steadied himself against the seat in front, quelling nausea. The train was slowing. I ain't any kind of hero, he said.

Kroch was laughing. The way you tell that story, I believe it.

I don't follow, Grant said without looking.

Kroch was close now, right up at his ear. You have got to convince yourself before you can convince other people, boy. You don't even say your name like you mean it.

Grant felt him retreat, felt his body rise from the seat. He turned fast and found Kroch in the aisle peering down at him.

It's my name, Grant said. People turned.

A smile discovered Kroch's face and warped it. Okay, Grant Person. Now you sound like a honest man.

The train moaned and stopped. Kroch kept his balance like a steel beam. People got up all at once, but Kroch was ahead of them, down the stairs and across the filthy platform.

•

He followed the other passengers through heavy glass doors into a room of stupendous size crammed tight with the sounds of footsteps and their echoes. It was like a cathedral where you worshiped by walking. He stood with his eyes shut while people arced around him from behind. He wondered if they would crush one another to death if obstructed, as sheep were known to do. His bag, bumped by passersby, tugged at his hand like a leashed dog.

He found a place on a long high-backed bench and caught his breath. In time a man and woman and child sat down nearby and he looked toward the woman and said, I want to get a train to New York City.

She wore a pink dress with frills and a hat with fake flowers on it, and her hand went to her child's shoulder and then her husband's.

What? the man said turning. You said what?

I want to get the train to New York.

The man was holding a cigar, rolling it in his hand. Well, you go to New York, soldier. It isn't any of my business. He brought out a silver guillotine from his coat and sliced the cigar end clean off. The cut end dropped to the floor.

Where? Grant asked him.

What!, now with the cigar between his teeth. The child, a boy, was staring.

Where do I get the train?

The man snorted, then pointed, shaking his head as if to fling Grant free of it. The woman stood, pulled her son from his seat, walked to her husband's opposite side and sat down.

The man lit his cigar. Well? he said.

⋆

There was a train leaving on the hour. He bought a ticket and was shown where to go to get on. While waiting he came across a machine that dispensed sandwiches and he put his coins into it. The carousel turned and he opened a door, then he thought better of his choice and quickly shut it. But the next door he tried wouldn't give, and neither would the first one when he tried it again.

Nearby two doors yawned into light and he could see cars moving on a street. He went out. The city looked like it did in pictures, except lived in, with buildings faded or crumbling from use and the cars nudging around one another with the scattershot instinct of insects. The order of city streets now seemed an illusion, like the smooth contours of rough land viewed from a distance. In each direction traffic lights changed abruptly, flashing red and then green between the buildings. A taxi stopped before him and a man dashed toward it and climbed in. Grant watched the taxi pull away. He was hungry.

The train stopped frequently at stations and sometimes stood still in lush countryside for no apparent reason. When it moved it moved slowly. Grant's compartment was full. He washed himself in a rural station bathroom and changed his clothes. When he learned the price of food in the dining car he tried to abstain from regular meals, but at times hunger overtook him and he ate without concern for money or manners. The men and women who shared his table didn't speak to him and he offered nothing to their conversation. He listened while they talked about Atlantic City. Men spent entire days making sand castles there, they said. One could witness a seven-foot shark in a glass tank and a horse that jumped from a great height into the ocean. This last seemed hard to believe. His fellow diners asked their waiter if he knew the city, and when he said he did they asked him if there really was a beach for coloreds and special entertainment for them as well. The waiter said that indeed there was, it was the hottest spot on the coast. One woman in the group occasionally met Grant's eyes with a kind look, and he thought of her soft features and long neck as he went to sleep that night.

•

By the time the train reached the station, Grant understood that he didn't want to be in New York after all. He considered the cars and lights he'd seen in Chicago and the thought made him very tired. For a while he sat on a bench much like the one he'd sat on there, and he closed his eyes and daydreamed about home. The routine that milled his days was absent utterly, like a cycle of weather going on halfway around the world. He wished he had a horse to ride. He would find the beach, and the horse would test itself on the shifting sand like a horse in a storybook. It would shy at first from the advancing water, then master itself and crash through the tide, leaving prints that washed away behind it. When he opened his eyes he watched his dining companions pass without noticing him. Once they had disappeared he made his way to a ticket window and asked how to get to Atlantic City.

He was told he would have to get a bus at Grand Central.

Which way? he said.

But when he went outside and saw the whole of New York he forgot the directions he'd been given. He watched travelers motion to taxis and tuck themselves inside and the taxis fold into the flow of cars. He took his money from his bag and counted it.

How much? he asked when he got in. The driver told him and Grant considered getting back out, but the driver was shrewd enough to have already started moving. Anyway he'd made his decision and ought to stick to it.

At Grand Central Terminal he paid all but three of his dollars for a ticket. The bus took him out of the city and along a busy road where identical housefronts crowded together like men lined up at a bar. They were traveling south, so he looked left in the hope of seeing the ocean. He couldn't. Soon they turned away from the evening sun, and sand began to appear along the road. Everything inside the bus turned to gold. Where the bus stopped he saw the backs of tall buildings and between them a mass of people walking. He heard the odd cacophony of a big band and smelled fried food. On the other side of a packed parking lot rose a flight of wooden steps. He went to them and climbed them and found himself on a wide wooden boardwalk, where people laughed and clutched one another falling down drunk in fine clothes, and publicly embraced in the backs of carts towed by running men, and pushed in and out of penny arcades and theaters and bars. Beyond all this was a cloudless purple sky that grew darker as it descended to the horizon. The horizon was flat and absolute, the authentic edge of the world. This at last was the ocean.

◆

He sat shoeless mere inches out of reach of the ocean's tongue, eating from a paper plate of pierogies. He had wanted meat but ended up buying the first thing he laid eyes on. Beside him his lemonade was already empty. He had two dollars and ten cents left and all his clothes were foul and wrinkled.

Night came sooner here, so back at home his mother was likely cooking supper for the men. By now they would have stopped wondering about him. Less than a week ago the house had been emptier at night than Grant could bear. Now, without him, it was emptier still.

He would not have thought it possible for an entire family to go wrong. They had been strong and abundant and lived in a valley that seemed theirs alone: when anyone entered, the dust they raised was visible for miles, and even unexpected visitors could be met on the road. Home was sacrosanct, permanent and unbreachable. In retrospect this seemed a childish way of thinking. Families die out, even the hardiest lines. No blood can resist bad luck.

Robert was the second to die. He turned six on the same June day in 1933 that Edwin turned twelve. That month a man just hired had fallen drunk off the back of a truck and for several weeks afterward walked with a crutch. The boys were poking fun out in front of the house, with Grant dramatizing the fall and Thornton looking on from under a shade tree, laughing appreciatively in his strange husky voice. Robert impersonated the remorseful hired man stuttering apologies and jerking his crutch about, using as a prop the shotgun he'd been hunting pheasants with earlier in the day. He had forgotten to engage the safety and when the stock struck his boot top something caught the trigger and a barrel discharged under his arm and nearly took it off his body. No one appeared at the noise. There were a lot of people on the ranch in those days and a lot of reasons to fire a shotgun.

Robert didn't fall, not yet. His shirt swallowed up blood like a patch of dry ground and quickly turned black. He held the shot arm with the opposite hand and dropped to his knees.

Thornton had continued to laugh after the shot but now he perceived something amiss and fell silent. Grant ran to Robert, who had pitched onto his side. He took the boy's gray face in his hands, telling him stay still, don't move. Then he ran to the barn screaming to his father to come hurry, grabbed a rotted wool sack and balled it up as he ran back to Robert's side. Robert had his eyes shut and his dry lips together. Grant shoved the sack under the bleeding arm and pressed it there to stop the flow. If this hurt Robert he made no sign. Bits of grease wool were poking from the sack and lapping up the blood and shrinking to slick strands with it. The shotgun lay in the dirt nearby and Grant snaked out a foot and kicked it away. Thornton sat blubbering in the shade. Their father arrived cursing, and Edwin behind him with a face that seemed already to have considered the possibility of such an incident and fully accepted its inevitability. Unlike their father, Edwin was not surprised.

And neither was their mother, when John returned in the truck with Robert's body to bury it. They had aimed for the hospital in Ashton but Robert died on the way. John didn't stop at the house, only drove across the bare dirt of the starveout to the corner where Wesley lay, and waited for Asta and the boys to follow.

She was not seen to cry then or ever again that Grant could recall, not even when Edwin shot himself in the stand of lodgepole they harvested from the hillside or when the soldier came to inform her that Thornton had perished at sea. The years those incidents spanned were compressed in Grant's memory like frayed patches on a coiled rope. Certainly there were other things in between, his childhood adventures and schooling and the reckless driving of gravel roads, but these recollections faded quickly in the intense tragic light and made his short life seem worthless and futile. When he thought of his mother her face bore the stoic glare she had adopted, a figurehead's face of the sort a person might contrive for staring into a wild wind, as if it was possible to find the source.

Night fell and the noises behind him died. The ocean crept up toward where he sat, and he moved himself back. When it approached a second time he stood and turned toward the city. The sand was treacherous, with broken bits of shell and rotting crabs that he could see in the light from the moon and from the buildings ahead. A sign was posted at the base of the steps that read SHOES MUST BE WORN ON

BOARDWALK. He sat down and put his on. A group of young men passed behind him singing. On a bench a man was kissing a woman. After a moment Grant took his shoes off again and climbed back down into the sand. The boardwalk was built on wooden pilings that created a sheltered space, and he ducked his head and situated himself in it, with a mound of sand as a pillow and his bag close beside him. He fell asleep to the sound of footsteps overhead.

•

It had to be noon, or nearly so. The traffic on the boardwalk was a relentless rumble and the air hot even here in the shade. He came out into daylight. People in various states of undress sunned themselves and leapt in the surf. Women's arms and legs were bare, and men walking along the water's edge held them close. A tall Negro was building a sand castle and had already finished one just beside it. Grant recognized the completed castle, from pictures he'd seen, as the Roman Coliseum. As he watched, two men approached the Negro and dropped money into a nearby paper cup, and he responded with a nod, not taking his eyes from the work. It seemed to Grant that the war's end had driven people to forget who they were and where their lives were leading, to relinquish their money and secrets as if now there would be an unlimited supply. He wondered what the day of the week was—he had forgotten—and if it mattered to anyone.

On the boardwalk he bought a breakfast of sausage and eggs and toast for one dollar and ate it standing up, under a colorful umbrella. He walked as far as the boardwalk would take him, peering down each extravagant pier through its gaudy archway, to the massive halls and costumed people passing handbills, and food stands and games of chance. Graceful dirty gulls swooped in loose formation around small children, who tossed bread in the air for them to catch.

Walking back he stopped before a small crowd of people playing ball and ring-tossing games, at a little concession that also included a burnt-out frypit and griddle and a shabby parrot on a perch. One game involved throwing a baseball over the wooden counter and into a shallow basket with a convex bottom. In another game players tried to yoke a milk bottle with a wooden ring. Both games were cheats. The ball reliably bounced out of the basket every time and the rings were too small.

But the parrot was interesting. One foot was tied to its perch with string. The parrot tottered back and forth on the perch, two steps one way and two the other, as far as it could go in either direction. It did this compulsively, silently.

Give him a coin, the proprietor said. He was ropy looking, with a crooked nose and a frayed straw hat, and his black eyes, which rapidly blinked, were like the parrot's.

Go ahead, he said. Give him a coin, see what he does.

Grant placed a penny on the counter in front of the parrot.

It'll take at least a nickel, the parrot man said. As if in agreement the parrot made a strangled sound, like a squawk.

Grant replaced the penny with a nickel. The parrot grabbed the nickel in its beak, flapped its wings and flew to the rim of a tall glass container standing behind the perch. The string went nearly taut. Having steadied itself the parrot dropped the coin. It landed with a dull sound on a pile of nickels, dimes and quarters at the bottom of the container. Then the parrot returned to the perch. Behind Grant someone applauded.

Hey, is that something else? the parrot man said.

Ain't it supposed to talk? Grant asked him.

The parrot man glared. He's supposed to do exactly what he just did.

Parrots are supposed to talk.

Well, this one does exactly what I tell him to, mister. He's supposed to fly over there and drop that nickel and that's exactly what he did.

Grant gave this some thought. All right then, he said, and deciding he'd been duped like everybody else, moved on.

He bought dinner. This left him with thirty cents. The afternoon passed and he considered that he might skip supper and sleep again on the sand, but what then in the morning? He went back to the parrot man and asked him if he had any work. Nobody else was at the stand.

The parrot man blinked. Do I look like I got any work for you, mister?

I just got here. I don't have any money.

What do I care? the parrot man said, but then, Where do you come from anyway?

As if to balance against future lies, Grant told him about Eleven, the nearest town to the ranch. It was no home town but it came close enough.

You fought the war?

Yes.

The parrot man nodded. I was a cook over in France. Boy, I don't ever want to pick up a fry pan again.

How about that cooking spot? Grant said, an idea beginning to form. The parrot paced, occasionally opening and closing its beak.

What about it? It's ruined.

What if I clean it up and try and get a little extra business going?

The parrot man frowned. I'm going to get myself some skee-ball for over there, he said.

Well up until then, Grant said. I'll clean it up free. You don't have to pay me nothing until I get it working. I'll take whatever you can give me, I don't want for much.

You're staying someplace respectable, right? The skin seemed over-tight across the parrot man's face, a chart of all the fretting he'd done in his life.

I got a room, Grant lied.

The parrot man paused to take somebody's money. For a minute he appeared to have forgotten Grant. Then he held out a bill and said, You go get something to scour it with and come back here. Tomorrow morning I'll get the truck to bring the food. You know how to cook, don't you?

Grant put the bill in his pocket. Sure.

All right, the parrot man said. He looked more worried now, as if he thought he'd made a mistake. Grant smiled at him but the parrot man took it wrong and scowled.

There was not much in the way of rooms. As he walked west the rates dropped. When they got low enough he walked north until he found a landlady who would let him wait until the next day to start paying. She was heavy and old with a pale expressionless face like a reflection in a china plate, and she sat in a wooden folding chair behind a grimy linoleum counter. A scratched glass bowl was sitting on the counter with a handlettered sign: DO NOT HAND ME YOUR MONEY PUT IT IN THE CUP. From an open door behind her issued the sound of a radio. She dropped a key into the glass bowl and Grant took it out. He had better pay two nights tomorrow night, she said, or she would send her husband up to kick him out. Grant told her he understood.

She leaned forward ever slightly and said in a low voice, This place is full of niggers. They will steal the fillings out of your teeth.

Yes, ma'am, said Grant.

The lobby was painted with what might once have been a cheerful yellow but had been corrupted by water stains and the husks of dead insects. A low table had old magazines on it and there was a dry astringent smell as if hundreds of newspapers were stored nearby.

He went to his room. It was about six feet by ten with a high ceiling and a narrow mattress bowed in the middle like a phantom boarder was asleep on it. There was a chair and a small table and a tiny closet with three wire hangers inside. A shallow sink had a sliver of soap on the rim and a square mirror above. The walls were stained but not too badly. His window overlooked an alley and a smaller building, and if he leaned to one side and pressed his head to the glass he could see a strip of beach far off to the north. For awhile he watched the strip of beach until the shadows of the fancy hotels threw themselves over the sand, obscuring its bathers. Then he lay down on the sunken mattress. It was not uncomfortable but he doubted its strength. He lay gingerly, trying not to move around.

The room was all right, though it had too much in it for its size. He looked up and considered the ceiling, where a specked length of fly-paper dangled from a nail. All that empty space up there with no way to use it. He closed his eyes and reviewed his war story. Japan. He pictured palm trees and little flat thatch houses, and the Emperor's men peering out of them with their rifles.

He should have gone. The local board had considered their defer-ment applications and told John to send one of the boys, one only. Max was too young to go, though he begged. Thornton had no idea what he was getting into. It ought to have been Grant who went and who was sunk in the South Pacific. But their father kept him, because he didn't trust Max to work reliably and because Thornton was the kind of help he could easily hire. With Edwin dead he needed to teach someone to run the ranch. Max argued that he could take Thornton's place, that he could go and call himself Thornton Person and pass for eighteen, but John would have none of it. I won't have my sons lying, he said, there's no honor in a lie.

No honor in staying home, Max said.

Grant might have said anything at all but he kept his mouth shut. It is awful quiet around here, Max said to him. Their father did not speak up in his defense.

I got work to do, Grant said and got up from his chair. They were all in the kitchen, the three boys and their mother, her back to them, washing a sinkload of dishes.

Hey Grant! Thornton said. Hey, where you going? We're just talk-ing. It was intolerable to him that they quarreled and intolerable that their father's will be questioned. The boys towered above John Per-son like miraculous crops.

It was never clear why their father mistrusted Max, who was fifteen in 1943 when Thornton was sent away, and who had never once appeared late to do his work or skipped school or engaged in any foolish thing that most boys were forgiven for instantly. But John dis-liked him. He made no effort to conceal it. Every time he opened his mouth in criticism of Max he would praise Grant before he closed it,

and while Grant had no use for this misplaced attention he was powerless to refuse it, the way a thirsty man can't help drinking bad water.
John acknowledged the rivalry that sprang up between them but did
nothing to set it right, believing the boys ought to be able to work out
their problems themselves.

John often said with apparent disgust that Max took after his
mother, and this was true. Like her, Max was competent and self-
reliant. She was the braver of their parents, Grant saw now, because
she never hesitated to love them and did not stop when they began to
die. She once surmised to Grant that she was chosen to lose her children because she was strong enough to withstand it, which gave
Grant to wonder if he then was chosen to be lost.

He had let Thornton go because he valued his life over honor, he
valued his life over Thornton's life. He had got what he wanted. He
was alive.

He returned to the stand just past dark with a soap bucket and
some steel wool pads from a grocer's. The parrot man was surprised
to see him. I thought you'd gone and run off with my dollar, he said. I
was feeling like a goddam fool.

Sorry, Grant said, and handed the parrot man the change. The parrot man counted it carefully.

He got to work straightaway, grinding off the blackened crust and
the years of grease glued up with dust and sand and salt. There was a
basket for dunking potatoes in the hot fat and he toiled at this for
hours, gradually exposing the steel mesh until it gleamed. When he
looked up it was late and the parrot man was watching him. The parrot was in a cage up on the counter, talking quietly to itself.

What's it saying? Grant asked.

The parrot man paused to listen. I don't know if it's foreign or if it's
something he made up himself. Anyway, I don't understand a word of it.

Has it got a name?

Who? Him? He crossed his arms over his skinny chest and his eyes
grew limpid and sad. You know what, I guess I never call him a goddam thing. I just talk to him. I don't call him nothing at all.

Grant cleared his throat. I need some money.

The old tight face snapped back into focus. You ain't cooked a thing yet.

You'll pay me tomorrow? My landlady needs her money.

The parrot man backed up a step as if he thought he was being tricked. You come in here tomorrow and fire up that frypit, you'll earn your money.

Grant nodded, satisfied. He and the parrot man swung down the boards that served as an awning and latched them in place over the windows. Then the parrot man locked the door. He took a key off his ring and handed it to Grant. You'd better be in early, he said. I got the truck coming here at six with your supplies, and you got to put up some kind of menu. There's going to be potatoes and pierogies and the like. You'll see it when it gets here.

All right.

The parrot man draped a purple cloth flecked with yellow stars over the cage, an artificial night. The parrot was silenced. For awhile they stood there, Grant waiting for further instruction. None came. He said goodbye and set off down the boardwalk.

When he reached the stairs down to the street Grant looked back at the game stand. The parrot man still stood in front, the cage on the counter beside him, staring off at the starlit outline of the sea. Grant raised a hand to him but the parrot man never turned.

◆

The next morning he unpacked the boxes that waited for him and stashed the raw food in the cooler. He dumped several blocks of cut fat into the frypit and fired up the gas. Then he found a grease pencil under the counter and wrote a menu on the back of the supplier's receipt. He raised the awning and hung his menu on a nail. Fifteen minutes later a man asked him for eggs and potatoes, and he made them and took the man's money. It was easy. At the day's end the parrot man tore down the menu and wrote up a new one, with higher prices.

The parrot man allowed him breaks, which he spent exploring the boardwalk. There was a hotel for rich people that looked like a wedding cake and a place where cars of the future could be seen and touched. And of course there was the horse, which as promised leapt into the ocean hourly with a girl on its bare back. The girl wore a bathing suit and smiled all the way down, even as the water came up to engulf her. Grant thought she must be brave and dreamed of meeting her, but he couldn't imagine how to approach her or what to say if he did. The horse, on the other hand, although it possessed a beauty flying through the air, up close proved old and tired, its coat coarsened by the salt water.

He sent a postcard home. It had a picture of the diving horse on one side and on the other he wrote:

> I am well here and have seen many amazing things. There is
> not a single hill anywhere. You can write me at this address.

And he gave the address of the rooming house. What he had written dissatisfied him, but it was his only postcard and he sent it without giving the matter much thought.

Business was often slow. It seemed there were plenty of other places to get fried food, most of them newer or cleaner-looking or with a larger menu. For this reason Grant's job did not feel secure. It was obvious the parrot man lacked much sense: it would have been easy to give the stand a coat of paint or pass out handbills or expand the menu, but instead he griped, asking Grant where all the customers were. Grant could only shrug. When idle he leaned against a post and watched the parrot moving back and forth on its perch. The bird seemed perfectly accustomed to this circumscribed life. Sometimes the parrot man allowed Grant to feed it a shred of lettuce, which the parrot accepted silently, champing on it for a minute or so until it was gone and then returning to work. Afterward Grant always lost interest in the bird and turned to face the ocean, another entity with a singular aim. Occasionally the sight of it sent him into a kind of trance, difficult to rouse himself out of. Sometimes he couldn't understand how people went about their lives in its presence. A thing so drastic, mocking them like that.

•

After one September night Grant woke earlier than usual and left his room to sit on the beach and plan or at least imagine what he might do next. Though it was before ten in the morning hundreds of people were out in the cool air, standing on the sand in their street shoes. There were no bathers at this hour. He walked through the crowd listening for clues to their purpose here, but learned only that something was expected to happen, some kind of show, and it would happen out at sea. The presence of these people on what he had come to think of as his beach irritated him and he found their proximity unnerving. Still, he chose a spot and waited.

Pretty soon a dot appeared out on the water and resolved into the shape of a boat. The static of conversation became a thrum and dropped off entirely as more boats bulged onto the horizon and drew into clear view, as if brought by the tide. From newspaper photographs he'd seen, Grant was able to identify these as transports.

It was in one like them that Thornton was killed. The ship had not been attacked but had suffered an explosion on board and sunk. It wasn't hard to imagine what this must have been like. The death was Grant's after all and had simply been lent to his idiot brother, who gratefully wrapped it around himself like a poisoned blanket. He imagined Thornton hunkered in his tiny cabin, straining to assemble in his mind all the evidence of danger; the deadened blast and the rushing water and the sudden darkness, the slide of objects from their customary places, and finally the ocean's blind hungry clench.

Just offshore now, the ships yawned open to frenetic applause, and from the guts of them came soldiers who knelt in the surf and fired upon the onlookers, and got up and ran, heavy with seawater, onto the hard wet sand and fired again. Women screamed and a few fainted dead away. Soldiers pulled up short and theatrically fell, writhing in mock death. And Grant knew genuine pain as the bullets entered him, even as he understood them to be imaginary; they found his heart and pierced it, tore the breath out of his lungs, swept his legs out from under him. They glowed inside him like irons. He was branded from within: the destruction his brothers had claimed was also his, was Max's and their mother's and father's.

He lay contorted in the sand forcing sobs from his body, oblivious to the sympathetic shadows falling across him, to the hands on his arms and back and head. He would not be helped. Instead he wanted to fill this ground with his tears and claim it as his own. He wanted to make himself an impossible promise, one he would sooner die than break but which he knew was already as good as broken, that he was never going to go back.

2

The parrot man fired him. It wasn't hard to see it coming and Grant had been prepared. By eating at work he had saved enough money to last him through several days of looking for a job. Nothing much had happened out of the ordinary, the parrot man had just finally had enough. He berated Grant, telling him he was a bad influence. The way Grant figured it, though, the parrot man had got it in his head to sell the frypit and griddle, which looked practically like new, and then use the money for the skee-ball game he wanted. Grant didn't blame him, much as he hated being shouted at.

I didn't do anything wrong, he protested, even as he untied his apron.

The parrot man's face swelled and darkened. It don't matter! he shouted. It's you! It's just you!

That night Grant washed his clothes in his room's small sink and hung them to dry in the narrow closet. The hangers there were rusted and the wallpaper soiled, so that the otherwise clean shirts bore crooked orange lines down the shoulders and a smear on one upper arm where the hanger butted the wall. To some extent these stains could be brushed off, and in the shifting colored lights of the street they were not easily detected. Tonight Grant had one clean dry shirt.

He put it on and went for a walk, determined to investigate the city's night life.

For a time he watched people shoot air rifles at wooden ducks. Winning the game earned them tickets which they could exchange for stuffed toys, gag items or small trophies. Later he sat on a bench facing the sea. Below him children played tag on the sand, lit by the bright city. But the activity around him only served to deepen his solitude. He felt like these people were stealing something, something he was unaware he had possessed or relied upon but which, once taken, seemed to represent a grievous and irrevocable loss. It was as if some integral, helpless part of him had been exposed and seized. When a group of young men passed him laughing he could practically see them reaching out toward him with greedy hands. Impulsively he leapt to his feet and trailed behind them to see where they would go.

There were four of them, pale bedraggled men with the weight of hard work on their faces like a heavy curtain. He could see that they were drunk. They left the boardwalk and entered an alley behind a hotel, where they vanished through an unmarked door. Grant lingered nearby. Voices, the smell of cigarettes. There was a bar in Eleven that Grant used to go to, all the time before the war but less often the longer he failed to enlist. Still, he felt at home among drunks.

He went in. It wasn't much different from the bar he knew. Dark walls and floor, the row of men's backs, a picture of the Sioux killing Custer. No music played. The men he had followed sat at some tables among girls and were already engaged in casual embraces with them. A woman served them all drinks which they set upon at once without looking up to acknowledge her.

Grant's entrance had brought no reaction whatever. He might not have been there at all.

At the bar he bought whiskey and sat facing the door at a table near the men. Behind him they cajoled and exclaimed and the girls laughed. For a short time he suffered in the wash of their voices, but before long the drink insulated him. He had no idea what he was doing here.

Someone bumped his table and Grant's hand shot out to steady his drink. 'Scuse me, buddy, the man said.

Grant looked up and answered, No harm done.

The man hesitated. He was big and full-bodied as a bull, but he had a frightened aspect, an incongruous nervousness around the eyes and mouth. He was one of the men Grant had followed. Whassat you're drinking there, he said.

Whiskey.

The man nodded and went to the bar. He came back with two glasses and set one on the table, leaving his fingers on the rim while he appraised Grant frankly.

After long consideration he said, Where you been, soldier? While he waited for an answer he licked his lips, pink and full like a woman's.

Peleliu, Okinawa, Grant forced himself to say.

Regular army?

Grant told him yes.

The man let out breath with obvious relief. I'm a navy man. Got myself discharged awhile back and couldn't wait to get back on a boat, if you can believe that. He pointed to the others. We're on a crew out of Boston, codfishing on the Grand Banks.

Grant nodded.

I bet you saw some action, the man said after a moment.

Saw my share.

Yeah?

Again Grant nodded, wary of where this was going and determined to keep it where it was. He said nothing.

Well come on over and meet the boys. We're just making some friends.

Grant joined the group. He finished his drink and soon another was put before him. He finished that one too. Everyone told him their names and he gave them his, but he couldn't keep straight who was who. Their personalities and faces ran together. A squared-off chin, a cauliflower ear, a round bosom under a cotton blouse. They asked him a lot of questions and he answered them, and sometimes they laughed at the answers. At some point one of the girls began to cry. One of the boys led her off and the two never returned. There was talk of fish and fishing and he must have told them about the parrot man, because that's what they were calling him by the fifth or sixth drink. Somebody shoved a crumpled paper into his shirt pocket and then he was alone on an empty street, and he was vomiting into the gutter underneath a flickering streetlamp. Next he found himself in bed, his hands gripping the mattress as if it was a raft asea. A certain water stain on the ceiling looked like a barren island. He bobbed around it as it spun above him and he vomited again, into the sink. After that he felt much better, and he cleaned himself up and looked out as the sun rose over the rumpled strip of visible beach. He brushed his teeth and noticed, in the mirror, the paper sticking out of his pocket. It was smeared and damp and read: CHALFONT HADDON HALL BACK ENTRANCE 8 AM.

Now he remembered. They were going to find him work, on their boat. He'd told them no, he was going home. That was his plan anyway. But he felt like a fool standing before the mirror, looking into his own drink-wracked face, he felt like he'd failed at whatever it was he set out to do. Here was a reason to wait: a way to buy time, the only thing he could afford. He wouldn't go back, not just yet.

He didn't know what time it was, he guessed five. He took off his clothes and washed them, then waited in his undershorts while they dried. In an hour he put on his one dry shirt and pulled on the pants still wet, and he packed the wet shirt and left. He dropped the key in the glass bowl at the unmanned counter. Out on the boardwalk he ate sausage and eggs and sat awhile to calm his stomach. He asked somebody where the hotel was, and then he went there. The rear entrance had a circular drive for cars and an area of white gravel with tropical plants growing in it. The seasons were changing and the plants were half dead.

They came in a black sedan without the girls. Somebody opened a back door and the men made room on the seat. Grant got in and shut the door and the car pulled away.

Holy Jesus, Parrot Man, what a night, someone said.

Hurts, was his reply. They laughed as if this was a joke. Then they exchanged stories about their drinking and about the girls. One said he couldn't get the dress off his.

Prude? asked another.

No, I mean I was too drunk. They laughed again. Meanwhile the buildings were shrinking outside and the sand thinning at the road's edge.

Where are we going? Grant said.

The driver was the bullish man who had bought Grant's drink. New York, he said. Fish Express.

Are we going to make it? someone asked.

Does Betsy have tits?

Their laughter died down and for awhile everyone seemed to be sleeping. Then they were in New York. The car was parked in a crowded lot. It had been rented. Pony up, one of the men said, and everyone gave him money. Grant counted out his share, half of what he had to his name. They shouldered their bags and walked dozens of blocks in silence. The sun was overhead and the tall buildings swallowed their shadows.

They arrived at a warehouse and walked around behind it where a train waited, its tank cars expelling a brilliant liquid like half-molten metal, which the afternoon sun shuddered upon as it flowed down troughs into the building. The liquid was fish. Grant stood and gaped as the others continued down the train's length. He had caught trout in streams but had never known such abundance of fish. They couldn't have been alive, nevertheless they roiled like a simmering pot. The hole they plunged into was black around them and they pulled the sunlight in their slipstream and reflected it from inside the darkness, like faceted gems.

Up ahead the men were signaling to him. He followed, ducking under the flowing fish, their scales rasping terribly against the trough bottom. The others were nodding to some men smoking outside a boxcar. Grant hurried to meet them. They climbed into the car and the smokers climbed in behind. The boxcar was equipped with benches bolted onto a rickety pine floor. Sunlight shone in strips through the narrow slatted walls and floor and spread across the car. The men found seats and smoked there, cleaved by the light.

There were maybe fifteen men altogether. They greeted one another with nods. Each had the pallid complexion and rimmed eyes of someone who had enjoyed himself to within an inch of his life. Some sipped from thermoses of coffee, a few ate sandwiches wrapped in waxed paper. Grant's breakfast had long since exhausted itself and he was simultaneously hungry and too nauseated to eat. He closed his eyes and fell asleep.

The movement of the train woke him. Men were starting to speak. They weren't all young as he was, most were too old to have been in the war and talked about other things. His companions were still on last night's girls. Grant had nothing to say at all and might not have even if he'd taken a girl home. He might like to talk to a woman but didn't see much point in talking about one with other men. He had dated when he was in school; there was a dance in a nearby town that once a year he rode to all day to get to, and all night to return. On those rides he liked the company of his own mind, liked to let it go where it wanted, to hypothetical situations and acts, perhaps with a girl he would meet that night. Sometimes he did meet a girl, but nothing beyond that night usually came of it. Mostly there was talking and some kissing. One time he met a girl with a reputation and she took him off to a riverbank for a couple of hours, and he often thought about that experience. He reckoned such a night could easily be had any time, it was what people liked to do after all, but he didn't care so much for afterward, when it could be hard to find anything to say. If he wanted to go to bed with a woman, he was going to have to find one he could talk with. But in his experience the ones who would talk didn't want to do it, and the ones who wanted to do it wouldn't talk. Maybe the two things simply did not go together. His mother had plenty of children but not much to say. He didn't want to meet a girl like his mother, so tough and unhappy.

Then again he didn't see himself meeting a girl at all. He felt very far from desire. Even so, he was lonely.

He looked at the men around him. Solitude hung on them like a soaking coat. And then he thought he could feel it on himself, leaden and cold, and suddenly he was no longer among them but with them, and of them.

Conversation waned. Some of the men peeked between the slats at what passed. From where he sat in the center of the car, Grant could distinguish bright sky from ground and ground from water, but little else. Instead he leaned forward with his elbows on his knees and watched the flickering railroad ties filled in between with gravel. This quelled his nausea and hunger, and from time to time, when the train crossed a river and the ground dropped away beneath him, a lightness overwhelmed him as if he was in flight.

They arrived at evening and leapt down onto a massive rail yard where freight cars surrounded them on every side. The men spread out and picked their way among the cars with the sun at their backs. At the yard's edge was a road and Grant followed the men along it. Gulls dangled overhead, tufted and greasy like dead wool, or stepped along the roadside in ragged regiments. The men turned onto a smaller road which led them to a wide and boat-strewn bay. Here the group wordlessly dissolved. Grant's companions led him around the bay's great arc to a ship of considerable size, as far as Grant could tell. They boarded via a gangplank that thundered with their footfalls. Men clinging to ropes that hung from the deck were scraping a barnacled crust off the hull. Once on board Grant was asked to stay where he was while the skipper was fetched.

From here it was possible to see where the bay emptied into the ocean, and the low land that curled back upon itself to admit it. Clouds massed to the north, and to the south the sky was slowly sinking deeper into blue. Behind Grant lay a huge city that until now had somehow escaped his attention. It had to be Boston. Sunlight careened through its buildings and they pulsed with an almost bodily translucence, like living things. All around him were men in unhurried action, coiling ropes (he would later learn to call them lines) and mending with large meticulous hands a vast sisal net threaded with glass bobbins. Cigarettes hung from their mouths. There was a sense of deep calm, as among pastured horses. He stayed very still, afraid of breaking it.

The skipper was short and thick and gave the impression of tremendous density, like he was full of lead. He arrived shaking his head no. Grant offered his hand and the skipper took it and held it for a scant moment, then dropped it suddenly so that Grant's surprised arm swung free at his side. Despite what he had been told, the skipper said, there was no work. But he knew a Brit who needed men.

It'll be trial by fire, though, the skipper went on. His crew took violent sick, there's hardly any of them left.

All right, Grant said.

You boys did good work over there, the skipper said with the tone of a man relating something he's just looked up.

Pardon?

Okinawa.

Thank you, sir, Grant told him and looked up and then down the shoreline, along the confusion of mastheads. Which way do I go?

There, I'm pointing at her now. She's the *Rose Adams*.

I'm real grateful.

Alone on the gangplank his footsteps made a disconsolate clang, and he wandered along the docks unsure of where on a boat to find its name. He asked passersby, some of whom pointed him so far one way or another, and at last he stood before the ship, and found his way aboard and asked an unoccupied man for the skipper.

You come to work? the man asked him. He spoke with an accent Grant thought might be French and wore his hair gathered underneath a black cap. A tidy ring of graying beard encircled his mouth and chin.

Yes.

The Frenchman nodded. For that you don't need the skipper, he said. He led Grant into a warren of steel passageways, through a lightless chamber full of tables and benches, through a low hatchway into a dim close hall lined with doors. The Frenchman opened one of these and motioned to Grant with an impatient hand.

Your bag, he said.

Grant gave him the bag and the Frenchman flung it onto the lower of two metal bunks. Each bunk was barely two feet wide, fitted with a thin cushion and two blankets, one for warmth and one folded as a pillow. A canvas belt was attached for keeping the sleeper in. Grant saw that he couldn't sleep here in the manner he was accustomed to, he would have to find a new way. There was a polished metal mirror in the berth and a low open sea chest on the floor divided in two by a board.

Come, said the Frenchman.

Grant followed him onto the deck. Here men were at work on a net much like the Americans', with bright golden-white patches gleaming among the dark sea-battered strands like late sunlight through a barn wall, the whole bunched across the deck and trembling under the sailors' fast hands. The net was woven of ropes in various thicknesses and in many patterns, with an obvious order that was nonetheless incomprehensible to Grant. He would learn this was the trawl, and that its use and care made necessary a vast new vocabulary that would become the core of his everyday speech. The trawl was as integral to this work as the ship itself. Even now Grant understood this: fish couldn't possibly have been caught from deep water until such a thing was conceived and fabricated. The Frenchman said something Grant didn't hear.

What?

The knot. You tie the knot? His fingers casually knitted the air in illustration.

No, I've never done this in my life.

There was no evidence that the Frenchman was surprised or annoyed. He nodded, taking Grant by the arm. They sat on lidded wooden buckets with the trawl on their laps and the Frenchman showed him how. As it happened he was not French but Belgian, and his name was Luc. The words eluded Grant but slowly he came to own them: becket, codend, belly, warps. They sat for hours until the sun was gone and then mended the trawl by moonlight. From time to time they moved to another section and Luc demonstrated, stringing the heavy iron bobbins onto the ground wire, repairing the frayed headline with fresh supple hemp. There were a dozen men around them, silent or whistling or singing quietly, speaking soft words to the trawl in accented English. They seemed to be from everywhere and nowhere, their foreignness a kind of commonality. They were thin, their motions sure. Grant pulled and wove the mesh slowly under Luc's eyes, aware the others' work depended on the strength of his own. For some reason this fact filled him not with anxiety but with clarity, like a sharp steady light. He tied and tested. Luc sat nearer than would be appropriate on land, touching the back of Grant's hand when it faltered. A boy named Brian with a narrow nose and large crooked teeth brought them coffee in a huge dented pot, coffee that tasted faintly of tea, as if the same pot was used for the two. The men whispered their thanks to him. He was the steward. Grant shook his hand and found his own fingers weak with pain. It would be three years before he went home.

•

The ship was a creature that lived on fish. It sailed to bitter and awful places, hauling fish out of the ocean, digesting them with its hands and knives. The Georges Bank thrashed it with storms and cold and tucked it away into epic fogs. It was flung and shaken by implausible waves, rolled by mad winds. Icebergs the men called growlers threatened to gouge them as they passed, and on calm days puffins sat on the water bobbing like buoys with the undulations of sea. There were many seas, some so flat and regular they seemed plowed, some violent and white as an avalanche. Calm seas changed color and texture from mile to mile, as range grasses thrived or foundered over the shifting character of soil.

As at home, life on the ship consisted of work and its consequences. Even the strongest bodies couldn't escape the pain of repetitive action. But the understanding among the crew was that work was preferable to repose. Rest meant less money. If this seemed a dreary kind of life, it could be said that few thought of it as life; rather the voyage served life, as it was lived elsewhere by other people. Though none of them ever said as much, they had come from the land and would always return to it. It was land they sought when they looked out over the water, however far away they knew it to be: land and its inhabitants: the people they hated or loved, who gave their lives meaning. And so much of the time that passed, heavy as it was with men's yearning, was dull. Dragging to and from port the men could find nothing to occupy themselves with, despite the crate of paperbacks that never left the boat and which few had read his way entirely through; despite the bottomless trough of personal tales they had brought which they told and retold and nobody seemed to listen to. The sea's cyclic fierceness murdered narrative. Instead it was superstition that gripped their imagination, a periodic terror fueled by the vagaries of nature. The behavior of birds and fish, the character of winds and waters, all were portents. Fear loved an idle man.

One man confessed he couldn't sustain an erection. He was the splitter, whose job was to debone and decapitate cod. He did this with such speed and agility that he frightened the others, some of whom confessed to nightmares about him and his knife. This man told them he had never made love to a woman, had tried but could not. A merchant he knew in Boston, he said, got him fresh ginger from Japan, because it was thought to be an aphrodisiac. He sucked slivers of it while he worked, occasionally stopping to chop off a fresh piece and spit the depleted one into the sea.

The chief engineer told them that he used to write daily letters to his mother, saving them in a velvet bag during each voyage with the intention of mailing them at once when he returned to port. On one voyage he argued with a Portuguese who beat him and flung the bag overboard. Now the engineer wrote no letters at all.

One man, the gogotier, who excised and preserved cod livers, never spoke at all. It was to his stoicism that Grant aspired—he didn't wish to tell his or any story. But Grant learned that he could be drawn out, and in the captive intimacy of the boat sometimes allowed himself to be. He revealed only the barest outline and the men filled it in with what they liked. By his silence Grant confirmed their versions of events. They made him into a marine of the Seventh Division and had him storming Orange Beach on D-Day. He fought bravely, and miraculously wasn't hit. At Okinawa a sniper nicked him. He showed them the rope burn and they held silent witness to it. Grant would hear of himself capturing and executing the sniper, would learn he had taken a Zero out of the sky. Over time the crew lost its veterans and took on younger men who had missed the opportunity to fight in the war, and these men held Grant up as a hero. It was thought that he had chosen this desolate life at sea as an antidote to the horrors of war. After awhile he began to act like this hero, speaking solemnly when at all, accepting without contradiction the respect of those he knew were his betters. Only the gogotier seemed to know the truth, or at least Grant feared that he did, seeing reflected in his hard hooded eyes the liar Grant knew himself to be.

He read his way through the crate when there were no fish to haul. The paperback mysteries, with their haunted heroes and wrecked lives, made his own life seem austere and pure, and the resigned French heroines of the pornographic novels filled him with a sick yearning. Like the engineer he wrote no letters.

By the change of seasons he could tell how long he'd been at sea, but the specific date was never clear. Time only mattered once the trawl was shot. Then, the roof of the water flashed under the projector's beam and they watched as the threads melted into it. Grant's heart learned to tick off each moment until the skipper called Let go everywhere!, and the boat levered like a jet underneath them and drummed full ahead. And then for two hours they ate flounders and drank coffee and the *Rose Adams* rolled through space.

They would wait on deck then, watching the winches turn until the beaded line of floats grinned on the water and the whole of the trawl outlined itself, humped beneath the surface like a grave. Boys at the gunwale hooked the trawl's fat body and the great boom swung out to pull the catch home. The bladder of fish climbed the hull and at last swung heavy above them, the terrible mass writhing in its mesh skin. Then Luc stepped forward and yanked the drawline and the fish flowed down and out around their feet, up to their waists, the cod's bulging eyes twitching against the caustic air.

Only then did work begin. They worked for eighteen sleepless hours at a time, sorting and gutting and salting the fish. Men went down into the hold where the cod were thrown and didn't come out until the following day. And on deck it was rarely a clement sky they worked under. This was the North Atlantic and the boat pitched and heaved like it was trying to slough them off. Waves washed the catch overboard or picked men up and flung them and knocked them out cold.

This happened to Grant. He remembered he was piking with the other men and next thing he knew he was sitting with them around a table, laughing at somebody's joke. He would discover that more than a week had passed. They told him he cracked his head on the outrigger. He fell unconscious, awoke in bed, recovered, went back to work and, when they had finished with the haul, spent several days reading books in his cabin. He never could remember so much as a minute of that week, up to and including the joke he'd been laughing at when he finally came to.

He visited countless port cities throughout Europe and North America. Sometimes he drank to excess and passed out in cheap motel rooms like everyone else. But mostly he walked through the filthy streets of foreign places wondering what living there would be like. He understood there was much to be learned by talking to the residents of these places, but could never bring himself to start conversations. Women came to the bars he visited and some of them were beautiful. Still he didn't approach them, for some irrational fear. He had a sense that he would be discovered, not simply his invented combat record but something terrible and empty that was inherent to him, some unsprung trap a woman might unearth and hold up inquiring before him.

One day he woke and saw his father's face in the mirror. He touched his lips and nose, the ridges under his eyes. A lock of hair formed a sleep-stiffened arch over his forehead, exposing the fine familiar lines there which deepened as he watched. Curiosity gave way to anger and he spat at his image. A ridiculous thing to do. As he wiped the mirror clean his throat burned with emotion, and he knew it was time.

The skipper was a rangy Englishman with an elusive kindness of face you had to search for to see. Whenever Grant encountered him, the skipper looked like he'd just heard a good story that he didn't have the time or inclination to repeat. On this day Grant found him alone on the bridge, staring into the wind as if calculating how it would turn. The hold was full of cod and they were headed for port in Canada.

I believe you have something to tell me? the skipper asked him. His prescience did not seem odd to Grant, only reassuring.

Yessir.

The skipper's thumb and index finger brushed against each other in a silent snap. You're leaving us, then? When?

In Halifax, I believe.

You have some plan? the skipper said.

Only to go home, sir. I got family I ain't seen in a long time.

Where is home? I don't remember.

I don't think I ever said, Grant told him. It doesn't matter.

The skipper nodded, his head aslant, listening to the sea. I don't suppose it does, he said.

As they drew closer to port a few of the men approached him to say goodbye. Luc gave him a compass he said he had gotten from his grandfather. Abashed, Grant accepted the gift.

But no one else came to him when they docked at Halifax. It wouldn't be a long stop and the boat had to be readied for another voyage. It was late summer now, and though the air here was clean and warm, the smell of habitation lay on it like a sixth sense, a mix of milled lumber and frying grease and automobile exhaust. The oddness of it was striking. He had smelled it in port before but this time he was part of it for good. He braced himself for contact with unfamiliar people. When he turned on the quay to raise his hand to the men, there was nobody at the rail. To them he was already gone.

A train brought him down the Canadian coast and all the way to Boston, where he ate fish in a seafood restaurant and spent the night in a familiar hotel. His bag held new things. He'd bought a carved whalebone box in Iceland. He had an ivory-handled flensing knife he won from a whaler in a card game. There was a corroded antique wristwatch he had pulled from a live fish, and Luc's compass, and his money, a thick sheaf of bills rolled up with an elastic band and stuffed into the toe of a black sock. He had made a lot of money in three years and spent nearly nothing. There might have been as much as ten thousand dollars, he didn't count it. During the night he woke in darkness and sat listening to the city. Tomorrow he would go.

•

But not home, not yet. First south by train to New York. There he bought a ticket west for two days later. Then he continued by bus to Atlantic City. He arrived after dark and carried his bag up and down the boardwalk, remembering. He'd thought he would never forget the diving horse, but the one diving now may or may not have been the one he'd known before. The girl riding it was different, that much was certain. The parrot man was also gone, the space he'd held converted to a taffy shop. The glass canister was still there, filled to the rim with gumdrops.

He walked inland. The shabbiness of the west side seemed to be creeping toward shore. The roll of bills glowed like a coal in his bag. He thought he was wandering, but soon he found himself at the door of his old boardinghouse, his fingers around the handle trembling with a child's anticipation. He didn't understand why. He hadn't been happy here.

The old woman was right where he'd left her, the glass bowl still in place upon the counter, the radio still playing in a back room. She looked up at him without recognition and he mustered a smile. She gave him the price of a room.

I used to live here, he said. About three years ago.

Looks like you're back, she said.

Just for a night.

Suit yourself.

He wrote his name on an index card and paid her in advance. She dropped the key into the bowl and he took it and headed for the stairs.

Hold your horses, she said. You got some mail. She rooted under the counter and brought out a basket of envelopes, then sorted out one, two, three of them and laid these on the counter next to the bowl. Name rung a bell, she said.

Grant went back and picked up the letters. He recognized his mother's handwriting on one and Max's on the others. His mother's had been posted some time ago, Christmas 1945. Max's were more recent. Holding them in his fingers, he thought they must be impossible.

His room was just like his old one except with a better view. Outside, the boardwalk glowed under a new profusion of lurid colored lights. He set his bag on the bed and sat down next to it. Then he opened the letters.

Dear Grant,

I hope you are well. Your father and brother and I are work very hard and the flock is pretty healthy. We hire an extra man but he is a drunk, so now we are looking for another. I hope it might be you but your father will not hear of it.

I do not know exactly why you left from home but I think I understand. Sometimes in life I thought I should leaving if I could, but I never did. But I have to ask you please to come home. It is important I know that you are all right.

My thoughts are with you.

Sincerely Mother

Grant

Mamas sick. A hired man is cooking the food and tending the cows and chickens, but she is very sick and you better get back. She is in her bed day + night and doesnt get up. Daddy yells at her to get up because he thinks shes faking and it is no good for her condition, despite that he is just a bastard all the time.

Dont think Im writing this because we need you to run the place because we dont. I could care less if you come back but Mother wants you so I am writing this for her.

Max

Grant

Mamas dead and buried here at home with the others. I wanted to bury her somewhere else but Daddy insisted. Enclosed is death notice in the paper. I thought you should know.

The letter was unsigned. He pictured his brother, pale and black-haired, bent twiglike over the old office desk in the shed writing to him. He read the letter again, making sure he had gotten everything right.

Grant unfolded the notice. On the back was half a coupon for whole cut chicken from a grocery.

PERSON, Asta, née Einarsdottir, died September 5 at home near Eleven. The deceased was born in Iceland in 1897 and came to the US with her husband John Person at the close of the first World War. She is survived by John Person and two sons.

He put the letters back in their envelopes and set them aside. After a time he lay back across the bed and later fell asleep.

In the morning he woke and took up his bag and went out, leaving the letters on the hopeless mattress for whomever might find them. He dropped his key in the bowl and walked to the beach. Dawn had broken and had begun to uncover the night's activity. No footprints marred the surf-dredged sand. Slick dark branches and clumps of seaweed dotted the shore, as if there'd been a storm in the night. Maybe there had been. He weaved between pilings under the piers and wandered onto a stone-and-cement jetty to look out at the sea.

He had meant to say goodbye to it, to the ocean. It was possible he would never see it again after today and it seemed right to take one last look. But the ocean he knew was nowhere evident. Here it had no character or identity. This was where it met the land, nothing more. He watched it advance and retreat then continued down the beach, still gazing out, still searching for its familiar faces.

On the far side of the Million Dollar Pier he saw a group of standing people staring down at a shape in the sand. There was a tall thin man, a Negro, wearing a straw hat and a cream-colored linen suit slightly too small for him. A white woman stood with a boy of about six. Grant came up close and saw that the shape was that of a man. He was heavy, short, his features bleached by the salt water. A gray pinstriped suit jacket and pants adhered to his body, but he wore no shirt underneath. His feet were bare. Sand was stuck to the suit and to his hair and three ragged bloodless holes gaped in his chest, another smaller one in his forehead. A large gold ring with a green stone was on a finger of his left hand.

Mama, that's a dead man, the child said, the words all run together as if they'd already been said many times. He tugged at his mother's hand.

No, she said, that isn't a dead man, now let's go. But they stayed. The woman was young and black-haired and stared helplessly at the body.

The Negro said, turning to Grant, That is a gangland rubout. I suppose somebody ought to be told. He was looking at Grant as if Grant ought to be that somebody.

Without thinking Grant knelt before the dead man and turned back the lapel of his jacket. In the inside pocket he found only sand and salt. The outside pockets were also empty. The trousers stuck flat against the dead man's legs and nothing was outlined in the pockets there.

When Grant stood up the woman regarded him with shock. She gripped her boy's shoulder and pulled him to her. He is, the boy said, he *is* dead.

Come, she said, and turned, tugging him along with her. He stumbled and fell in the sand. Wordlessly he picked himself up and followed her toward the boardwalk.

This city ain't the same, the Negro told Grant. I was a boy during the prohibition. You expected to see this kind of thing in those days, but now we're supposed to be in another sort of era.

Nothing'll stop a body from dying, Grant said.

That ain't what I mean, came the terse reply.

Grant left him there and walked up the beach a ways before heading toward town. The dead man's waxy face followed him as he walked, a terrible face, Grant thought, that might not have been improved by life. Its features were spread flat as if pressed into glass, the mouth and nostrils wide and black and the chin smoothed over, by fat or the effects of water he didn't know. The face was so unlike his mother's. Her fine features barely registered, like quick strokes of a pencil. She could never occupy the same state as this man, her flesh never take on the mass, the burden of death.

The boardwalk seemed tainted by false optimism, its proprietors brisk and enthusiastic in their preparations. They reminded him of farmers he'd known, steadfast men who believed that God and the land would provide. He remembered his father, who had left his home country and never returned, in his struggle to live having lost the opportunity to do so. Obligation pulled Grant and he grew eager to leave.

He walked west until he found a diner, where he was served black coffee and a thick slice of moldy cake. When he complained the waitress reached over the plate for his fork and took a sizable piece into her mouth. She chewed it and swallowed and said she didn't taste anything funny, so he took her at her word and finished the rest himself. It seemed important to have faith in her opinion.

There was nothing left for him here. He paid and went to the bus station to wait. So far the weather had been fair but now a cold wind picked up and chilled him. He pulled a jacket from his bag and put it on. The world was still, the sun steady in the sky.

He wondered how they got his mother into the starveout. Probably his father and Max lifted the casket up onto the truck and drove there, with the box clattering on the bed behind them. And then what? Did anyone else come for the burial? There were ranch women who when they went to town were greeted and talked to and touched, but his mother had never been one of them. It was possible that none of these women went to pay their respects or even sent condolences to the house. They may not have known she was dead until they read it in the paper. This is the way their father would have handled the matter. He needed them now, his living sons, both of them.

Some hours later a bus came and took Grant to New York. He ate and slept at the station, his fingers tight around the handles of his bag. In the morning he bought a newspaper and found a story about a body washed ashore in New Jersey. The deceased was thought to be a minor mob figure. No other details were provided about the man, save the peculiar shambling walk he was known for when alive. It was unclear who killed him or in retaliation for what offense, but an investigation was being opened by the police.

Grant inspected his fingers where they had touched the dead man's coat. There was nothing unusual about them. Even so, he felt defiled by his involvement, peripheral as it was. He felt that something of the dead man had seeped through the skin and was running now in his blood. He flexed the muscles in his fingers and watched his hands open and close like machines.

When the train came he folded the newspaper and stood. The events of the world were unimportant now; all that mattered to him was his place in it. He threw the newspaper into the trash and climbed on board.

3

He woke before Chicago certain someone had taken the seat beside him and was gazing at him with malevolent intent. But it was an old woman, seemly and upright, staring straight ahead. He blinked. In his ebbing sleep the world was all stirred up, its visible parts set off strangely against one another. He sensed that he'd dreamt but could not remember what.

The train was moving west. Though he had passed by here before, the towns outside looked flat and alien, the light dimensionless. He felt with his feet for his bag and found it under the seat, right where he'd left it.

It would have been easy to get himself a berth to be alone in. He had the money. But this would have seemed a waste, and he'd have wished he was out among the other passengers. Solitude was polluted; he'd had enough of it. He could smell fish on his clothes: there was nothing to be done but throw them out and buy some new. He wondered how long until Chicago and asked the woman beside him if she knew the time or where in the world they were. She examined the back and then the palm of her small white hand, then told him she was afraid she did not know.

As it happened they were very near Chicago. Grant disembarked with some relief. He bought a basket of fish and ate it on a bench next to a trash can. The fish wasn't fresh and had been cooked in old grease, and he could smell spent cigars and discarded lunches in the garbage, but there were no other benches in sight and he was too tired to stand. He was the first to board the train home. The seat he chose lacked adequate leg room, though by the time he realized this the train was full. He stayed there for the next day and a half.

Twice he was gripped by strange fears. The first came as the train left Chicago. He was watching the stockyards the tracks snaked through, the animals inside them so unlikely against the backdrop of warehouses and tall buildings. The wheels moaned, and suddenly he believed he had left something behind on the platform. He panicked, his hands flew to his bag. Again he found it where he'd left it. But this gave him little comfort, even though he hadn't carried another thing since he left home three years before; and for much of that first day his legs ached and twitched, yearning for the station and whatever it was he had abandoned there.

Then, that evening, he looked up and saw a small pale face regarding him from outside the cabin. Its eyes were in shadow and it raced alongside the train. But it was night and the compartment dimly lit, and the face proved to be another passenger's reflected from across the aisle.

The train couldn't be stopped at Grissom except to pick up a new traveler, and since there was none he would get off at Ashton, a city of about twenty thousand that lay an hour's drive from Eleven. It was just as well, there would be no one to pick him up in the ghost town, nor any telephone to call for a ride. Ashton was where the hospital was, the one Robert hadn't reached in time. Their lambs went to market in Ashton and the wool was graded and sold there.

It was late September, still warm. A wind lashed the Ashton depot that in January could freeze a man to death. Grant stepped off the train and leaned into the gale, his bag and arm with it driven out behind him. Men staggered past in city dress, clamping their hats to their heads. The streets seemed abnormally wide and the cars more

and newer than he remembered. He went into the Ashton Dry
Goods, bought new clothes and changed into them. The old ones he
left behind, in the trash. He entered a steakhouse and ate a steak.
Then he turned back toward the station, walked several blocks along
the tracks to Ashton Supply, and pushed through the door. He looked
up and down the feed and seed counter for anyone he knew. Only the
proprietor, bald, narrow-eyed, was at all familiar.

You know of somebody headed for Eleven? Grant asked.

The proprietor's eyes took in Grant's new clothes and landed
finally on his face. What's your name? he asked, as if he ought to have
known it but had momentarily forgot.

Person.

Person, okay. Your people was here not long back. But no, I don't
believe nobody is headed out that way.

I just got off the train.

Looks like you have, he said. Tell you what. There's a dude around
here somewhere who I bet'll take you where you want to go. I believe
I seen him putting on every hat we got.

Grant thanked him. He found the dude as promised, standing
before a window trying to discern his reflection in the dusty glass. He
was tall, about thirty-five, with the rumor of a yellow beard and fresh-
bought ill-matched clothes. But there was a tragic leanness to him,
and a sharpness of eye that marked him as smarter than he looked
from a distance. One of his hands adjusted the hat on his head and the
other held a folded-up map.

Pardon, mister, but I been told you might give me a ride.

The dude twitched. His map rattled in his hand. Me? Really? he
said. The hat had a price tag attached to it which lay against his ear on
a string.

I need to get to Eleven.

The response was an apprehensive glance. He unfolded the map
and turned it around in his hands.

It's right the other side of the flats, Grant said, here. He leaned over and put his finger on the place. The dude had a scent to him, a boozy sort of perfume.

Well, that isn't on my way.

Where're you going?

He fingered the cuff of his coat, lambskin with wool on the inside, too hot for the weather. Nowhere, really, he said.

◆

The dude's name was Ted Purcell and he came from Peoria, Illinois. He seemed to name the town not with the expectation that Grant would recognize it but to impress upon him the great distance he had come. People from the east had a tendency, Grant noticed, to consider travel by car or train or airplane rigorous and brave. Knowing what he did about life there, Grant supposed this was a sensible thing for them to think. Still, he only gave Purcell his name and offered no congratulations. They were riding old route five in Purcell's new red Ford pickup, its elaborate radio failing to draw a clear station. Purcell had bought the hat and was wearing it now, the thong cinched tight under his chin.

So what do you do out here, Grant?

Raise sheep. But I been away awhile.

Is that so? I'm away myself.

Grant could only nod in answer.

You could say I'm on a little vacation. I'm a salesman, not door to door, or rather I go door to door you could say to big companies, and sell them the numbers they need to operate. I sell information, statistics. That might seem funny to you.

No.

Oh? Purcell said. Okay, good.

He reached out and turned off the radio, but by now the static had fused with the sounds of the engine and asphalt, and its sudden absence shocked them into silence. It felt like they had taken flight. A while later a truck with a wide wooden bed clattered by, heaped with hay bales. Some of the hay fluttered against the windshield and Purcell ran the wipers, though the hay had already blown away by itself. White-faced sheep were clustered on a distant hillside. Breeding season was long under way, and a current of emotions roiled through Grant, dizzying and strange. His palms and forehead perspired.

A kind of vacation, Purcell said. Usually, since I travel a lot with my work, I take my vacations at home. With my wife and daughter. I'm married to a terrific lady.

He held up his ring for Grant to see.

But this time I don't know. I just don't know what I'm doing out here, I really don't.

He continued: It's beautiful country out here, don't you think?

I don't tire of looking at it, Grant admitted, and this was exactly what he had been thinking, that to see a hillside covered with sheep filled him up near to overflowing. He licked his lips, sitting straight as if to keep from spilling.

Purcell said, How much farther along here are you?

Not much.

The first buildings came into view a good two miles out, wind-raked board structures half leaned over and filled with weeds. It was as if Eleven had tried to grow once, but its extremities had shriveled and died of their bloodless distance from the town's weak heart. There were probably old men who could tell him who had lived out here. Now cattle were grazing around and in the wasted buildings.

Here were a couple of farms run by drunks, with their ragged mongrel stock rooting in the trampled pastures. Whenever Grant's father culled a ewe with a bad jaw it was to these men he sold it cheap. And then came Eleven itself, low, blown dry, its paint peeling. Patchy-looking bored horses foraged out behind the post office and market and garage. Grant signaled to Purcell to pull over in front of the bar, marked as such only by the chipped tiles set into the front stoop which crookedly spelled out the word BAR. Purcell obliged and shut off the truck. Stillness settled over them like a tarp.

Wow, Purcell said. This is your home town?

Not strictly speaking. It's the nearest town to it.

A couple of men had come out of the bar and were gawking at Purcell's truck. Grant knew them. One he had finished high school a year behind. The other was the first one's father. They owned the garage across the street, but the bar was where you had to go to pay for your gas.

I appreciate the ride, Grant said.

Purcell flicked his finger at the keys where they hung from the ignition. Are you going in for a drink? he said.

In fact Grant had thought he'd just ask somebody for a ride home. Some part of him didn't want Purcell to know exactly where he came from. But as his hand tightened around the door handle he told Purcell that he could stand a drink.

I believe I'll join you then, if you don't mind.

All right, Grant said. But lock these doors. My bag.

The father and son looked them over good as they passed. Their name was as lost to Grant as he imagined it was to others, but it didn't matter. One could be identified with respect to the other—the son, the father—like a couple of undistinctive boulders notable for lining up in a particular way. They were a landmark, a point on the map.

Inside, Grant discovered that a radio had been added to the bar. A Maddox Brothers song was playing. Nobody danced. Instead there was a rhythmic sort of drinking, a methodical scrubbing away of all memory of work. It made a sound, a throbbing human static of brittle voices. He knew the sound pretty well but in his absence it had taken on a humorless intensity he didn't like. He recognized men who had been in school when he left town, whose eyes, in the interim, had crystallized into malevolent little pearls. All this he appreciated in a matter of seconds, a few steps beyond the threshold of the bar. He stopped Purcell with a hand.

I ain't leaving with you, he said. Don't get caught short in here. Some of them come in looking for a dog to kick, and you don't want to be it.

This is really something else, Purcell was saying. Wow.

Grant saw two men looking at him from a table, one seated and one standing. The sitting one was named Cotter. He was a towering hand of about sixty with an exhausted, disproportionate face, who had occasionally worked at the ranch. The other man fixed things, Grant couldn't recall his name. This second man had been getting up and now he walked past them and out of the bar.

Grant met Cotter's eyes. I'm gonna talk to that man there, he told Purcell.

Okay, go right ahead.

He went to the table and sat down. Working for my father these days? he said. Cotter had a glass of something black and viscous-looking in front of him. His eyes tumbled over Grant's face.

Up until recent, he enunciated, like they were foreign words from a book.

You quit?

Cotter smacked his lips. Been away, have you?

Yep.

Where to?

The Atlantic Ocean. I fished out at sea.

You want to know the truth? Cotter said. I'm still working at your place. But I ain't working for your father no more, cause your father has gone and quit this county, just like you done.

Grant waited a moment before saying, Quit where to?

I ain't with him, so I don't know.

I'm coming back, Grant said, and since it didn't seem like enough added, I'm back for good.

Cotter nodded, examining him as if he was some rare animal, subtly different from the common variety. If Grant remembered right, Cotter had a wife once who quietly walked out on him. He moved onto the ranch and worked there two years, frequently neglecting the animals and buildings and pens and fences he was supposed to maintain, in favor of a lot of private drinking. During the second winter he nearly froze to death, after which he was fired. Grant might have been ten at that time. Cotter said, Who in the hell is that you come in with?

A man who gave me a ride from Ashton.

Looks like he needs a wet-nurse. He turned to Grant. And you look awful pretty yourself. A smile seemed to be thinking about appearing on Cotter's face, but it never arrived.

Grant opened his mouth to reply but the new clothes were too complicated to explain. Already he was changing his mind, wishing he had asked Purcell to take him all the way. So are you headed out there? he asked Cotter. Out home?

If you could call it that, Cotter said nodding.

But you're going.

Wouldn't be in such a hurry if I was you. He leaned back in his chair. You had better drink something.

Grant obeyed. They sat and watched Purcell as he fell in with a couple of show riders at the bar. The riders were lanky and polished, kids by the look of them, shooting glances at one another behind Purcell's back. They were buying him whiskeys which he haggled over with the bartender, demanding he bring the bottles up close so he could look at the labels. The riders had a great laugh at this and slapped Purcell too hard on the back.

Grant fell into a protective frame of mind. Plenty of people were laughing in this bar tonight but all of it seemed to be at somebody's expense. At every roaring table was a man with his chin in his lap. Just once, Grant thought, he'd like to hear a good joke. He would enjoy a good gentle kidding.

His mother used to be funny, before Wesley took sick. It was no specific memory that told him this but a general sense of absence, like a room shut for winter that nobody remembers to open back up. In fact he couldn't place a smile on her face in his mind, nor could he recall the face entirely, only its individual features, without particular expression. He could remember the sound of his own high laughter, and Max's strange chuckle, knowing and sharp for a child of two.

Cotter must have come the spring after Wesley died. The chinook ought to have brought them some kind of hope and instead it brought Cotter. He arrived on foot having got a ride as far as the crossroads.

Grant was playing on the front porch with the younger boys and Cotter simply walked up the road and asked for their daddy. It was never clear how the men knew each other but John Person must have owed Cotter a chance. In any case their mother didn't like him and never once looked him in the eye. And here Cotter had outlived her, against all reason.

By now Purcell had put on a talking load and was audible where Grant sat, not in sense but in tone. The riders asked him questions and Purcell blurted answers, slurring and spitting his words. The three of them seemed to come to some agreement. They headed for the door, Purcell in the lead and the riders behind him with their fingers twitching at their sides. Grant didn't like the look of it. He was angry at Purcell for coming in here and angry at himself for letting him.

He got up and Cotter followed. Outside Purcell was fishing in the glovebox of the truck. The riders leaned against the bed waiting, one with his boot on the runner, rubbing the toe back and forth over the bright paint. They regarded Grant with proprietary glances but turned away entirely when Cotter filled the doorway behind him.

Grant said, Purcell, what in the hell are you doing?

Got to show these fellas something.

He turned around holding a gun. It dangled in his hand like a rag: an old-fashioned revolver, something he might have got at an antique store. He said, It's this thing I've been working on. Okay, where do we go to do this?

One of the riders motioned for him to follow. Grant put his hand on Purcell's arm and Purcell trained a dark look on him, a thing outside common understanding, intense and prophetic like a ewe in the bloody heat of birthing. It occurred to Grant that a man ought not to remind him of a sheep. He tightened his grip.

Leggo, Purcell said and jerked away. He turned to the riders. Okay, fellas, come on.

Cotter followed the three of them but Grant stayed behind to lock the door of the truck. Only while slamming it shut did he notice through the window a busy ring of keys splayed on the seat.

They went around back where beyond a half-acre square of weeds lay a dark and empty pasture, grown over with the baked bloomless stalks of wildflowers. They climbed a split-rail fence where a beam had slipped out of its notch and under moonlight gathered around Purcell while he fiddled with the gun. Off to the west a long hill was humped like a spine. Behind it lay home.

Okay, you ready? Purcell asked. He must not have expected an answer because he lifted the gun and started firing, pulling the trigger with a spasmodic motion and bringing his open palm down on the hammer for another round, a flip-cock, like a movie actor: one, two, three and four almost at once, five, and he staggered back on the sixth. His heel struck a clump of earth and he fell, and the shot went wild, straight up in the air. In the long seconds after, as the last report decayed, Purcell moaned and stirred and patted the ground around him for the gun. Cotter was the one who stepped up and moved it out of reach with his boot. The two men regarded each other. Under the moon Purcell's eyes were clear, and he blinked and a smile spread over his face like a stain. Then the riders laughed and one of them made a kind of rodeo holler, and Purcell sat up and shook his bare head. It was not clear what had become of his new hat.

He extended his hand, and there was quiet again as Cotter clasped it and began hoisting Purcell up. Then they all heard the whickering whistle and felt a sharp snap conducted through the ground to their feet. A little cloud of dust leapt up six inches to the right of Cotter where the bullet had hit.

Cotter paused to glance at the dust cloud moving off, then he pulled Purcell closer with one hand and used the other to knock him back down again. No insects were chirping in the wake of the shot, and the blow made a clear wet crack like a piece of meat hitting an iron pan. Purcell stood his ground a moment until Cotter let him go, and then he folded over and lay flat out on the ground. Cotter bent down, prised the slug out of the dirt, and tossed it onto Purcell's chest.

Maybe the riders had anticipated beating Purcell themselves. Their dejection was plain as they cleared their throats and turned back toward the bar. After a minute Cotter left too, and so did Grant. He felt bad for Purcell but what the Peorian had done was stupid.

In front of the bar Cotter was getting into a truck that Grant recognized as his father's. When he asked Cotter to wait, Cotter glared at him. I thought you wanted a ride home.

My bag, Grant said. It's locked up in his truck.

The two of them stood looking in Purcell's window awhile, at Grant's bag and the keys on the seat. Cotter said, How bad you need that bag?

It's got a lot of money in it.

Cotter nodded. He went over to the stoop, where he asked a couple of sitting women to move. They did, and he pulled a loose wedge of cement from the step. Then he turned around and flung it through the truck window. Glass splashed across the interior. He reached in and pulled out the bag and tossed it onto the bed of Grant's father's truck, then carefully replaced the chunk of cement.

I got work in the morning, Cotter said, let's go. He got in behind the wheel.

Grant wanted to rouse Purcell or at least put the keys in his pocket for when he came to. But his bag had been moved and he realized the necessity of moving with it. He took a last look at the bar's open door and got in the truck.

·

Cotter drove fast enough to kill them both. They climbed the hill obliquely and crested after several switchbacks, then briefly followed the ridge and angled down into the valley. The road ruts gripped and expelled their tires, flinging them from side to side. Whitetail deer leapt in the grass behind a roadside fence, and when the fence disappeared the deer came in slow motion across the road. Cotter missed them and swore. Grant didn't know if this was due to the close call or because he'd half hoped to strike one a deadly blow and bring it home to slaughter.

He felt the turn with his body's memory before Cotter spun the wheel to make it. They came to a stop in front of the gate and Grant got out to pull it open. When Cotter had driven through, Grant shut the gate and climbed back in. The road was deeply furrowed and uncared for. Grant's teeth knocked against each other and he understood for the first time how distant this place was from the one he used to know. On either side, beyond the headlights, the land was swallowed by darkness, as if the moon had been extinguished. Fixed above them, it was like a moon in a painting, illuminated without casting light. The land rose in front of the truck, and then the rise was behind them and the ranch stood blackly, outlined by a less comprehensive darkness. No lights shone in the windows. Cotter pulled up and turned to him and said, Good night, boss.

I ain't your boss, Cotter.

You're gonna be. The wound of his mouth took on a grin's shape. Don't get on your high horse and fire me.

Grant was left holding his bag in a still cloud of blue smoke near a dry tire-carved trench in the yard. The buildings were beginning to etch themselves into a sly clearness around him. Off to his left was the sheep shed, and he could tell at first by scent and then by sight that the animals were in it. Ewes spilled out along the fences like snow-clumps, sleeping. Beyond the shed the rams were likely penned, as the ewes by this time had been bred and would be coming down out of heat. Pretty soon they would go to winter pasture.

Up ahead at a bend in the road was the equipment shed and to its left the horse barn with the chickens penned up beside it, and a small yard. Rising on the right, hugged by the road, was the hill that ran up behind the house; past that was where the hands were quartered. On the hill was the pasture and starveout, where nothing was moving that Grant could see. The house stood at the base of the hill like a wagon that had careened down it and never again been touched. It lay barely held together by force of habit alone. Grant entered it, passing the woodpile arranged beneath the eave. The pile was insufficient to last the winter. He would have to go up the hill and skid down some logs as soon as he was settled. Inside, the house was cold and dark. He moved to the stove by memory and touched it. No heat.

Surely Max was here. But the house seemed empty, emptier than it ever had when he was the only one in it. He breathed the stagnant air and it smelled arid, like the outdoors. His quick breaths made him cough. The cough echoed.

He skirted the tables and chairs and felt his way up the stairs. At the top he found the hallway lit by that painted moon, suspended in the exact center of the paneless window at the hall's end. Two doors on each side, all shut. His own was on the left, nearest the window, with Max's across the way. The room that had been his parents' waited for him behind its warped door. A layer of dust coated the hall floor, with a scuffed track leading through it, ending at Max's room. Grant stood still listening and could hear neither his brother's breathing nor the movement of his body in the bed.

His own door yielded to a gentle push and cracked open with the small sound of a breaking seal. Bitter air flowed out. It was as if the room had preserved the cold from winters past especially for his return. He left the door open and went inside.

Nobody seemed to have been in here while he was gone. Enough grit had coated the windows to render them near opaque to the moonlight, and his bed was made in just the formal manner he would have made it were he planning to leave for a time. A couple of Indian arrowheads lay on the bureau, a folded handkerchief, a jawbone shaped like a crooked finger with a few teeth adhering to it, which he had found on the range and believed had come from an antelope. He set his bag on the bed and opened the dresser drawers. There were his clothes, and a few rocks with the shapes of ancient shells and leaves embedded in them, and a pack of cards depicting a tropical beach scene, and a photo of a girl he had gone to a dance with once and who had died of pneumonia not long after. He took off his clothes and dropped them on the rug, a crooked gray thing his mother had made out of rags, and put on a red union suit and a pair of woolen socks with holes in the heels. He shivered while his body warmed the fabric. Then he pulled the stale sheets back and got in under them, and stared at the wall at the bed's foot where a pencil picture was tacked. Max had drawn it as a child. It was a picture of the doglegged U of the valley with the house and the grounds nestled in the middle, from the vantage point of the hill out back. He put himself in the drawing, here in this bed under the northeast roof corner, and imagined himself to be asleep there, and soon enough he was.

•

He opened his eyes to the sight of Max in the doorway watching him. His brother was narrower than he was, his dark hair parted in the middle, his face stern and shaven and watchful with the clear blue eyes of their mother. He had the artificial stillness of a sitter in an old photograph. It seemed to Grant as the sleep left him that Max had likely been planning this meeting for years, and it was part of the plan that Grant should speak first, so he did.

I got your letters all at once. It was after everything happened. And then, when Max's expression failed to break, he said, I'm sorry.

Max raised his arm and rested it on the jamb. He was wearing his jeans and stocking feet and a wool shirt, and he sniffed in the way he always had on cold mornings.

Dad ain't here.

Cotter told me. Grant sat up and the dust came off him and the bed. Where's he got to?

Damned if I know.

How long's he been gone?

Couple of weeks.

Grant swung his feet out from under the bedclothes and set them on the floor. The boards chilled his heels. So where are we then? he said. We got a herder still? They ready to go to range?

Max met the questions with a hard glare and Grant saw how it was going to be. It ain't my problem, Max said. It ain't my goddam problem because you are on your own here, brother. Because I am planning to disappear myself.

Grant got up and pulled his pants on. Max had turned twenty this year, if he remembered right. Okay, he said, where are you off to?

Damned if I know, Max said.

There was not much of their father in Max's face. Some, though, at this moment: a studied expressionlessness which failed to conceal his satisfaction that things had gone bad in much the way he'd anticipated. But mostly Max was a ghost of their mother, with his high smooth brow and small mouth and thin nose that drew the eyes close together. In fact he might have been called feminine if not for the way the flesh gripped the bones in his face. If Grant squinted he could almost see her, waiting in the doorway for him to leave the room. This is what Max was doing, waiting. Grant obliged. Max led him down the hall and set his hands on their parents' bedroom door. He pushed it open.

It was me and Dad and Doc Lafitte, he said. Dad over on her left side there and Doc holding her by the wrist on the right, and I was in this chair at the foot. Just so you know exactly how it happened.

The bedclothes had been left mussed, the chairs off true in their places as if they'd just been got up from. The little closet was open and her handful of dresses hung up in it, a big straw hat on the shelf above them and shoes on the floor. The bureau that had been filled with their father's things was partly emptied, the drawers gaping, his wallet and comb gone from the top.

I think I got the picture, Grant said.

Max went back to his room and came out with a suitcase in one hand and a paintbox in the other. The box had an easel attached that could be unfolded and set up out of doors. Max had gotten this as a gift for his fourteenth birthday and occasionally took it out and painted pictures with it, but rarely had he offered to show them, nor had anybody asked to see. He passed Grant, who still stood at the open door, and vanished around the corner of the stairs. Grant went down after him.

Max was sitting on the floor pulling his boots on.

Who's the herder? Grant asked from the bottom of the stairs. Is it still Murray?

Yep.

He's coming?

Said he was.

Grant went over and stood by his brother. How about the record books? They out in the shed?

Max said, I ain't touched 'em. He stood up and took his coat off the hook and put it on.

How about the flock? Grant said.

Max grabbed his hat. He turned to Grant, putting it on his head. I would have to say the flock has seen better days. But like I said. It ain't my problem. He bent down for his box and bag and grinned without particular scorn. Maybe you'd like to open that door for me.

Grant opened it.

Cotter was outside standing by the idling truck. Behind him the sheep were bleating on the browsed muddy grass and the sun was beginning to ignite the ridgetop on the opposite side of the valley.

Grant called out to Cotter, You're coming back?

So long as you can pay me, I'll be back.

Max had set the suitcase down and was sticking out a hand for Grant to shake. Good luck, brother, he said.

Grant's hands were under his arms against the cold. Suddenly angry, he kept them there. This is what you really want to do? I don't know what there'll be for you when you come home.

Max's smile remained but lost its carelessness, tightening up at the edges, showing signs of effort. Didn't say nothing about coming home, he said, his hand falling. And he walked out to the truck.

Grant watched it pull away and over the rise, and then he was alone. He blinked at the gathering light. The sunline was creeping down the mountainside. More ewes emerged from the shelter and jostled one another looking for a clump of uneaten grass. He went to the fence. Here it had come unfastened from a post and gaped out like an old boot top. He pushed the wire up against the pine and bent a rusted staple around it, and when he let go the staple gave way and rattled on the freed wire. He ran his tongue over his thumb and tasted the pitch there.

He did not know where to begin.

•

Cotter set to work as soon as he came back. He parked the truck directly in front of the barn and released the horses into the pasture behind it. Grant called to him that he would be in the shed seeing to the books. Cotter nodded and continued working.

The equipment shed housed a rarely employed tractor, fencing, feed, paint, water pipes, tools for shearing and the collapsed wooden pens for lambing and a lot of rusted junk. The lights still worked. Grant slid the door shut behind him and picked a path to his father's desk. There were shelves bolted to the walls with ledgers and manuals lined up on them. A lamp with a cracked green glass shade leaned over a tin cup full of pens. The calendar his father had used for a blotter showed the month of June.

The oaken chair at the desk was worn smooth around the seat and armrests, and when Grant sat down on it the joints adjusted soundlessly like a man's. He opened the desk drawers. One was packed with files marked by year with that year's tax forms inside. The other drawers had tools in them or machine parts.

He reached up to the shelf and took down the last few years' books. Each began with a penciled inventory of land and stock and feed, followed by all bills outstanding and accounts unsettled. Then came the year's receipts and expenses and a record of production. John Person had run the ranch on a cash basis and the numbers ought to have been simple and clear. But for some reason the books had gone slovenly in recent years, with question marks appearing at the ends of columns and some not filled in at all, the penmanship itself staggering above and below lines and the totals at year's end left uncalculated. The erratic accounting dated from before the war and only intensified in the years Grant was gone. In the column marked STOCK for 1946 there was a barely legible notation—

circling 80? 100? 120?

—meaning, Grant guessed, that a hundred or so head had been killed by an infection of circling disease. It was bad that the sheep had been lost but worse that his father couldn't figure out how many.

He saw that a solid inventory of stock had been taken in January, one of the few sure figures in the ledger. The number was a full third less than five years before. They appeared to have under a thousand head now.

He took out a stack of files and read the tax forms of the past three years. They looked clean. He didn't see how they could be correct but there was no use worrying about that now. Instead he spent several hours estimating what they were owed and what they hadn't yet paid, and made a list of names of clients and creditors. These he wrote right into the ledger. The figures came out crooked from his unpracticed hand which had written near to nothing for a long time: the muscles remembered their fishing work and let him know they preferred it to this. In the end he came up with two figures, bound to be wrong: $2,100 and $9,700. The first was what was owed them, the second what they owed.

The men he spoke to on the telephone were brusque and polite, reading the numbers off to him without judgment. He didn't tell them whether they would soon be paid and they didn't ask. Grant made the calls sitting on a kitchen chair, and while he waited for responses paged through a four-year-old Montgomery Ward catalog hanging from a nail on the wall nearby. Somebody had bored a hole in the upper left-hand corner of the catalog and threaded it with twine, thinking to do exactly what Grant was now doing. Grant guessed that not much had ever been ordered from it.

The kitchen and supper room were all of a piece, the kitchen floor fitted with narrow dark boards and the eating area with cheap pine planks. Once the entire floor had been packed dirt, up until Wesley died. Soon afterward, Edwin got the idea that his brother's death was attributable to dust and vowed to raise the kitchen floor up off the ground. He learned how to cut and fit floorboards from a book and worked sporadically on the project for seven years, until he shot himself. The floor was never finished. For some time the table stood half on the new floor and half off, with cement blocks propping up the orphaned legs. The pine planks had been nailed down since Grant left. They were poorly measured and a gap of several inches between the wall and floor ran along the far side of the room.

Not long before his suicide Edwin confessed to Grant that he believed he himself killed Wesley, by whispering in his ear that night during supper. Though Grant begged Edwin to tell him, he never learned what it was he whispered.

By the time Grant finished his calls it was one in the afternoon. He'd been slightly wrong about the figures. They were owed less than eighteen hundred and had fallen almost eleven thousand behind. That he could use the money he'd earned to settle nearly every outstanding account seemed a fitting penance, but the decision to do it was slow in coming. It was also possible to sell the ranch and everything on it, but this raised the problem of finding their father, who owned it. Or he could keep his money against future catastrophe and run the outfit as if he had nothing whatever to his name.

He might have decided right then had the door not crashed open and the herder appeared. His dogs rushed in around him and stood sniffing the air, bristling with suspicion.

I'm taking the flock, Murray said. He gazed at Grant, seeming not to register who he was or who he was not. Confident now that Grant was no threat, the dogs came to him and smelled his open palms.

Let me come have a look first. I been away.

Murray blinked at him as if he couldn't see the point. He turned and walked out into the yard.

Grant put the ledger down on the table and followed. There wasn't much to Murray, a snarl of dirty black hair, brown trousers and vest, a nervous little face that looked like it had been out in a lot of bad weather. Around him hung an air of physical weakness and ill health. But in fact he was strong as an ant, able to perform without effort tasks a man twice his size would need a machine to do. Grant had seen him lift up a sheep and dunk it in the insecticide, the pasty bare arms holding the struggling animal in place for the requisite time, and then hoisting it back up and out of the tub as if it were an infant and doing this over and over for hours, without anyone's help. He was powered by will, violent and potent.

Now he was inside the fence with his dogs, and the ewes moved like blown smoke to the back gate. Murray called out to the dogs and they came around the flock and lay down by the fence. The sheep stood at anxious attention; a gentle wave of baas rippled over them. Murray stood with his hand on the back gate waiting as Grant came in the front from the road.

The sheep were Rambouillets and crosses, mostly white-faced, some black. They cleared a space around him as he entered, sidling almost, seeming to pretend that it wasn't Grant's presence but some random whim that made them go. Grant found himself ill at ease among them. From a distance of several feet they didn't look good: he saw long necks and paunches and patchy fleece. There were surely culls here, ewes that oughtn't to have been bred but had been bred all the same. He caught one by the neck and dock and moved her out of the band. Her head was scurry, the chest bony and thin. Others had weak or crooked legs or showed signs of disease.

One year could not have done this to them. His father had been letting them go bad for some time, at least since Grant had left, probably before.

He walked through the front gate and around the fence to Murray, who was letting the dogs lead the ewes out the back. Beyond the property Murray's piebald horse was hitched to his camp wagon, a rickety thing in a half-barrel shape fitted with truck wheels and a high stovepipe. The sight of it angered Grant, it seemed to speak to the whole rotten state of the outfit, and he said to Murray, It looks like a goddam hospital in there.

Murray swung his red face around and replied in a mutter. I bring 'em home at least as good as when I come for 'em. Whatever happens happens when I ain't here.

He didn't look at Grant while he talked. His mouth barely moved to let the words out.

I don't care a whit for you or your brother, he went on, his brogue like a marble in his mouth. I used to been working for your father and now I'm working for the sheep. When you got 'em they're your own responsibility. That's all I care to say.

He moved off calling to the dogs. When he reached the wagon he mounted it and led the flock out across the valley floor. Grant watched him awhile and then went back in the house. Upstairs he took the roll of bills from his bag and stuffed it into his shirt pocket. Then he collected the record books from the table and brought them back out to the shed. With the sheep gone the yard seemed deserted. Neither Cotter nor the truck was anywhere in sight. The horses stood flank to the sun in their pasture. Inside, at his father's desk, Grant found a box of envelopes and wrote a name and an amount on each. When he was through he counted out the bills and sealed them inside.

4

It was evening when he next approached the house. He could hear the unfamiliar voices of two men behind the door, one of them talking and laughing at something, the other one hoarsely mumbling back. He stepped up onto the porch and the boards creaked. The voices fell silent. After a moment he opened the door and walked in.

They were seated across from each other at the table with a deck of cards spread between them face up and scattered, as if the game was long over. Both looked up at Grant, one smiling and the other with a stubborn sort of incomprehension. The smiler wore a felt hat which he took off and set on the floor by his chair. The other one had his chair tipped back. He pushed himself forward and the legs struck the boards with a hollow sharp crack.

I'll bet you're Grant Person, the smiler said. He was about forty, lanky and coarse. His had been the mumbled voice. It put Grant on edge, seeming with each word about to give way to a cough. The other man was half the smiler's age. He looked down at the table and began pushing the cards into a little pile in front of him. His big still shoulders and hung head gave him the appearance of a stump that had begun to grow back.

Grant stood on the threshold, cool air sweeping in behind him. He leaned back out and collected some firewood, then dumped it in front of the stove and shut the door with his foot. I don't believe I know you, he said.

Kittredge, said the smiler, and raised up a hand like a calling card. It was the left and was missing its middle finger at the first joint. Obviously it was the man's habit to present the injury baldly, in order to preclude discussion of it. Grant was sympathetic to this tactic but wondered how a man could lose a middle finger without doing any damage to the other ones. Kittredge gestured with the hand toward the younger man and said, Petey, you ought to give Mr. Person your name.

Pete Neeler, he said without taking his eyes off the cards.

We're in your kitchen, see, Kittredge said, because this is the usual time supper gets eaten. I suppose your brother has took off, has he?

Yes he has.

I wonder if Petey and me even have employment to look forward to.

At this Neeler raised his head and gawked at Kittredge. We sure better, he said. God damn we better. Even if we don't we got some money owed us, that's for sure.

Grant decided to ignore Neeler and direct his inquiries at Kittredge. He said, You two been staying out at the quarters?

Yep.

Is it just the two of you and Cotter out there?

Kittredge nodded. Your brother brought in some Mexican shearers, and there was some men helping out at breeding, but now it's just us all. No dogs, no girls. And he smiled again, or rather widened the grin that seemed to be the natural state of his mouth. Grant found himself returning it by instinct. It struck him that he hadn't had occasion to smile at anything or anybody for more than a week, and he remembered that a week ago he had in fact been out on a boat in the Atlantic Ocean. He thought that he might have an ally in Kittredge.

Well, he said, there's always enough work that wants doing. I don't know how long I can pay you to do it though.

Fair enough, said Kittredge.

Somebody's going to need to bring down some firewood. And I ain't been up to the ditch yet, but how's the headgate looking?

Could use cleaning up, I'd put money on that.

Okay. Okay, we ought to get that taken care of before the freeze. So there's some work for you.

At this point Neeler reared back and looked clearly at Grant for the first time. Out of the corner of his eye Grant saw Kittredge go rigid in his seat.

Your brother said you was in the war, Neeler said. You took a long time coming back, didn't you? Where you been, then?

It was possible to believe in the innocence of the question, judging by the voice alone. But Neeler had a challenge in his eye even if he didn't know its full import. His eyes were set far apart under wild thick brows, his face was a knot, pocked and blunt and dumb. Grant said, I was doing some work on a boat off the Atlantic coast. I didn't fight in any war.

But your brother said—

He wasn't talking about me. He was talking about our brother that didn't make it back. Grant gave Neeler a minute to register some remorse or at least embarrassment but his face remained vacant. So what do you like eating, Grant said, and maybe I can try fixing it.

Your brother makes beans with bacon and good biscuits, Neeler said. And coffee.

That so? Grant asked, directing the question at Kittredge.

Kittredge nodded.

Well, that is something I can do, anyway, Grant told them and moved to the pantry for the food.

◆

That night Grant found the broom leaning up against a wall of the pantry and began to sweep the dust out of the house. He did the kitchen and his own bedroom and then Max's. Max had emptied his bureau drawers but left much of what hung on the walls, drawings he had done in pencil, watercolor paintings of things Grant recognized from the valley, such as a certain rock set into a hillside or water flow-ing out of a spring. The pictures were spare and haunted, rendering the land as a scattering of crisscrossed lines and colored fields. Grant didn't know if they were good, only that they didn't represent his own understanding of the place. When he left the room he shut the door tight behind him.

He swept the hallway, erasing footprints: his own, Max's, maybe their father's. Then he moved into his parents' bedroom. He worked quickly, jabbing the broom into the visible spaces and pulling out the dirt. A presence here was urging him to finish the work and leave. At first he identified it as his mother's. But he trusted her death now and knew there was nothing left of her here. Not until he was through and the door was shut behind him did he understand: the presence was his father's, the presence of his absence, of his inevitable return. The house, the ranch belonged to John Person, and surely he would come back to it and would condemn Grant for what he'd failed to do, as he never had years before.

Before Wesley, Thornton had shared Max's room, and Robert, Grant's. Only Edwin had his own. This was the room still unswept, and Grant hesitated to enter. The window at the hall's end framed a moon barely changed from the night before. Its cold light threw the tendons and veins of his hand into sharp relief, into a landscape lunar in character. He wiggled his fingers, putting shadows into motion, and finally pulled the string that brought the hall light to life. The moon was lost in glare. Grant pushed open the door.

Only Edwin's bed remained, supporting a bare lopsided feather tick and surrounded by chairs, as in a theater. He recognized the chairs. They had come from the kitchen. As many as fifteen people had eaten there once, when the family was larger and there was more work to do, and someone, probably their mother, had hidden away the unoccupied chairs when the extra hands disappeared. Against the bare walls the chairs looked penitent and skeletal, locked outside time. The sight of them made Grant think of the men who had sat on them, gone from his memory until now: the haggard truckster who

came with week-old city newspapers and left a day later with wool, a
chore boy who carried water and kept the woodboxes stocked, the
extra herders and camp tender, men whose names were lost to him
but whose faces could be recalled piecemeal: a knobbed drunkard's
nose, a drooping gotch ear that came from sleeping flat in the dirt and
never washing, a row of yellow teeth with a laugh behind it. Then, he
could not have imagined running the place without them. But they
had made do when it was necessary, and when a brother died they did
without him too. When Grant left they did without even him.

Now it looked like they hadn't done well enough. The ranch was
dying, there was no getting past it, drying up under a thirsty sun, and
no simple ministrations would set things right. He would send away
that money in the morning but this was a mercy, not a cure.

Or so it seemed to Grant. It was best to avoid much hope. He
backed out of Edwin's room and shut the door, leaving the chairs in
their lifeless attitudes and the dusty floor undisturbed.

·

There was a light above the front door, cobwebbed beneath the eaves,
and when he went out Grant switched it on. The yard came into view
around him. He walked up behind the house, through the pasture,
until he came to the starveout fence. The rusted wire bowed as he
climbed over and stayed bowed when he was past. No grass grew here
and the dust shifted underfoot like sand. He followed the fenceline
up over the rise until the house was out of sight and the headstones of
his mother and brothers shone like open palms under the moon.
There was a gate, which he opened. Beyond the graves the hill
dropped off into a coulee and it was here that a night wind struck the
bank and crept up over its lip. Grant was standing in the wind's path.
His pantcuffs shackled his ankles. His mother lay under him.

They had paid for a properly engraved stone, same as they had for
the others. Just her name and dates. He crouched and ran his fingers
through the cuts. The ground was gently mounded but likely had been
more so, not long before. He thought they ought to have covered her

with boulders to keep the dirt from blowing away. The other stones stood pitched forward in the wind, all but Wesley's, which somebody had piled the dirt back around and tilted windward as a precaution. It appeared to Grant that the graves were creeping closer to the bank, and in fact a fence post already hung by its staples over the edge.

He peered down and then lowered himself into the creekbed. Rocks half buried in the bank were blown smooth. A few desperate patches of brush clung to the loose dirt. Above them he could see something else jutting, a split plank with a nail head protruding, another one a few feet past it. He realized these were the boxes that contained his brothers, the ground around them eroded away. He stood on tiptoe to touch the wood. Blown grit had sanded the varnish off a corner of one box and much of the lower edge of another. The one exposed longest was worn so far through that soon there'd be a hole and the coffin would fill up with dust. He pushed his fingers into the earth and pulled away a clayey lump, which he pressed against the corner, trying to make it stick. But it fell off and scattered around his boots. The hungry wind thrashed at his back. For a minute he let it press him to the bank, and he smelled the dirt and felt the ground strain against the punishing wind. Then he reached up and seized the hanging post and pulled himself back up onto the hill.

•

When he got back to the house, Kittredge was waiting for him with a bottle in his hand and an apology on his face. He said nothing until they were at the table with glasses in front of them.

I'm real sorry about all that. He ain't mine but I got no choice but to keep him, y'see. It was with some embarrassment that Kittredge said this, his eyes averted, his jaw taut.

You're only responsible for what comes out of your own mouth, Grant told him.

Well, it sure don't hurt nobody for me to try keeping him in line.

Whose is he? Grant said, as if Neeler was a child. But that seemed to be how Kittredge regarded him.

A woman I used to know. She died of a tumor in her belly and she asked me would I look after Petey for her when she's gone. Well, I told her I would. That must have been about eight years back. I believe he's a little bit slow. Didn't seem that way when she passed on, but I suppose seeing as he was her boy and not mine I wasn't paying much attention, y'see.

You wouldn't of said no even if you knew what he was like.

No, that's right, Kittredge said nodding. You're right about that. Her husband lit out a long time back and nobody seemed to know where he was at. I wouldn't leave a boy to be no orphan, that's true.

Kittredge drank in little sips with his mouth barely opened. The two of them listened to the wind coming down on the house. Then Kittredge said, Petey didn't have no respect for your brother, maybe because they was the same age. I wouldn't put it past the boy to twist around his words.

Grant took his time replying. Our brother Thornton went instead of me, he said. His ship got sunk. My brother considers me to be a coward and I can't say I blame him.

Kittredge received these words without evident judgment. He nodded. My daddy died in the first war. Ain't no shame in keeping alive's what I say.

That's kind of you but it's not the full truth.

I don't suppose.

Grant could have argued further, he had it in him. But he kept silent. Without even trying he had befriended Kittredge and there was no point in riling him. They continued to drink as the house shuddered around them.

Nothing was worse to an easterner than silence. He would see in their eyes while he was talking that they were only half listening to him, because they were busy working out what they were going to say back. And if after they finished talking he tried to think through what he was going to say, they wouldn't give him time, they would just go right on ahead and say something else to fill up the empty space. Grant couldn't have said why this should be so but he guessed it was too much like dying. For them, being with another person without talking was like being side by side in the ground.

But he had gotten used to it, so much that Kittredge's silence seemed heavy with significance, and he turned an eager face to the older man. Kittredge smiled, confused. Grant realized he was going to have to watch himself while he got reacquainted with the customs of the region. His mind raced with the ugly sound of his own voice as he said, How long you been working here?

Two years, Kittredge said.

You were here when my mother died.

Kittredge looked into his glass and turned it slowly on the table-top. I kept myself out of all that, he said.

Grant got the message: Kittredge wanted it kept that way. But he had to know, he had to find out what he could. And my daddy? he said. You were here when he left? He say if he was coming back ever?

Kittredge wiped his tired face and got up from the chair. I just came by to apologize is all. If we're gonna be working together, I just want to let you know how it is with the boy.

At the door he turned back to Grant, still at table, and spoke. One day he just weren't there no more. He didn't say nothing to me. Horse came back from town on its own.

Good night, Grant said to him.

Kittredge pulled his hat down tight and nodded. G'night.

•

It was hard sleeping in the familiar bed. The house complained in the wind. Every sound carried clearly through the old dry boards. Surely he would have woken his father leaving here that night. Grant could see him: propped on one elbow with Mama asleep beside him, he would have remained still and alert for hours, waiting, and then given up for good the second the sky lit. Going to town his father would have been ashamed of him, even more than he'd been during the war.

Grant rarely went to town in those days, once Thornton was dead. He usually let Max and his father go alone. Then, when it was just him and his mother at home, he would find a reason to go into the house and talk with her. By this time her hair was white but she still pulled it back in a ponytail like a girl. She sat at table mending something or making a list, her hands doing the work with what seemed excessive strength, the needle or pencil jabbing purposefully and calmly. She was calm even in grief. She asked him about whatever work he'd done that day and he told her. Sometimes he asked her about life in Iceland, but she only nodded as if it was a yes no question and said that it was no easier there than here. Until he was fifteen he didn't know the names of his grandparents, Einar and Finna, and by then they were long dead.

He believed he was the person closest to his mother, closer even than his father was. There was little evidence for this, their conversations could not have been called personal. Nor were they affectionate: she touched him only when he was sick or hurt, and when the rope cut his leg she held his hand while the doctor applied a stinging poultice. She held him after Robert's funeral, or he assumed it was her, he could only remember being held and not who was doing it.

For no reason he remembered a textile dealer in Eleven who used to bring his mother an orange on her birthday. Maybe he did this for all the ranch women, to lure them into town to buy cloth, Grant didn't know. But nobody else had ever brought his mother gifts. He realized he would never again see her peel and eat an orange.

He was cold, so he got out of bed and took another blanket from the bottom bureau drawer. Under the blankets, he considered that come winter and the real cold, he would have little trouble keeping warm. There were many blankets in the bedrooms and all of them were his now.

•

He woke before sunrise and went down to the kitchen. The moon was gone and the house had purpled in the near-light. He lit a fire and set water on to boil. Into a handled sieve he folded a clean cloth and he shook coffee from a canister kept out on the counter. When the water was hot he let it trickle through the grounds and into a cup until it brimmed over. He brought the cup and a kitchen chair out to the front stoop, and he sat there and sipped the coffee as the day brightened around him.

In time the far hill came into clear view and with it a moving dot on its face, following the lumbering trajectory of a bear. He watched it descend. It came in a zigzag, switching back here and there with the folds of the hill. For awhile it dropped out of sight beneath the slight rise of the nearer land, and Grant forgot it. But then it returned, visible between the sheep shed and barn, in the unmistakable form of a man afoot. Soon it had topped the rise and started down toward the fence. Grant leaned forward in his chair and brought the coffee to his lips. It was cold now. Could the man be Murray? If so, something bad had happened which had separated him not just from the flock but from his dogs and horse and wagon as well.

It wasn't Murray. This man was fat; his body swayed as he walked. When the man had nearly reached the fence Grant could see that he was wearing town clothes, a suit and no hat. He started to get up to meet him, but changed his mind. Any city man who'd walked down off that hill and come all the way here could take the extra few steps onto the porch. The sun was just starting to climb the hill behind him and its first rays to strike the distant ridge, and unless he missed his guess it had been fifteen or twenty minutes he'd been out here watching. Which was funny, because he couldn't fathom a man making it down off that hilltop in under an hour.

The man was in the road now, twenty yards away. Grant was almost grateful when he realized that it was the dead man he had discovered on the beach in Atlantic City.

He was much the same as before, corpulent and white, his eyes eaten raw by the salt water. He soundlessly mounted the steps and stood still before Grant, drawing no breath. Grant sipped his cold coffee.

So what'd you come for? he said.

The dead man's lips had retreated and two brilliant rows of false teeth arrayed themselves across the opening. An arm rose and the bleached hand at the end of it pointed to Grant's cup.

Grant looked down into it. The coffee had spilled over his fingers and clothes and patterned the porch underneath him. Suddenly it seemed to be burning. He dropped the cup and coffee fanned out over the boards. Full day had broken and Grant could see clearly now that it was in fact blood.

When he woke it was still night. Dread gripped him as he considered having to get up and go through it all again. He sat up in the bed panting. In time the dream lost definition, and he went down and made coffee in much the same way he'd dreamed. It was his mother's method, most of the men boiled theirs. When the sun came up he pulled on his boots and walked up around the back hill to the hands' quarters, a little row of plank shacks with chimneys sticking up out of them. Smoke was coming from one chimney and Cotter was out in front of another cutting wood with an ax. His breath formed clouds that hovered over him, and steam poured off his hands and out of his collar. Grant said, I got to go to town to pay some bills.

Cotter looked up, then went over to the truck and opened the door. He reached in and pulled out the keys and tossed them to Grant. Grant passed them from hand to hand while Cotter returned to splitting wood. He wondered if he should address Cotter as he would a friend or just tell him what to do. The latter, he supposed. They had nothing in common but work.

You got any particular plans for today?

No, Cotter said.

How about fixing up the sheep shed? Mays well get it out of the way before the cold.

Cotter nodded. He looked old in this infant light. Grant put the keys into his pocket and called on Kittredge.

It was Neeler who answered the door. He wore no shirt and his hairless chest looked stove in. Grant couldn't understand what he was doing here, there were two unoccupied cabins and he could have his own. Neeler stood staring at Grant until Kittredge came to the door behind him. Grant said good morning and suggested they get up on the hill and start skidding some logs down for firewood. He told them he would join them when he got back from town.

Okay, Kittredge began, you want we should—

We already got wood enough for our ownselves, Neeler said.

Petey, said Kittredge, stepping forward into the light. Neeler's hands were on the jamb and he filled up the opening, keeping Kittredge behind him. The boy's eyes were on Grant, as deeply interested as Grant had yet seen them.

Grant said, I'll barely fire up the cookstove except for your breakfast and supper. So you've got a responsibility. I'll meet you up the hill when I get back.

All right, Kittredge said quickly, sounds good to me. But Neeler stayed where he was, saying nothing, until Grant turned to go.

The truck still worked the same, turning over with a couple of coughs and a tap on the gas. He stopped it in front of the equipment shed and went in and got the envelopes. The ones that were going to Ashton he had written addresses on and the others he planned to deliver by hand. The sun lit up the windshield dust as he topped each hill, and behind it the valley shone like a haunt. On the county road he passed a brand-new rig he didn't recognize, but he raised a hand in greeting that the driver returned.

His coffee was rolling in his gut and refused to go to his head, where he wanted it. The dream had soured him. He put on the wipers and the dust streaked across the window and blew off. The radio said frost. Town came into view and he pulled over by the Sunrise restaurant and went in.

All six people there were familiar to him. Jean Tate was cooking. She was the sister of the girl whose picture he had in his bureau drawer, the girl who died. At the counter were the father and son drunks from the gas station. Three others shared a table, an old man and his sons. Grant knew the sons. All of them looked up when he came in and then turned back to their breakfasts. He sat at the counter, leaving a stool empty between himself and the drunks.

Welcome back, said Jean Tate. Want a couple of eggs?

Please. He turned to the drunks beside him and said good morning.

The younger said, A lot of coming and going up at your place these days.

It was uncertain if Grant was to take this as meaning, among other things, his mother. He chose to see it as an indiscretion and didn't pursue it.

Afraid so, he said. There was an Ashton newspaper on a nearby stool and he picked it up and read a few headlines.

Your amigo left here with a hell of a headache, the young drunk said, that pretty boy you brought in the bar. There was a certain wistfulness to his voice, as if he wished Purcell was still here to ridicule but would have to make do with Grant. Grant turned. The father slurped his coffee, wincing. He made no sign of noticing the conversation. Booze had seemed to loosen his skin and his face sat low on his skull. It was easy to see the son going the same way, in fact it was starting already, his features in the early stages of slipping off.

That so? Grant said.

The son laughed. Where in hell'd you pick him up, I want to know.

Ashton.

He snorted. Could of guessed as much.

Across the room, the old man and his boys got up. The old man threw a few bills onto the far end of the counter. The three nodded at Grant as they left and Grant nodded back. One of the boys looked over his shoulder as he passed through the door, and it wasn't clear to Grant who he was looking at, the drunks or him.

When Jean brought out his food she met his eyes. You ready for winter? she said.

Nope.

He ate in silence and left while she was cleaning up in back. The truck was still warmer than the air. He drove out to the grocery and paid Mrs. Healy in full, and she gaped at him as if he'd just handed her his own head. The horseman Klopfer counted out every bill right there in front of him. The man at the farm supply only nodded and said thanks. He saved the drunks for last to give them time to get from the Sunrise to the bar. It was there that he handed the old man his money. The old man took a single bill out, turned in his stool and gave it to his son, then he folded the envelope once without looking and shoved it into his coat pocket.

The rest he mailed at the post office. The clerk was a young man Grant didn't know, but Theroux the postmaster could be heard in back shouting bets into a telephone. Grant got his receipt and stood out on the sidewalk looking at it. It was done now, the money was gone. After awhile he went back to the Sunrise. Jean was alone with the paper spread out on the counter. He sat in front of her and she looked up.

How's your mother? he said.

Okay, she said. Daddy's all right. I'm living up above. She pointed at the ceiling.

You're making a living on what Nellie pays you?

Nellie's dead. I bought the place.

He nodded. It took some effort to say what he was thinking. Maybe I could come into town some night and see you.

Yeah, okay, she said simply. She looked like her little sister around the eyes and nose, except that her face was full like her mother's where her sister's had been sharp. She'd survived the same pneumonia that killed her sister. Grant was surprised she wasn't married to somebody. Maybe she had been.

What night?

Just show up. I won't be anywhere special.

When he got back to the ranch he could see Kittredge and Neeler up on the ridge at the edge of the trees. Kittredge jerked his arm and in a second or two Grant heard the rattle of a chainsaw. Across the yard Cotter was at work on the sheep shed. The sun had burned the clouds out of the sky and Grant was getting hot standing under it. He took off his jacket, went to the barn and saddled a horse. It wasn't one he knew but it let him on easy. He rode up the hill along a trail that had been there since before his parents came, worn by the home-steaders or the Indians or whoever came before them. The trail led him across the bald stumped hillside where the forest used to be, creased now with dry shallow ravines. A few of these had dugways cut on either side to let the horses through. Others he had to goad his horse into crossing. He came upon two horses tied to the ground, too close in his opinion to a cliffedge. He dismounted and peered over. Maybe twenty feet down. He went back and looped his reins around a stump, then continued to where the men were working.

Kittredge was cutting and Neeler sawing the branches off the felled trees. Logs were lying about along the treeline, too puny to have bothered with. The noise of the chainsaw stopped.

I'll start skidding them out, Grant shouted. Move into the woods a little and get some of the big ones.

Kittredge nodded. If he thought this suggestion a slight, there was no sign. But Neeler looked down at the tree he was sawing and then up at Grant as if comparing the two. Grant went back for his horse, tied a rope around a log and dragged it down the trail. He left it in front of the house and returned for another. They worked in this man-ner until two, when Grant made them dinner. Cotter had already come in and left an empty bean can behind, with a crusty punched-tin fork sticking out of it.

After dinner they worked until sundown, and all the next day. Sometimes the sun was covered by a cloud but mostly it stood out naked and fierce. It burned them and so did the wind.

That night Grant went back to town with Cotter, who was headed to the bar. When they got there Grant turned and started to cross the street. Cotter asked him where he was going.

I'm meeting Jean Tate.

Jean Tate? he said, as if he didn't know who it was.

Grant stood embarrassed, his desire exposed. But it was of no con-cern to Cotter. He shrugged and continued to the bar.

The Sunrise was open but it was a skinny kid working there, his scoliotic back straining over the grill. Grant went around behind the building and found a lighted door. He knocked twice and went in. A flight of stairs led him up to another door, standing slightly ajar, a thin strip of light from inside illuminating the stairwell. He knocked again and the knock forced the door open another inch. From inside came a voice too faint to understand. He pushed and the door gave way onto a simple apartment with a bed and chair and a radio on a round table. There was a sort of alcove with a stove and sink in it, and she was standing there cooking. He'd already eaten but when the smell reached him he felt compelled to eat a second time.

Eaten? she said. She had a wooden spoon in her hand and an expression on her face that neither welcomed him nor fended him off.

No, he said.

She reached up and took a plate from a doorless cabinet and set it on the counter next to another like it. Then she emptied a boiling pot into a colander and the colander onto the plates, and covered the noodles with whatever was in the pan.

Sit down, she said, and put the plates on the table. I'll be right back.

When she was gone he sat down. A sort of stroganoff. He was near to pitching over onto it, he was so hungry. It was as if all he'd eaten an hour ago got lost on its way to his stomach. This was a familiar kind of hunger, he'd felt it time and again on the *Rose Adams*, when a twelve- or eighteen-hour shift came to a close and his body suddenly remembered that there was such a thing as food. He strained to think about something else while he waited for her to return. What he thought about was kissing her. He had kissed her little sister, who slapped him and then kissed him back.

She came in with two pint glasses. They all know you're here, she said. They gave me hell about it.

Probably think we're up to something, he said.

Aren't we? She gave him his beer and sat across from him. Round-faced, small-breasted, shoulders wide for a woman, she looked like an owl. She shot him an owl's look, surprised and puzzled, like she'd just tricked herself.

I admit that crossed my mind, he said.

Eat, she said. They ate. The food was almost good enough to make him cry. It had been a long time since he'd eaten anything with seasonings in it. Neither of them looked up until they were through. Then she came around to his side and took him by the hand over to the bed.

•

I'm not ever marrying nobody, she said. I got myself engaged to Claude Miller, did you know him?

A little, he said. They were still in the bed, the sheets half on them.

He's in college, studying veterinary doctoring. Anyway, once we were engaged he made it pretty clear he didn't approve of my living by myself, and he said while he was at school I'd go live with his mother. She had a room ready for me. Well, I had to tell him to forget it. In fifty years I'm going to be in this very room, smoking a cigarette and looking out that window at what's left of that street. Mark my words.

Reminded of cigarettes she took a pack off the night table and lit one. The apartment was dark and the orange glow of the match danced over her skin. Grant wanted her again. But she said, Did you and my sister ever do it? She spoke in a low quiet voice, almost as if he wasn't supposed to hear. He considered how to phrase his answer, unsure of what kind she wanted. People aren't very sturdy inside, he thought; there are a hundred things either of us could say that would break the other. People shouldn't have that kind of power, they ought to have strong walls and no weapons. At least it seemed so at the moment.

We had a little tussle once, Grant said. But nothing came of it.

She opened up her mouth and closed it again, then burst out crying. He put his hand on her thigh. She said, Oh, hell, I was going to say I wish you said yes, so you could tell me about it. Then I thought better of saying something like that. She laughed.

You miss her.

Claude might not of seemed like such a terrible idea, she said, if I had her to talk to.

He said, Did you see my brother much while I was gone?

Her breath caught. She released it slowly and the air filled with smoke.

Not like this, she said.

He laughed. No.

She cradled her chin in her hand. I guess this town hasn't got whatever it is he thinks he needs. He never much liked the kind of talk that goes on around here. Folks look at him as funny, and I think he looks down on them.

You know he's left.

Heard it.

He said, You think he'll come back?

You did.

He moved his hand over, and into her. I did.

Don't get comfortable, she said.

◆

That fall they did a lot of work, and by the time it snowed the fences and buildings were fixed and a little money was coming in. Kittredge said that he and Neeler were going to Colorado to help out his mother. Grant drove them to the bus station, dreading a winter alone with Cotter.

Sometimes he saw Jean, never consistently, never once calling her first. The telephone was connected up with a lot of other people between here and town and somebody was always listening in; and though he didn't care what any of them thought about him he considered it unfair to subject Jean to their scrutiny. Besides that, she seemed satisfied with this arrangement. He would just go down to the Sunrise and eat dinner at the counter, then go over to the bar. After awhile he'd come back with a couple of glasses and they would drink them and then go to bed. Jean was solidly built, he liked the way she felt under his hands. Sometimes when Cotter wasn't along he'd stay the night and drive back in the morning.

He supposed he preferred her company to nights alone in the empty house. But mostly it felt like a cheat—it'd be wrong to rely on the pleasure of a temporary thing. She never said what she thought of him and he didn't want to know.

He did learn a lot about her dead sister. Claire had worn mud on her face nights. She tried to learn the piano but had lacked the aptitude. She'd been a fair cook and a good rider and had aspirations to own her own store, a dry goods or the like. Jean had the idea that she herself had only won her independence because Claire never got hers.

I wasn't made for leaving home, she told Grant. Not until she was dead did I start thinking I might. I can't explain that.

I don't guess you ought to.

She asked him if he felt the same way about his dead brothers. For some time he considered how to answer. The way he saw it, there wasn't much point in worrying about what might have been, not just because it's never going to be but because you're bound to be wrong anyway. All he felt about his brothers was that they were gone. He wouldn't have done some of the things he did if they had lived, but for all that, he might have done something even worse.

No, I don't, he said finally.

The answer silenced her a moment. I expect it would be different for you, she said.

Only once did he ask her if she wanted to come out to the valley with him. A kind of curtain came down over her face and she said no, she would have to be back at the restaurant real early. Of course he could have had her back in time, but it was obvious she would never spend a night in his house regardless.

That suited him. There was no need to get closer. Death had darkened the air between them and neither wanted to see the other too clearly.

Around Christmas one afternoon he stood in the road by the house and noted a certain blankness of sky to the north. It was coming on four o'clock and what sun they'd had that day was near to gone in clouds. Snow covered everything and the air was uncharacteristically still. He didn't know what his eye was telling him. December, blank sky. Nothing to get surprised at. He went in and lit the stove and cooked his supper with the radio playing. He tried to hum along to the holiday music but it made a hollow sound and he stopped. In awhile he'd finished with the food and prepared two plates and sat down at the table. He ate his dinner and thumbed through an old magazine. Then he got up and looked out the window. Beyond the swell of hill there was only blackness, not a single star in sight. He had stood here this morning and the sky had been clear and blue for a long time before it clouded up again. He pulled his boots on, went outside and walked up the road. It was cold and he wanted to fold his arms against it, but even alone after dark he wouldn't, ashamed for no good reason to be moved by weather. Halfway to Cotter's shack he realized what had brought him out here, and he ran. Cotter's door was slightly ajar. He pushed it open. Inside, the stove was cold and Cotter lay on the floor beside a fallen chair and an empty liquor bottle. He had pissed himself and vomit stained his shirt. Grant watched his chest until he saw it rise and fall. There was a pile of wood by the stove that Cotter must have brought in and forgot. That was what he'd noticed—no smoke. Grant got the wood lit and stripped Cotter and covered him up with bedclothes. He wiped his face with a wet cloth and tried to pour water into his mouth. Cotter sputtered and coughed as the fire took on life.

Grant pulled up the fallen chair and sat over Cotter, giving him water every few minutes and staring into the stove's open door. In half an hour Cotter opened his eyes. They came to rest on the fire as well. Grant handed him the water cup and he took a few sips. Then he rolled over wincing, scrabbled his fingers until they found the liquor bottle, and swallowed the few drops left inside. He blinked and sat up.

Get me some clothes.

Grant pulled a few things from a pile on the bed and handed them to Cotter. He got dressed, his back to Grant. There was a scar beneath the ribs, whether a doctor's or attacker's Grant couldn't tell. When he was done Cotter took the water from Grant and drank some more of it.

Why don't you move up to the house, Grant said.

Cotter shook his head no.

Plenty of room for you.

Them rooms belong to other people. It ain't my place.

Grant stood and went to the door. With his hand on the latch he said, Don't feel much like my place, neither.

Longer you live, Cotter said, the more it'll feel like yours and the less it'll matter to you. I can make myself at home anywhere. This here's fine.

He waved a heavy hand at all that was around them, the smoke-brown windows and walls, and the dirty sheets and the stiff sick-soaked clothes in a heap on the floor. Grant nodded and opened the door and the winter rushed in, fanning the fire.

Good night, Cotter, he said, and stepped out into the cold.

·

In January of that winter he rode south over the government land to check up on Murray. It was a good day's ride and he counted on having to camp somewhere for the night. He knew a few outcrops that could pass for shelter. With him he brought a bottle for the herder and a mystery book to read. The hills were lower and more narrow and jagged to the south, as if a great fist had come from the east and struck at Eleven, bunching the land all up and down the Post Range.

Why these mountains had that name depended on who you talked to. One story had homesteaders fencing a pasture when Indians killed them and bound their bodies upright to the posts they'd been driving. Mostly this story was used to scare children, to keep them from getting lost in the hills. Some people thought the name referred to settlers' outposts once built on the ridgetops, now gone. There had also been a mail route through here which was often attacked. It was true that people used to find decaying letters scattered through the passes, though Grant himself had never seen one. The Indians had had another name for the range that meant surrounded by rivers, because its boundaries could be marked by the streams that flowed around it. Now and then you heard old people call it by that name.

The folded land offered long changeless channels of astounding length. Over years Grant had learned to mark the distance he'd gone down them, the way long study of a clockface can make detectable the hour hand's motion. When he was younger he would pass the time on long rides by imagining attacks by animals or Indians and devising ways to defend himself against them. If he was alone he might take a few shots at a tree or rock, for fun.

He left in late morning. By midafternoon the flock came into view in the distance, languidly shifting, a gray stain on the snow. The sight reminded Grant of the carpets of seaweed that spread just beneath the ocean's surface, swelling with the currents. Murray's wagon punched a dark pinhole in the white beyond the sheep. Its chimney emitted a thin line of smoke that rose straight up in the windless air. Grant's horse snorted and quickened. A pan and cup clanked together in the pannier.

When he was halfway down the incline two dark shapes broke away and moved toward him on a swift parallel path. Soon they sharpened into dogs. Grant slowed to give them a chance to smell the horse. When the animals seemed satisfied with one another, the dogs led him down into the valley.

Against the trampled white the sheep looked jaundiced and sick, their bellies stained by mud. They were eating grass through the snow. Grant believed he knew this area and thought he could remember a cutbank running east-west beyond Murray's camp. He rode down toward it and the dogs followed as far as the wagon, where they waited to see what Grant would do. In a minute he pulled up short a few lengths from the bankedge, acting on intuition alone. He hadn't seen it and would have fallen over had he kept on. He dismounted and looked down at the ground ten feet below. It rose to about twenty feet off to the west before the lower ground came up to meet the higher. The undisturbed snow below rendered the drop nearly invisible. He rode back to the wagon, the dogs picking him up halfway and trotting intently beside him.

There was no door on the wagon but for an elkskin tacked across a sidewall of sheet metal. Without mounting the buckboard he rapped on the metal and felt rust flakes scrape his knuckles. He called out Murray's name.

The herder pushed the skin aside with a rifle barrel which came to rest aimed at Grant. Grant could hear the dogs growling, suddenly anxious. Murray looked at him with eyes shielded by colored glasses. Behind the lenses the eyes were small and wild, like poison berries. It occurred to Grant that Murray didn't recognize him.

It's Grant, he said. Grant Person. Come to see how you're doing.

Murray stepped out and hopped to the ground and Grant backed up to admit him. The rifle barrel did not waver in its aim. Murray had grown a beard which had filled in unevenly, leaving bare rough skin at the corners of his mouth.

Grant said, Flock's all right, is it?

'Sfine, Murray said. His Adam's apple quivered high on his throat.

You know there's a little cliff a quarter mile south of here. You'd best bed down beyond it on the low side. So the sheep don't wander over the edge. Don't you think?

Nope, Murray said, keeping his eyes full on Grant.

In this blinding white landscape, Grant figured, every foreign shape has got to shake a man deep. He suddenly remembered the names of the dogs, Cootie and Mitch. Assuming they were the same dogs. He felt like a fool with this rifle pointed at his chest and the silly dogs behind him.

How about you put that thing down, Murray? I ain't armed. My rifle's still in the scabbard. He pointed to the horse but Murray didn't look where he was pointing. There's nothing to get upset over.

Murray lowered the rifle and blinked, as if waking up. One of the dogs came over and stood by him.

You all right? Grant said.

Aye. He looked south. I don't see no cliff.

Look where the grass stops. A quarter mile. It's a ten, fifteen foot drop.

Murray leaned a little forward. Aye, I see it now. I mean to take 'em there tomorrow.

Grant wanted to suggest he take them there today but he said nothing, not yet. He understood these were too many sheep for one man, this man in particular. Looking out over the flock Grant felt the burden of owning it and wished for the first time since returning that he might find some other endeavor broad or deep enough to absorb him. As a child he would ride out far enough so that he couldn't see the house anymore, and the largeness of his surroundings would make him feel larger himself, and it was possible to believe it was all his: that he had subdued it, and everything he could see was under his control. Now the sight of the flock alone filled him with feelings of powerlessness, and all the human influence he had seen in the east, all the evidence men had fabricated to prove to themselves they existed, seemed little more than a brittle crust that would one day be scoured off the earth. In the world of men, in buildings and on streets and under the influence of commerce, maybe it was possible to see it differently. But here it no longer was, not for him.

He camped that night cupped by a cretaceous overhang eroded under, he guessed, by pooled ice some fifteen thousand years or so back. Nearby stood a cairn of rounded stones herders used to stand upon to watch sheep. He didn't know how old that was, it had been here when he was born. He built a fire and ate bacon and beans cooked over it. The grease left over went into a tin cup, and he dredged a lampwick through it, which he held upright while the grease hardened in the cold air. When the fire went to embers he wrapped himself in his sougan, lit the wick and read his book until he couldn't feel his fingertips anymore. Then he blew out the flame and covered up his head and hands.

The virgin world he woke to didn't seem so oppressive and he found his confidence in the herder renewed. He had left Murray his bottle of booze and promised to bring him the mail, if any came. Riding back home he made a model in his head of each day of the coming year, through the winter and into lambing season and shearing and on to fall. There was some solace in the anticipation of work, and punished hands and feet and the inevitability of injury and illness. But he dreaded restoring ties to the market. Either he would not be remembered by his buyers and thus susceptible to swindle, or remembered as the one who had left and come back, and thus the object of their disdain.

Regardless, there was satisfaction in the planning, in the imagined days darkened with instructions on his imagined calendar. It had a different picture above each month, of one idyll or another, a silhouette of a man among animals or a sentimentally lit landscape.

When he got home he read his book and fed Cotter, and he worked in the morning and on subsequent mornings and read and ate and listened to the radio, and in this way he passed through the winter.

By spring he had convinced himself some change was imminent, but it would be another year before Max returned.

·

It was a year of holding on. In spring Murray came back thinner. He said he had run out of food. Grant suspected him of slaughtering a ewe but didn't mention it. He plied the herder with a little extra money to keep him working a few days longer, to get the flock ready for lambing, and with Cotter they tagged each ewe and clipped the hair around her teats. The lambing pens had long been set up in the barn and they stocked each with good clean bedding.

When the lambs started coming the men eased into the work as into cold water, tentative at first and then later without even knowing they were doing it. Cotter and Murray, near drunk, gentled the ewes like mothers. Murray kept a washtub warm with boiled water from the house, and carefully dipped chilled lambs up to their necks and rubbed them dry one after the other. When it got to be too much for the three of them, Cotter went into town and brought back a couple of men from the bar. Grant didn't know them, a husky teenager with bloodshot eyes and a Crow Indian named Charlie, who spoonfed orphaned lambs with a nurse's steady hands. When once a ewe nudged its teats against a stillborn lamb, they watched Charlie lift the dead animal from the pen, slit it throat to dock, pull it out of its skin and wrap the skin still bloody around a wobbling orphan, which suckled at the mother as if she were its own. All of them had seen this before, but never done so swiftly or with such gruesome kindness, as if the Crow was dressing a child for school.

Some of the dead lambs were born amputated, without hooves. Some curled up like oak leaves, their bones bent against the rigid muscles. Living lambs lay shaking themselves to death or stood paralyzed until they perished on their feet. Among the dead and dying and newly living animals the five men worked without speaking to one another, sometimes lying down right in the dust and sleeping. Half awake one night with his head inches from a newborn lamb, Grant believed he was among his brothers, all grown and familiar beyond the necessity for speech. When he woke fully he held back tears and touched the weariest man, the teenager whose name he'd already forgot, and the boy filled Grant's shape in the dirt, as if this spot, once occupied by someone else, was therefore now more acceptable as a bed.

Grant would forget the boy's face within weeks, and the Indian's not long after. The intensity and intimacy of these days would bleed in his memory into similar days of other years, until no particular recollection could be extracted from the ones that surrounded it. Soon after they were finished Grant would sense his memories losing definition in just this manner. Alone in the barn he would struggle to retain them, believing that what they had done should seem, years from now, more essential, more particular, than other days among other men. It should have created between them some uncommon affinity. But Charlie and the boy he would never see again, and Murray and Cotter were not inclined to reminisce, and he would allow his memory to erode as it always had, leaving him with only the contour of the thing, a kind of haunting, which came to him in odd moments like a draught from a previous life.

On a day when they were near done, Grant stepped from the barn to find a warm and cloudless spring evening. The light was like an heirloom taken out of storage and spit-shined. He rolled up a cigarette and smoked it. Almost eight months he'd been home and only now was the last piece of him truly back, as if it had taken the bed and body of Jean Tate and the blood of the birthing ewes to root him at last. After awhile the other men joined him. When they had all gone in and eaten, Grant counted out their pay and Cotter drove them back into town.

Murray would return in a week to take the flock onto spring range, and Kittredge and Neeler would come at shearing. But for the moment Grant was alone, and his past, which before had seemed like a fierce intractable living force, reminded him now of the herders' cairn on the hillside, something cold and inert he could stand upon to see what was coming.

Later he would wonder how his imagination had failed him. But for now there seemed nothing in front of him that wasn't simple and familiar. His life's odyssey was over and he was where he'd always be. Such were his thoughts on this impossible first warm evening of the year. In four days he would be twenty-seven years old.

PART TWO

AFOOT

5

A year later he came back from riding the ditches and saw, standing on the sill of an upstairs window of his parents' bedroom, a square bottle of blue glass catching the late-afternoon sun. He pastured the horse then returned to the yard to stare at the front door he was going to have to walk through. A blue glass bottle in the window. It would be casting a long shimmering colored shadow across the floor and bed. He entered the house as if nothing was out of the ordinary.

You need to get an electric refrigerator, Max said. He was sitting at the table with a bottle of whiskey in front of him. A cloudy shard of ice poked up over the rim of his glass. He swirled it around with his finger. Sawdust, he said. It gets in your drink.

When'd you get here?

I got a ride out from Reese Hamlin. He said you had something going awhile back with old Jean Tate.

Grant sat down and took his hat off.

Have a drink, Max said.

I might at that. He stood up and got a glass. Do I want to know where you been?

I don't know. Do you? Max looked different. He was wearing

clothes a city laborer might wear, his head bare, his face thin but soft, gruel-fed.

You been to the city.

Max said, New York.

You like it much? Grant asked. He sat down and put his empty glass on the table.

You meet a different breed of people there, I can say that.

At this, the groan of a mattress sounded from just above them, their parents' room, and then light footsteps. Grant hadn't heard such a sound for nearly five years. Max was grinning now, but not for Grant: a private grin. His eyes were somewhere else entirely.

You bring somebody along?

Sophia, Max said.

Sophia, Grant repeated.

She came down the steps wearing a black dress, though Grant understood this to be a city style and not mourning clothes. Nonetheless the sight of it reminded him of his mother. The girl was barely there, a bending branch wrapped in a twist of rag. Her skin was white and lucent, like the open palm of a candle which held the melted wax. Her nose was long, her eyes dark and large and far apart. Long hair tied back onto itself. Face fearful and unbeautiful.

Sophia, my brother Grant. Grant, Sophia.

Ma'am, said Grant.

She snickered. Oh boy, she said, a woman's voice filling the room. I can't believe this.

We met in the city, Max said. Her daddy sells radios.

He's a retailer, said Sophia. She blushed.

Grant let his eyes stay on her a moment. The oddness of her voice had seemed to amplify it, he could hear it still.

Help yourself, he said to her and nodded at the bottle. She went to the counter and took a glass without hesitation, then sat down at the table. In a moment Max took his eyes off her and asked how the outfit was doing.

A lot had been done, the flock culled and bred, repairs made around the place. Grant told him this knowing that pride was creeping into his voice, pride he knew his brother would be listening for. Max's face maintained a kind of imitation attentiveness: but this was Max, you never saw the whole of him. There was the face he was showing you, which stood for what he thought you wanted, and there was the real face you could only see when the other one slipped off by mistake. Looking at his brother and at the girl and back, he saw that Max had a hidden beauty, something about him almost womanly, the pale ears and the softness of his skin. It took a woman's presence to bring it out, or at least this woman, who looked gripping her whiskey as if she'd fight you for him and expected she might have to. Her glass was empty. With a start Grant noticed that his was too. He'd never filled it up. Sophia said, Did you show him your paintings?

Max coughed. He just got in, he said a little loudly.

Grant watched Sophia. A change in her posture told him she was nudging Max with her foot. She turned to Grant with an underhand grin.

He isn't telling you he's been painting. That's what he's been doing all this time—she turned to Max—haven't you? He's the real thing, she said now to Grant. No kidding.

He looked at his brother, glad to have her out of his sight.

Yeah, Max said, and here was an answering look, dirty and conspiratorial. The girl didn't seem to catch it.

You were always good at art painting, Grant said.

She snorted. He sure is!

Then they were silent. A raven's cry broke through a window and across the room and was rebutted from someplace distant. Grant was looking at Sophia and her entire mien split wide open, as if in the birds' calls she had heard a scrap of her own tongue telling her she was farther from home than she knew. And like that she sealed back up, and whole again punched Max in the shoulder, and laughed.

Grant had seen the truth. They hadn't told him yet, but they weren't planning to go back to New York.

◆

Sleep was next to impossible with other people in the house; it cried out as if changing size in the night. And in fact it was: huge when Grant was a boy and small when he left, large when he returned and small again tonight. Voices came to him from Max's room distorted by space and by walls: Sophia's in the shape of desperate queries, and Max's, curt replies. She was feeling around the edges of her situation, he guessed, a blind woman tossed in a cell. Max, reluctantly, would be telling her how it was going to be. Earlier, when she was sleeping off her drunk, he had walked with Max around the yard and Max told him all he'd done in the city. For the first week he slept on benches and bought hard rolls and bottles of milk at a bakery. Then he found this bar where the famous painters drank and he met Sophia, who bought him liquor and introduced him to important people. She set him up in a warehouse her father owned and he got a job washing dishes for some Greeks at a diner. At night he went to jazz clubs and drew pictures of the players and sold them the drawings. He painted with watercolors because they were cheapest, and when he had no money he found scraps of paper in the warehouse to paint on or else went out in the street and tore broadsheets off walls. He told Grant he tried to paint a certain horse a thousand times and never once got it right. Once a week he took a shower at the YMCA. After awhile he moved into a room with Sophia and her father quit talking to her. One night somebody discovered his things in the warehouse and threw out his paints and easel and everything he'd done, and after that he had to paint in the tiny apartment.

So what are you doing here? Grant asked him.

For a minute it seemed there would be no answer. Then it came fast, spat out. There's something fake about those people, those painters. They pretended like they were dock workers. Half of them are rich off art and they can't even paint a goddam picture.

They think much of you?

How in the hell should I know, Max said, sounding like he knew all too well. The two of them had been leaned up against the sheep fence where the strongest ewes and lambs were walking, and Max shook his head and went alone to the equipment shed and poked his head in the door awhile. For a few minutes he disappeared inside. Then he came back out and approached Grant with his hands in his pockets.

Hear anything from Daddy? he said.

No.

He nodded, unsurprised but seemingly embarrassed to have asked. Grant said, You planning to stay long?

Max was looking up over the house at the grinded-down hillside, grimacing at its wasted brightness. Might, he said finally.

She gonna stick it out, you think?

I expect. Ain't much for her in the city. Her daddy cut her off when she moved out.

How old is she, Max?

Plenty old. Nineteen.

I wasn't suggesting anything funny, Grant told him.

A mirthless smile cracked Max's lips. Maybe you ought've, he said. There's plenty that's funny.

Now, in the room at the end of the hall, Max and Sophia had fallen silent. The house still shivered around them as if trying to expel them all. Grant wondered what his brother had told her she was going to be able to do all day long. He could feel the panic in her, in city people, their crushing need to keep themselves occupied. Now that the sod was giving up its freeze there would be plenty of work, especially at a shirttail outfit like theirs, with the lambs here and summer ahead of them, but he guessed none of it was anything she'd be willing to do. He bet she didn't even have a decent pair of shoes.

Minutes passed or maybe hours. The moon soared up out of sight over the house. Coyotes cried and he thought of the sheep on spring range, where Murray'd take them soon, and he hoped they'd be as lucky this year as last. Listening to the coyotes he doubted it. In awhile their cries grew faint and a closer sound reached him, which he recognized as the sound of floorboards straining under somebody's weight. The footsteps were in the hall and they stopped outside his cracked-open door. He could see a figure there darkening the threshold and he sat up in bed with the blankets spilling off him.

The door opened and the figure stepped in soundlessly and shut it. Outside, the coyotes again took up their barks. He spoke his brother's name into the darkness.

In response the figure moved closer. The room's only light came from the moonglow the hillside reflected. Its intensity was insufficient to show the visitor's face.

Sophia, he said, much quieter now, and the figure stepped forward into the light. Grant saw the smooth sleeve of a suit jacket. A bead of water collected at the cuff and fell, and it thudded on the floor like a bomb. The dead man's face came toward him, a bloodless wound cracking its cheek.

Sssh, the dead man said. Grant was very still. A cold finger reached out and touched his lips. The touch froze and sealed them. He woke frantic, his fingers in his open mouth and then over his eyes. He began to forget. Suddenly exhausted he fell back to the bed and into dreamless sleep, with his face cradled in his hands.

◆

Yearling lambs had to go to market. They'd be trucked to Ashton and from there to Denver for slaughter. Lambs were too valuable to eat on the ranch: maybe once in the spring, a skinny or sickly one they couldn't have got much for. Otherwise the animals they slaughtered here were past the breeding age. They ate mutton or sold it in Eleven, where people didn't so much mind the flavor and texture of mature flesh. Grant woke to find the house still quiet and innocent as a contrite child. Downstairs it was cold. The door had been left open, or had blown open in the night. Out in the road ravens paced, peering in. He shut the door and lit a fire in the stove.

He'd made arrangements with a man named Teabow, who owned a truck, to come help them haul the lambs to Ashton. As the kitchen warmed this was who he phoned. Teabow said he would be late. He would have been later still had Grant not called. They would get better prices for their lambs the earlier they came in the day, but there was nothing more that Grant could do. He hung up the phone and set to fixing breakfast.

Through the window he could see Cotter hitching their trailer to the pickup and bringing it around to the yard, near the shed gate. The lambing pens could be rigged to create a chute to drive the lambs through, and this is what Cotter did next. Then he came in to eat.

Cotter had not been around, having taken a few days off. Grant put his eggs in front of him and said, He's back.

Your daddy?

Max.

Cotter put his egg in his mouth and chewed it, thinking. He said, We could sure use him.

It was true. The work would take all day. When Cotter was done eating, Grant said, He's brought a girl with him.

What kind of girl? Cotter said. He stood and put his plate and his coffee cup in the sink.

From the city. New York. That's where he's been.

Cotter crossed his arms and let out a breath. He pursed his lips and appeared to think it over. He ain't gonna work a lick, he said.

They went out and spent some time looking over the ewes they planned to keep. Grant went into the shed for a notebook and pencil and came out to the chute where Cotter had chased a few ewes and wethers with a stick. Cotter opened up the gate and Grant ticked them off as they went through. The trailer filled and Max still hadn't appeared. A few times Grant looked up at the corner window but nothing was moving there. Eventually Teabow showed. He was stooped at middle age like he'd been living in a burrow, and his eyes bulged and blinked unceasingly. The three of them filled his truck and gathered in the yard a moment to smoke. Grant wanted to get moving, they could smoke in Ashton. But the break only seemed fair.

It's gonna freeze again yet, said Teabow.

Can't argue that, Cotter said.

Teabow turned to Grant. Them sheep look better'n last year.

I'm trying to grade them up. How's your missus?

Teabow shook his head. He had got a Mexican bride, who had registered with a marriage bureau in the hope of finding somebody more well-to-do than was locally available. Teabow had chosen her off of a list. He'd gone down there and picked her up and they got married on the way, somewhere in Arizona. She was a nervous woman to begin with—whether this was her regular nature or on account of marrying Teabow nobody seemed to know—but had not come to town much at all lately and was thought by a few to be sick in the head. It was rumored that her mother had been shot or stabbed in some kind of bar fight, and that Teabow may have misrepresented himself as a wealthy rancher. For this reason people felt some sympathy toward her, strange as she was. The Teabows lived on the far side of town, out on the flats, and raised a few animals. She pretended not to know much English though Teabow said she spoke it good.

Grant had inquired after her in the hope of getting things moving, but now he regretted bringing her up at all. Teabow looked hurt and Grant had a sudden sense of his desperation, of his shock and puzzlement at the unexpected turns his life had taken. He saw himself years in the future, driving south in the blue pickup to meet his own catalog bride. Teabow said, Aw, she's all right, she's a little barn sour, is all.

Maybe we ought to get going, Grant said.

He rode with Teabow in the cab of his truck. They didn't say much except to comment on the weather, which was unremarkable. Grant wanted to apologize for asking about Mrs. Teabow but he knew it would likely compound Teabow's embarrassment. Now he would always be the man who had said that, and Teabow the man it was said to. That words couldn't be taken back was simple and obvious, a feature of passing time, but the idea filled Grant with despair.

When they arrived in Ashton they had to wait for another outfit to unload its stock. A good half hour passed. Finally they drove in the sheep. The price was lower than expected. Grant tried to haggle up but his heart wasn't in it. They got back to the house after noon and Teabow wanted dinner, so Grant figured he might as well make it. In the kitchen he found Max and Sophia sitting at table as if waiting for him. Introductions were made.

We got to get Sophia some shoes, Max said. You going back into Ashton?

Grant said, Well, what do you think?

I'd guess you are.

All right, then.

But the two of them stayed inside while the trailers were loaded, and only when the work was finished did Max lead his girl down the steps and across the muddy road. They got in the pickup with Cotter.

That's a real pretty girl, Teabow said to Grant out on the highway. How long them two been married? I didn't hear nothing about it.

I don't know that they are married, Teabow.

Well! Teabow said. That seemed to hold them until Ashton.

Max and Sophia slipped away when they got to the market and came back later with her new clothes. In work boots and dungarees she looked like a toy, her legs spread slightly as she walked and her hands stiff and open at her sides. Men stopped what they were doing and gawked. Grant was embarrassed for her—their stares were mean—but something told him she wouldn't have cared what they thought. When she smiled at them, most of them smiled back.

They returned too late in the day for another run. Grant told Teabow he'd handle the rest himself in the morning, and paid him cash. He watched Teabow's rig disappear over the hill. Cotter had been backing the trailer around the side of the shed and now he came to join Grant where he still stood in the road. Grant said, You were right about Max. He didn't lift his little finger.

Can't say I blame him.

Grant looked at Cotter but the face betrayed no especial hostility. What's that supposed to mean?

Just what I said.

Grant kept looking at him. Cotter hitched his shoulders and sniffed, and finally added, Hell, I ain't never blamed you for nothing, did I. Let's drop it and go eat.

All right, Grant said, and they went in the house.

•

Over the next few days Max and Sophia seemed to be spending a lot of time out in the equipment shed, moving things around. Now and then Grant went in there for something and noted that a space was growing in the back, by the desk. One afternoon he found that the desk itself had been moved, the shelves taken down and stacked on it. Max was kneeling on the cement floor banging something together out of old boards. Sophia stood off in a corner holding one of Grant's mystery paperbacks in front of her face.

What're you working on? Grant asked.

Easel, Max said.

Plan to do some painting out here, do you?

Yep.

Grant looked over at Sophia, who lowered the book and met him with a smile, the one she'd given the ranch men in Ashton. It was common, like a knickknack, something she'd learned to do somewhere. Yet Grant found himself returning it. Embarrassed, he walked out.

When they came in the house that night only Sophia climbed the stairs to her room. Max sat down at the table with Grant. When she was gone Max said, She's bound to run out of books pretty soon.

Max had picked up an air of complaint in the city which Grant didn't much like. You're gonna have to go down to Ashton and get some more then, he said back, too harshly. Max got up and poured himself a drink. He looked at Grant, gesturing with the bottle, and Grant nodded. Max put the drinks on the table.

Looks like we're drinkers now, Max said.

Looks like.

Max drew breath and let it out. We're clean out of Sophia's money, he said. It took most of what she had just to get here. It was a long time coming with her and her daddy. She was supposed to enter into girls' college last year and she never got on the train. And then I met her. He shook his head and drank.

Grant said, You're going to have to pull your weight. You know how it is.

Mama asked for you every day she was dying, Max said suddenly.

It was so clumsy a weapon that Grant couldn't even get himself angry over it. The words sat there orphaned between them. Max swirled the drink around in his glass and held it up to the light. Then he went on.

Sophia says she can cook. She taught herself a couple of things. She can take over for you, and wash the clothes and such.

Get her a library card.

I believe I'll do that, Max said. So. The lambs, did they go high? No they did not. And it wasn't me that made Mama sick.

No, Max said. It was Edwin and Robert and Thornton and Wesley. You didn't have a goddam thing to do with it, did you. No, you're right.

I'd best turn in, Grant said standing.

You still got whiskey there.

I'll leave it to you to pour it back. Or you can have it yourself. That'll be your first job. And he pushed in his chair and went quietly up the stairs, pretending to Sophia that he thought she wasn't listening to all that, that she was trying to go to sleep.

◆

They were lucky to own their spring range outright. This was the gentle clump of foothills to the north, close to home and at this time of year covered in lush grass. John Person had bought the land from a Norwegian homesteader who couldn't hack it and was moving to Minnesota to find a wife. He'd got it for next to nothing and paid it off by the beginning of the war. They started out with a hundred and fifty head and added every year, creating more work for themselves as they went. The extra children—Thornton, Robert, Max, Wesley—were supposed to make up for it.

Grant expected Murray back in the morning and woke intending to get a good breakfast together. When he got to the kitchen he discovered Sophia already there. She was wearing an apron, his mother's which she had found in the pantry. The apron was bleached white but Grant could remember it spattered with blood as his mother stood hacking at a knot of meat. She had made it herself out of tarp canvas. On Sophia it nearly reached the floor. Her booted feet poked out from behind it.

Max'll be down, she said. He was up late getting his studio finished.

You mean in the shed.

Yeah. So I guess I've cooked a little, before. I mean, I know my way around a kitchen but I don't know how you do things around here. So maybe you could get me going.

Grant said, There's five of us this morning and I was going to make some potatoes and eggs.

Okay, I think I can do that.

One of your jobs is gonna be the chickens. You know how to get eggs from the henhouse?

No.

He led her out across the yard to the henhouse. Inside she made a face at the odor in spite of her obvious efforts not to. He showed her how to tell if a hen is setting on anything or not, and how to reach under her and get the egg. They brought twenty or so inside in a bucket and he got her cracking and scrambling them, which it looked like she'd done before. He told her how to clean potatoes and cut them up. While she did that he made the coffee.

Cotter came in with milk frothing in a pitcher and set it on the table. He gave Sophia a long look. Her new trousers were hanging off her narrow body. She said good morning and Cotter nodded. Grant put a cup of coffee in front of him and Cotter poured the warm milk in.

Grant took some fat out of the can and melted it in a skillet. Then he fried up the potatoes and added the eggs. She stood close and he felt her eyes on his work. When he was finished she put the food on plates. By then Murray had walked in and Max was on the stairs.

He came up behind her and grabbed her around the waist with a hand coming up just under the breast. The men watched him do this, abashed and transfixed. How's it going? Max asked her.

Oh, you know.

He didn't let go of her until Grant took the plates and set them on the table. Let's eat while it's hot, he said.

They all sat and ate, and drank the milk and coffee out of good chipped china. Murray looked a long time at Sophia and at last asked Max who she was. The question seemed to please Max but it was Sophia who answered. She stated her name, staring Murray straight in his eye. Shocked, the herder turned away, and the other men laughed at his discomfort and at their own.

Grant couldn't remember anything the herder had ever laughed at, though he'd seen him smile at something said in a bar once or twice. Maybe he laughed when he was by himself. Sophia looked up a couple of times while they ate, as if making sure it was all right not to be talking. He could hear the meal through her ears, the uncivilized chomp and smack of people who had better things to do, and he slowed himself down. She was still wearing the apron.

When they were finished Grant sent Max to help Murray move the ewes out, and he showed Sophia to the animals and them to her. She seemed to regard them with a fearful respect, as if she was encountering them in the wild. In the barn he sat her down and made her milk the cow. The cow kicked and complained. Sophia slipped backwards off the stool, alarmed. He helped her up, taking her hard round elbow in his palm. He explained the routine of feeding and milking and cleaning.

What about the horses? She looked at him frankly. I'm afraid of horses.

Cotter takes care of them. But you ought to learn riding.

It had never been Grant's role here to instruct or advise; he felt funny telling somebody what to do. You couldn't live comfortable with a person you knew too much more than. It wasn't a balanced kind of life. Sophia threw things off, made him take note of how he looked and sounded, and that scrutiny of himself, not in his nature, made him long to be alone. She cast the ranch in a new light: she wasn't of them, she was an envoy of the larger world that also wasn't of them, and without even trying she made them an object of the world's judgment. Of Max's judgment.

That was the real difference. The opinion of a girl from New York City didn't mean much to him but his own brother's did. Max had a critical streak the east hadn't put in him. He was always like that. Edwin had been too, and their father. But there was something different about Max. He measured them against his own fledgling consciousness and seemed to find them lacking. It wasn't their actions or lack of them that bothered him but unseen, inherent flaws, things over which they had no control. They were powerless to please him.

Why had Max come back, and why had he brought this girl with him? Was she a keepsake of his failed escape, or was she here to bear witness to him, to the spectacle of his indecision? Grant would have wagered that Max never had this picture in mind, of the poor girl slapping dust off her skinny backside, standing in fear of a cow. It was almost funny, or would have been if he didn't know so well the shape of his own meager heart: the very shape of this valley, a bleached-out miniature clenching in his chest.

•

That night Max and Sophia turned in early, so Grant went out to the equipment shed to see what they had done. The easel stood in the center of the empty space, a wooden cross with a narrow ledge to support a painting. From the ledge hung a little tin bucket with paintbrushes poking out of it. In front of the easel there was an upturned fertilizer drum covered with a tarp, he guessed a place for Max's subjects to sit. A lamp had been rigged, a bare bulb on a long cord slung over a ceiling beam, which exposed the tarp and the gray cement floor to a naked unrefined light. Grant crossed the space to a far wall where four thick cases were standing, cracked leather portfolios with taped-up handles. They must have dragged these onto the train with them, or the bus. He opened one up and spread its contents on the floor. Paintings, drawings on paper, smudged and torn around the edges and in some cases creased twice from folding. Here were the jazz sketches, wandering lines of ink that suggested the outlines of things: drums, a horn, the glow of a spotlight on a slick forehead. The pages were nearly blank, so minimal were the lines. But somehow the empty space stood for darkness or light or the sound of music. They were hurried and sloppy to Grant's eye. But their birth under his brother's hand chilled him. He didn't understand why.

The paintings were of gray city buildings and the stairstepped V of light the street cut between them. There were nudes, distorted and sexless, arched across sofas or floors like caught fish, their flesh the color of sinew and bone. He believed he recognized the body as Sophia's, or maybe that was only a suggestion his head was making to his eyes.

He gathered up the papers and put them back into the open portfolio, then leaned it up against the wall with the others. Afterward he sat on the barrel awhile staring at the darkened space behind the easel where Max would stand.

Grant knew what it was to be looked at: a kind of mirror, a way of seeing his own foreignness in others' eyes. He felt it when an animal he was hunting turned its head and regarded the hole he made in the landscape. He had felt it on the *Rose Adams*, when they called him a hero. He wondered what his brother saw when he looked at him, what Sophia saw.

But there was no point in contemplating what he had no way of ever knowing. He reached up and switched off the light. Then he stood still in the total dark for a moment, listening to the sound of nothing.

6

Coyotes came down out of the hills. This was early April, when the snowline was retreating up the hillsides leaving good grass in its wake and pulling the sheep up after it. A clear moonlit night brought the first kill. Grant heard the animal's screams from his bed and the blast of a rifle after it, and he got up and went downstairs to look at the clock. It was four in the morning. He went back up and dressed and as he passed Max's room he heard them stirring in there as well. By the time he'd got the coffee going Max was on the stairs and Sophia behind him rubbing her eyes. What's going on? she was asking.

You heard it? Max asked.

Yeah, Grant said, and to Sophia, Coyotes.

She went to the cupboard and set to work with a reluctant air. When they had eaten, Cotter showed up and Grant asked him to go get the poison out of the shed. Then he readied the provisions for a night's vigil.

Max watched him. I'll be sleeping here tonight, he said.

Grant could picture them in the bed together, his brother's hand at rest on her hip, her arm dangling off the edge. It won't get done in a day, he said.

Sure it will. We'll track 'em and dig out the den. Nothing so hard about that.

Grant said, We're out of practice.

He went to the shed and packed their bedrolls while Cotter rigged up the horses. They met Max in the yard. He was rubbing his hands together. Shit, it's still cold, he said.

Cotter handed the strychnine tablets to Grant in a candy tin which Grant slipped into his shirt pocket. Then they got on the horses and rode out over the hill following the sound of the dogs. Murray was circling the flock on his horse, a rifle under his arm and his colored glasses on a string around his neck. He was still cursing when they got to him. A bloody gash was on his lower lip where he appeared to have bit himself. I nicked 'im, I nicked 'im, he was saying.

Murray led them to the carcass. A back leg was broken and stripped to bone, and the ewe was torn open through the anus with its innards spread out on the spongy earth. He pointed up the hillside where the grass was bare. Fleeing, the coyote had avoided the snow until it was out of sight around the south side, leaving no visible tracks.

Grant dismounted and sliced the ewe open along her belly. He cut out rough cubes of flesh and slit them down the center, then pushed a tablet of poison deep into each. He handed some to Max and kept the rest. The dogs, quiet now, circled around them smelling the air.

Keep the dogs back, Grant said to Murray.

They took off in opposite directions around the hill, dropping the poisoned meat above the snowline. To the north Grant found a scrub pine that had been pissed on, but the tracks, clear in the shade, had melted nearly to nothing out in the sun and wind. At this altitude the sun had already risen and he had begun to sweat under his hat. He rode up among the rocks looking for further sign. But there was neither scat nor tracks.

When the meat was gone he rode back around the hill and met Max down in the canyon. Grant told him about the markings under the tree.

Might be looking at the wrong hill, Max said.

Doubt it. He wouldn't go off south if he didn't have to.

Max looked up at the hillside, brilliant now in the sunlight. Murray's kidding himself about that shot. We would of seen blood.

Maybe, Grant said.

They ate dinner with Murray in his wagon, where they could sit down without getting wet. Grant had never before been in it. It seemed larger than it did from outside, with a miniature cookstove and a wooden bench and a man-sized space on the floor where Murray could unfold his cot, which hung from pegs on the wall. The smell was of old meals and the herder's unwashed body. A lantern that hung from the ceiling was the only light. Grant imagined that in winter a man could go mad. When they'd finished eating he suggested Murray move the flock over the next hill while they hunted the coyote. He was surprised when Murray agreed. Then they cleaned up and stepped out into the daylight, which fell on them now with unusual intensity. In the still air it felt like a summer day. Murray called the dogs, and the sheep looked up and began to gather on the hillside like droplets of oil in a pan of water.

Grant and Max mounted and again circled the hill, this time higher up past the snowline where the rocks were larger and broke out through the ground. Twenty minutes later Grant heard his brother's whistle and moved ahead until he could see Max afoot on the western slope, standing over a shape in the snow.

The shape was the front half of a mule deer eviscerated by a coyote. Its dragging tracks came around from the south accompanied by the coyote's pursuing trail, its prints spread out and staggered in a casual walk. Alongside the trail was blood. From his saddle Grant took a shovel and shotgun, and they followed the trail up and around, back to the eastern face, which by now was in shadow and cooled by a wind. The snow had a crust which their boots crunched through as they walked. They were led to a gap among rocks, where the burnt-meat reek of the animals was drifting. Max stuck out his hand and Grant gave him the shovel.

No, Max said. He took the shotgun and jammed it in the hole and flicked off the safety.

How much good you think—Grant said, and Max fired. A single scream followed the shot's echo out across the canyon. Grant's bowels loosened at the sound and he crouched with one hand in the snow to keep from emptying himself.

Let's dig 'em out, Max said.

It was hard work. The ground was rocky and they had to roll big boulders out of it to get to the den. In a few hours it was exposed: a mother and six pups, most of them wounded by the shot, the mother glasseyed and panting, bleeding from the face and flank, and the blind pups squirming like mice underneath her. She tried to snarl. The shotgun lay next to Grant on a flat rock. Max pointed to it.

You want to finish them off? Or else hand it to me.

Grant bent down and picked up the shotgun and reloaded the empty chamber. He walked to the exposed den and aimed and the mother's eyes turned up to him. He saw that her legs didn't move, the shot had paralyzed her. He looked in her eyes and it was like looking into the night sky, at starlight that has taken a thousand years to reach the earth. He fired one barrel and killed her, then turned her over with his foot and finished the pups with the other.

When the echo died out Max stepped up and pushed the animals around with his boot. That's a goodly amount, he said.

Grant's eyes were on the dead pups. He said, He's still out there somewhere.

Drop bait ought to get him, don't you think?

Ought to.

Told you we would do it in a day.

Grant looked up and faced him. Max was grinning and the grin filled Grant with a rage he neither understood nor felt able to control. He was still holding the shotgun. Max looked down at the barrel and quit grinning and walked up to him. His boots dislodged a fist-sized rock that went tumbling down the hillside, skittering over the crusted snow. He grabbed the shotgun and Grant's hand loosened to let it go.

Without it his palm felt the cold and suddenly he could feel the cold all through him, in his joints and his gut and throat. He said, I think I may be coming down with something.

That must be it, Max told him, their eyes locked.

By nightfall Grant was feverish and by midnight he could barely stand up from bed to get a drink of water. He must have slept because at some point it was morning and his throat was a burning log, and a dark-faced man he recognized as Doc Lafitte was looking into his open mouth. Lafitte's strong features betrayed nothing, his big fleshy ears and bent nose, the dark smears under yellow eyes which had the lifeless appearance of things that were tacked to a wall. Figures flitted behind him: Sophia, his mother. Grant remembered that his mother was dead, declared so by this very man. Or was it Lafitte who had died?

Doc, he croaked. His throat swelled and contracted to a tight agonizing point.

Lafitte's hand drifted to Grant's forehead and then felt up under his chin. Grant shied away from the contact and a new pain exploded in the back of his head. Last night, the doctor said. They tell me you are having a terrible dream.

Grant remembered no dream and tried to say so. He opened his mouth and some air made it through but the words were lost in pain. Then it was night and moonlight was heavy in the room. He sat up. On the bedside table was a water bowl with a sponge in it, and a pill bottle and a glass of water. He sipped from the glass and coughed some of the water out. Then he put the glass down. From somewhere he heard the sound of someone sitting up in bed. Next he found himself flat on his back again with a screaming pain in his head and neck. After that time seemed to pass and it was morning again and there were eyes staring down at him. Sophia's. He was hungry.

I'm hungry, he said.

You look a lot better. She was wearing his mother's robe over a nightgown and her bare feet were flat on the plank floor.

My throat, he said. My head hurts like hell.

Here. She gave him the water, put it to his lips though he could have held it himself. Some of it dripped down his chin and neck and she wiped it dry with her sleeve. He smelled his mother's scent. Sophia stood up from her chair.

I'll make you some toast, she said.

Eggs, he said. Meat. What time is it?

Ten o'clock. I don't know if you can keep all that down. My daddy always eats a big breakfast the day he gets over being sick, and it always comes back up. A look crossed her face like it was on the way to somewhere else: rueful, repulsed.

If I can get it down I can keep it down, he said. Her answering expression was wary. He tried to remember. How long's this been going on? he asked.

Two days, she said. Max said not to worry but I thought you were going to die.

She looked at her hands, which were white and knit together. You had some kind of fever, she went on. Since you went to sleep last night it's been holding steady and it broke sometime this morning. The doctor gave you aspirins. You should take more when you eat your food.

Hair was growing on her ankles, a fine dark stubble. The toes curled and made a cracking sound.

I shot those coyotes and got a chill.

I know. Max told me.

Where is he?

Out working. Doing my chores, I guess. I said I would stay in and look after you.

That's real nice of you.

She blushed. I'll get your breakfast.

He listened to her going down and after awhile smelled bacon cooking. He took two of the aspirins and choked down a little more water. Then he got out of bed and went to the kitchen. His own body smelled of the sickness. She had the door propped open with a chair and sunlight was bleaching the room. The light was on the table and floor and her face at the window. She was looking out at Max working with Cotter in the yard. When Grant sat down she jumped.

Holy Moses, you scared the crap out of me, she said.

Pardon.

She turned back to the stove, moving quicker now, banging pans and dishes and spilling coffee over the counter. She muttered an oath and poured his black. Then she put food in front of him and sat with her legs crossed while he ate. When he was through she took the plate away and poured him more coffee, then rolled a cigarette from the makings in the pantry and smoked it sitting across from him.

There milk for this? he said, raising his cup.

She shook her head. Besides, she said, in your condition you don't want it.

Thanks for looking after me, he said.

She shrugged. How're you feeling?

Weak. I'll go out later.

You ought to stay in bed.

He could feel the food sliding into his stomach and his stomach reacting with a kind of astonishment. He closed his eyes. Maybe you're right.

You had brothers, she said suddenly. You and Max.

Four, he said.

She was looking past him at a corner of the room. They died. What happened?

You ought to ask Max about that.

He's told me.

Ain't anything else I can tell you then.

She was silent a long while. He wanted to get up but the breakfast was pinning him to the chair. He watched her because there was nothing else in the room to look at. The sun blazed behind her and he could see the outline of her scalp, round and helpless like a newborn's.

So, he said. You got any?

Sure, she said. Brother and a sister. Both older. My sister's a lot older. She's got a family. They live in the city but I hardly ever see them. My brother's married too. He lives in Chicago.

I've been there.

She smiled. Then the cigarette burned her fingers and she yelped and tossed it on the floor. It smoldered and went out and she cleaned it up with a rag. She threw the rag into the sink, and when she turned to him he could see tears forming in her eyes. They didn't fall.

I don't know how you can stand this place, she said.

Nobody's keeping you, he said. It came out angrier than he meant it, owing to the headache which only now was beginning to subside. But it was as if she didn't hear him.

Never seeing a soul except each other, she said, it's nuts.

It's a certain kind of living.

An idea seemed to occur to her. Where's the closest city?

Ashton's an hour's drive, he said.

Ashton! And she was up and past him and climbing the stairs.

When she came back down she was dressed in work clothes. She sat on the floor by the door and put her boots on. Just bought these, she said, and already they look like hell. She laughed. Of course they weren't so pretty to begin with, were they? She laughed again. Then she got up and faced the open door.

I'm sorry, Grant found himself saying, though none of what she'd said was on his account.

But she didn't answer. She turned her tight unhappy face on him for a moment and went out into the light.

•

He read and slept the entire day and dressed to eat dinner with the rest of them. Cotter and Max nodded when he came down, then turned back to their meals. This had a strange effect on Sophia. She looked from one to the other, asking them why they didn't so much as inquire about how Grant was feeling, her voice offended as if they'd failed to notice something she herself had done. Max said Grant looked pretty all right to him, no need to inquire, and the subject was left there.

Grant quit taking the aspirins. It didn't sit right with him. He slept uncomfortably and dreamlessly that night. In the morning he dressed straight off and after breakfast went to town for supplies, groceries and nails and meal for the chickens, because going to town wasn't too hard and could take up the time. His hunger of the morning before would not subside no matter what or how much he ate, and he was beginning to think the fever had undone something in him permanently, had hollowed out a place and sealed it off for good so that nothing could satisfy him. He ran through his errands and invented a couple of extras to keep from going home. When he'd truly run out of things to do he parked in front of the Sunrise and sat down at the counter.

Jean didn't say anything to him but when she brought his sandwich there was a plate of potatoes beside it that he hadn't ordered. He peered at himself in the napkin dispenser and found his reflection a little wan, the cheeks sunken, though that could have been the metal distorting him. He read the newspaper through the lunch hour and didn't look up until everybody had left the place. Then he saw Jean's eyes on him and watched as she went to the door and turned over the sign to read CLOSED. She stood and waited for him. He put down the paper and followed her upstairs, where she undressed him and then herself.

It seemed to take hours, like all goodbyes. He knew even as she moved under his hands, her flesh was somehow heavier, as if the lightness of passion had gone out of it and it was only a human body now, living but unpossessed. They lay listening to dogs barking outside and she told him all of what was going on in town, who was selling out to a cattle company, who was cheating who, an appearance of Mrs. Teabow buying bread at the grocery. Grant told her that Kittredge and Neeler were coming back from Colorado in a few weeks, he'd got a postcard saying they'd buried Kittredge's mother. He told her about the coyotes, and his fever.

What about the girl, Max's girl?

What about her, he asked.

There a story behind that? Or did she just appear out of nowhere?

He told her what little he knew. She thought the girl wouldn't make it very long. Grant couldn't disagree. But he didn't want to be talking about her like that, as she'd treated him kindly when he was sick. Instead he reached for Jean and she kicked off the bedclothes for the last time. During it she pinned him down and looked at him hard and said, You watch yourself, you don't look too good.

I don't feel quite right yet.

No, she agreed.

When he left her she said goodbye and shut the door behind him. He sat unmoving in the truck awhile, staring out at the filthy street, feeling the ghost of her under his fingers. He was hungry.

•

In the beginning of May Grant drove to Ashton to pick up Kittredge and Neeler. Kittredge had phoned the morning before to say they were coming by bus, and he was sorry if they were coming early but he was awful anxious to get out of Colorado. Petey's a little agitated, he said. He and my mama didn't much care for the other and we had a hell of a time down there. And then she passed on, Kittredge continued, and it just seemed to me it was time to get out.

Grant said, That's all right.

We finally got her trailer sold, though if you ask me we got skinned on account of we wanted the quick sale. Anyway it's no trouble if you ain't got work for us yet. We can put in our share for room and board if that'll help matters some.

Don't worry about that now, Grant said.

Well, I'm much appreciative.

Now the May sun was hot and dry and it chased the road dust through the truck window and muddied his throat. He thought he might get himself a bottle of pop in Ashton and drink it on the way back. Off to the south the mountains were indistinct, blazed and blurred by snowcaps. A man could be standing up there, Grant thought, with nothing but air between you and him, and still you could barely see him. For a moment it seemed strange that distance could render a thing invisible, that a man standing on the mountain could go unnoticed from the road. He thought about Kittredge, saddled with that fool boy, putting his mother in the ground. He could imagine what that felt like, but it was only his own memory he was thinking of, his own experience of death. The actual contour of Kittredge's pain was as distant to him as the mountaintop.

The bus station was an exposed wooden enclosure in the dirt lot behind the Ashton Supply. When he got there, nobody was in it. He parked the truck and walked in the back door of the store. Kittredge was folded into a metal army chair, tired as a rag blown up against a post. His hair was whorled across his scalp in a thumbprint's pattern and appeared brittle and gray, the hair of a much older man. Neeler'd gotten a haircut and was sitting on a shoe salesman's stool violently pulling on a pair of red Justin boots with fancy stitching up and down the sides. Grant took a chair.

Oh! Kittredge shouted. He plucked Grant's hand off the armrest to shake it. We got in a little early, he said, and Petey wanted to take a look at some boots—

I'll take these here ones, Neeler said without turning toward them. There was a slickness about him now, his shirt buttoned up to the collar and the red boots on his feet.

Hell, Petey, Kittredge said to him, they ain't worth nothin' for real work. You'll just rub out all that bric-a-brac.

They ain't for work, came the reply. They're for me.

Hey, look at who you're ignoring here, it's Grant, come to pick us up.

Neeler tilted his head halfway in Grant's direction and nodded once, a slow rote thing he must have seen in the movies.

Truck's out back, Grant said, I'll just meet you there when you're all finished. He saw their bags between the chairs and he picked them up and walked out. Funny how he had got used to wordless Cotter being the only one around; the population was doubling and tripling. He laid the bags in the back of the truck and went around to the front of the store, where he got a cola out of a machine. He stood drinking it a minute then went back to the lot to wait. Not much later they came out, Kittredge first, fingering his hat brim, and Neeler ten feet behind him wearing a new pair of brown work boots. Kittredge opened the passenger door and got in, leaving a space for Neeler. But Neeler jumped in the bed with the bags. Kittredge shut the door and Grant started the engine.

God damn that boy, Kittredge said with an uncharacteristic vehemence, still wearing his flat smile as if it was the only thing his face could think to do. God damn him, I don't know what's his problem. I ought to just cut him loose.

Grant steered them out of the lot and onto Main Street, slowing for the blinker. Why don't you? he said.

I can't. I can't, Kittredge said sighing. You ought to see him some nights, balled all up in his bed like a baby, it'd be like putting a gun to his head, it sure would. I'll tell you what, I feel sorry for that boy, I really do.

Out on the highway Grant took a draught of the cola and put it back between his legs. Max came back, he said.

Kittredge looked at him. That so? Where's he been all this time?

New York City. He was painting pictures.

Kittredge squinted out over the hood at the coming road. Painting pictures! Well why'd he come back then?

Same reason anybody does, I guess.

There was a knock on the cab window. Neeler was pointing and making a gesture, drinking from his thumb and little finger. He had a look on his face like something'd been stolen from him. Grant drank from the bottle once more and then held it out the window, and Neeler leaned over the side and took it. Through the rearview Grant saw him empty the bottle into his wide cracked mouth and fling it out behind them, where it bounced and shattered on the black macadam. The glass receded, glimmering like a liquid.

He drove them straight to their quarters. Come up the house when you're ready for some dinner, he said. In fact they were late, it was after two and Sophia'd likely cooked it and left it, if she'd cooked it at all. Neeler beelined to the cabin empty-handed and Kittredge humped their bags to the door.

Back at the house he found himself alone. He buttered some bread and sat down to eat it. His eyes moved to the kitchen window. As he watched, Sophia came out of the barn slapping dust off her clothes. She looked up and saw the truck and then turned her head to the window Grant was looking out of. With the sun above and behind her reflecting off the house, he doubted she could see him there, yet she stood frozen for long seconds before she went into the henhouse.

Ever since he was sick she'd been striking up conversations, at first asking him practical questions about the animals and later inquiring about him personally, about their childhood here and his years at sea. Initially he was reluctant to discuss either, but since they were often on his mind he came to think there was no harm in it. Now he wasn't sure. Talking about a thing, he'd learned, could freeze and focus the memory, sharpening some parts and obscuring others, as in a photograph. He didn't want his memory to be like a box of pictures, a set of little truths that didn't add up to a life. Yet he kept talking to her, trying to ignore what he was saying, because he found he liked her brand of talk, liked the company of somebody who wanted to hear.

She told him about her girls' school in the city and all its pettinesses and trivialities, which struck him as absurd, the way they taxed and strained the emotions. It made him think of his own school, the one they went to before the new elementary was built in Eleven, a single brick room under a crumbling roof which now stood slumped and empty along the road to town. Their teacher was a tiny lady from Eugene, Oregon who had married a local cattleman and had used to play in an orchestra. Half of every day they spent practicing on musical instruments, whatever ones the students could find, harmonicas, flutes, a concertina, a fiddle. A dented trumpet that had a shivery, addled tone like the bleat of a goat. They played in concerts for their families, though only when the weather was fine and they could do it outdoors. There was no room in the school for both performers and audience. Grant had learned to play a borrowed flute and Max a guitar. Sometimes there was a girl singer. A passing truck might pull over to listen. It seemed a strange way to occupy schoolchildren, though nobody questioned it at the time. The teacher would be sad to know that he no longer played music, and to think of it made him a little sad himself.

When he talked, particularly about things he'd done with Max, Sophia sometimes sat up suddenly or spoke a wordless note as if she was amazed, even at such plain recollections as a hunting expedition or fistfight. He got the sense that she was remembering it all for some future purpose.

They didn't ever talk about Max directly, and when Max was with her she didn't say much to Grant. Instead she directed what she said to Max, who might look at Grant to include him or might not. For awhile Grant didn't notice this was going on, not until he'd begun to speak to her in private, and he began to wonder whether Max knew the two of them spoke at all, so different was she in his presence. Only when he was alone, out riding or lying in his bed, was Grant fully at ease, when he could forget and didn't have to keep track of who was around him and who wasn't, and what he could say and how he could say it. Yet at these times he missed her, anyone's, company.

Now he got up from the table and went out to her and asked if she could fix something for Kittredge and Neeler to eat. I'm sorry to miss you earlier, he said.

You didn't. Max and Amos wanted to wait.

It took him a second to register this name: it was Cotter's. Where are they? he asked.

Shed, she said scattering meal on the ground for the chickens. Her eyes were on the work, her movements dismissive, like she was shooing him. He went to find Cotter and his brother. They were in the shed as she told him, examining a canvas tarp for wear.

Christ, Max said to him, you have got to get some rat poison out here. He waggled a finger through a round hole that had been chewed in the tarp.

I've done it. It doesn't seem to do much good.

They'll get into my things, Max said.

Grant shrugged. They were expecting the shearers soon, a band of Mexicans who worked their way north following the season, up into Canada in summer, visiting outfits like theirs who didn't have the time or skill to do it themselves. There was no permanent shearing shed here, so the lambing pens were nailed together and covered with a treated tarp to keep the rain out. This was the tarp Max and Cotter were working on.

You hear from the Mexicans? Grant asked.

Max let him wait for the answer while he fished in a metal box for a roll of gray tape. He tore off a length with his teeth and fitted it over a mousehole. Called from Gillette while you were out, he said. They ought to be in tonight late.

Grant wondered when Max had been planning to tell him this. He said, You get the rooms done up?

Max treated the question like an accusation. Don't I look busy enough already?

Cotter caught the tone and lifted his head. He turned to Grant to see what he would say.

Only asking, Grant said and a split second later made an error in judgment and added, You're near to boiling over, Max. Maybe you ought to tell me what's going on.

Max stood.

Grant said, It ain't my fault I got sick. I'd've liked to be out here helping you—

That's right, Max muttered, nothing's your fault, is it. Everything just happens.

His hands seemed to be shaking. The sight of them filled Grant with remorse for everything he'd done and said, the way seeing a quaking tree branch can bring on the instincts of winter. He shivered without moving. He wasn't sure what was happening.

Cotter moved suddenly and the both of them turned as if they'd forgot he was there. He was holding a set of pliers and stood framed by the painting tools behind him, the easel and the model's platform. In the dim light, by a trick of perspective, he looked to Grant like a giant, the subject of some myth.

What! Max barked, and Grant felt himself twitch.

Cotter coughed. I was just thinking, he said. When you two was boys you used to pretend you was fighting, remember that?

He was turning the pliers over and over in his hand. A bent nail fell from their grip and rang out against the cement. He put the pliers in his back pocket as a man sure of his safety holsters a gun.

No, Grant said.

That was your way of fighting, pretending a fight. One of you got mad, the other one would get his dukes up and start scuffing like it was some kind of joke. He looked from one to the other and let out a laugh. You'd think from looking at you that you was afraid of killing each other.

Grant turned his eyes to his brother but Max wasn't looking back. He appeared to be in a trance. Grant remembered now, the bogus dustups out in the barn. They'd got started because of an incident when Max was seven or eight and Grant thirteen. Robert was two years dead, they were arguing over something of his, maybe it was a saddle. Max was cleaning off a knife or sharpening it on a stone, and Grant came over and took the saddle from nearby for some reason. And then—he couldn't have explained why, maybe Max was entertaining some fierce possession of the saddle in his mind at that moment— Max came up behind him with the knife and stabbed him through the side just below the skin, so that the blade sunk in under the ribs, pierced the fat and came out again a couple of inches beyond at the front side of his flank, never going more than a fraction of an inch deep. He couldn't have said what Max had been thinking to do when he got up off his stool. Probably not what he ended up doing. But Grant had half turned when he heard him coming, and the knife went in hard and smooth and easy. Max's face was bent in a theatrical fury that Grant had sometimes seen since Robert died, when Max thought he was alone. He was only a little boy, Grant remembered, barely beginning school and already with two dead brothers behind him.

The two had stood still, regarding the knife sticking out of Grant, the blade clean where it met the hilt and streaked with blood where it emerged. After a silence of seconds Max began to cry and Grant dropped the saddle into the dirt, or must have, because he used one hand to press the wound and the other to pull out the knife. Afterward Max helped him to disinfect and bandage the cuts, his only apology. At the time, Grant's impression was that Max had no idea what he'd done, or even that he'd done anything. They told no one. From then on their skirmishes were faked.

It was strange. A kind of animal readiness came over Max, his eyes grew wild. Grant learned to drop whatever he was doing and take him on. They batted at each other and rolled on the floor in a feral clinch. Max always held on longer, even when Grant loosened his grip and tried to roll him off. In due time the aggression drained out of the embrace until, in its greediness and desperation, it began to resemble an act of grief. Max bit him, sometimes breaking his skin through the clothes, and Grant held him until at last he grew limp in his arms. This went on a month or two until Edwin shot himself. After that Max began to teach himself and Thornton the rudiments of work, and what peculiar intimacy he'd shared with Grant was gone.

How Cotter had managed to see them doing this, Grant had no idea. They had carried on in private. But Cotter, who they'd not thought of as real, had seen and remembered, and he had them now in thrall, like a magician.

Cotter bent over and pulled another nail out of the plank he was working on. The sound of his breath shook them awake. Grant hazarded a glance at his brother and Max fixed his eyes on the floor where the tarp lay crumpled. His hands were still. It was obvious he was waiting for Grant to go.

I'll go fix the rooms, Grant said, and he left the shed for the house to get the linens.

⋅

He hadn't been in his parents' bedroom since Sophia had come to occupy it. Little was changed. A photo of some girls, Sophia among them, was thumbtacked to the wall; a scarf hung over a lampshade; the bureau was covered with small things, perfumes he hadn't known her to wear, letters, jewelry. He picked up the blue bottle from the windowsill. The glass distorted and discolored his fingers. Some tonic had been in it once, he could smell the astringency and make out the antiquated type on a half-gone label. The sight of his shriveled hand made him think of Wesley. He put the bottle back. From this window he could see the road vanish beyond the rise and reappear as it climbed up out of the valley.

The extra linens were kept in the closet, folded and stacked in a far corner behind the hung clothes. This was the only upstairs closet and it had been his mother's alone for as long as he could remember. It wasn't in her nature to be especially private or possessive, but it was understood in this house that the closet was all she had to herself. He opened the door and took note of what Sophia had done. Her few clothes—an extra pair of dungarees and several work shirts of Max's, a few dresses too fine to wear and which he had never seen her in— hung on the right side with more than six inches separating them from his mother's. His mother's dresses she had not disturbed. He widened the gap to see where the linens lay and the back of his hand brushed the waist of a dress, Sophia's. He pulled the hand away like he'd been shocked. Reluctantly he brought it to his face. After a moment he took the fabric between his thumb and finger and leaned forward to breathe through it. The air trapped inside smelled of her powerfully, a concentrated scent he knew from passing her. It reminded him of the ocean, not for the specificity of the fragrance but for its intensity, its separateness from the smells ordinarily around him when he worked or slept. It was like looking at photographs of a place he knew he would never go to, someplace foreign and lovely. For a moment he missed the sea and the man he had been then; their distance from him filled him with longing. Not that he would prefer to be there now, to be that man. He had not been happy. But he longed for the inevitability of those days, the impossibility of leaving the boat, the certainty of some hardships, the necessity of other people. He let go of the dress but allowed it to brush his face when he bent down to pick up the bedsheets, and he closed the closet door firmly behind him.

In the shearers' quarters, fitting the narrow beds with sheets and inhaling the old woodsmoked air, his concentration left him and he envisioned Sophia posing for his brother, undressed before the cold corrugated metal walls, and he sat down on a freshly made bunk and for several minutes held his face in his hands.

•

Max rode out over the hill to bring in Murray and the flock, and by the time the sheep were back in their shed, clouds had begun to mass over the mountains to the north. By nightfall Cotter had the shearing shelter assembled in the yard. Grant woke that night to the sound of the Mexicans' truck and the near-silent swipe of drizzling rain on the windows and roof. He dressed and went down to meet the men. There were five of them, all small and muscular. Their reticence and similar build made him believe they were brothers. Each had some English but it was the oldest, Jorge, who spoke for the group, and when he met Grant he clasped his hand and pointed at the sky. Grant nodded, telling him the tarp was patched and sealed and the flock under cover in their shed. But he knew the shearing would be hard in rain. Though these men were professionals who could each get the fleece whole off two hundred head in a day, the wool couldn't be bagged wet and there would be a delay as each sheep was toweled off and the towels dried. Grant was ashamed of their makeshift shelter, he dreaded ushering the workers into it. To Jorge he said something to this effect, and the smaller man shrugged and said it was okay because their ranch, unlike most, had good beds. Elsewhere the flock was given the better roof. Somewhere in this comment Grant thought he could hear a slight, but one so oblique and blunt-edged as to be inconsequential. He nodded and pointed them toward their quarters.

The rain picked up as the truck's lights receded into mist. Grant thought about what they would need to combat the rain: every towel and blanket in the place, a barrel they could start a fire in and scrap wood to burn, another good tarp to keep the water off the gas generator that would power the electric shearers. It couldn't have been much past two A.M., but he turned back to the house to wake his brother up.

·

By morning the rain was a steady torrent under a black sky cut at intervals by lightning. But the shearers seemed oblivious to weather, going at their work with silent determination, the fleece loosening itself from the sheep in thick intact mats. Max rolled the fleece and gave it to Neeler to examine and stuff into sacks; Neeler rushed the sacks to the equipment shed. Kittredge and Murray and Cotter led the shorn sheep to their shed, wrestled each into a dipping vat and let it loose to huddle with the others. Grant was rubbing the unshorn animals dry as fast as he could, trying to wick the rain off the fleece without pressing it deeper down, and Sophia ran, frantic, to the fire and back, trying to keep the towels dry enough to do him some good. But they were losing. They would need to empty out the bags and air the fleece, it was inevitable. Sometimes Grant looked up and saw one or two of the shearers standing idle, somehow smoking a cigarette in the awful wet, and he understood that they wouldn't be finished by nightfall, that there would be at least another half day, and though the shearers weren't union workers Grant had promised them union wages because they were better than the local men. It was more than he could afford. By noon Neeler had begun to complain that the fleece was giving him a runny nose and making his head ache. Sophia traded jobs with him. But after that the towels came to Grant still wet, and the shearers looked up from the damp animals annoyed at the sudden change. By late afternoon the shearers had their shirts off and were using them to dry the sheep a second time. Throughout, the roar of the generator filled the air, punctuated by the crash of thunder and the occasional frenzy of barks from Murray's dogs.

All of them took supper together. Grant went up to Edwin's room and brought down the chairs, which by seven o'clock were again occupied by brothers. Max finished eating first and said, in a hoarse disgusted voice, What a goddam mess.

No kidding, said Neeler, rubbing a handkerchief under his nose and looking at it.

Max went on, ignoring him. This cheap shit won't work, he said. A few of the shearers looked up. All that goddam work for what's going to be a rotten soaking load. I seen 'em going in, the wool's all taggy and grimy. He threw down his fork. We got to start bringing them in before lambing.

He hadn't been looking at Grant, but it was for Grant the words were intended. It's too cold before lambing, he said.

Too cold for that slapped-together shack, maybe.

Jorge was sitting beside Grant and touched his wrist with two thin fingers. Maybe you build a permanent pen next to your shed, he said quietly. With wood floor. And a chute that come up to it, with a roof. Not so hard to do.

No money, Grant said.

Sophia came up behind Max and spooned food onto his plate. Max turned his head and pushed the plate away. She paused a moment and moved on to the Mexicans, who nodded their thanks.

Grant's arms and fingers ached from working the towels over the animals and his eyes were red from exhaustion and cut fleece. It seemed they might all be at this table forever, so powerful was the disinclination to move. Sophia sat down in front of her empty plate and looked at it, keeping a distance between herself and Max. Some time later Jorge cleared his throat and stood up, and the other shearers followed him to the counter where they left their plates in a neat stack. Then they went out into the rain for another few hours' work. Not long afterward Cotter got up too, and then everyone else.

•

The Mexicans were paid and gone by midafternoon of the next day, and while Sophia slept, the rest of them tore down the shearing shelter and dragged the pieces into the shed. The sun had arrived as if it had been waiting for them to finish. Shorn sheep were wandering out into the light. Cotter and Murray went to give them dry bedding and feed. In a few days they would be on summer range.

Kittredge sat on a fence rail rolling a cigarette with shaking hands. Grant watched, wanting to take the paper and tobacco from him and do it himself. When Kittredge had finally got it Grant went to him and asked if he wanted to go get some sleep.

Nah, Kittredge said without elaboration. He looked peaked. He rubbed his forehead with the stump of his missing finger, still shaking but less so now that the smoke was in him.

Maybe you'll want to take a little rest, Grant said. Stay here and heal up some. I wouldn't ask you anything for the bed but if you could get some of the food when—

Nah, now all *that's* done—he pointed with his thumb in the direction the shearers had gone—it'll get easier around here, ain't that right?

Sure.

Unless you can't keep us on here, that's a different matter, I understand that.

No, that ain't it, Grant said, though it was. He owed again, a few hundred here and there. The fleece would cover it but beyond that he didn't know. Once the fleece went to market Kittredge and Neeler were no longer necessary. Kittredge's free hand gripped the rail steadily, but the hand he smoked with still shook. He tried to keep the arm pinned to his side. It gave him a winter look, like he was protecting himself from weather. Grant said, I just thought you might use a break, that's all.

Kittredge nodded. Maybe, he said. Maybe soon. I think right now I'll just smoke this here cigarette.

Grant left him there. Murray and Cotter were tending to the sheep themselves now, salving shear cuts and guiding the animals out of the sun to spare their skin. He remembered he'd sent Neeler into the shed to air out the fleece. When he went in he found it unrolled across the floor, much as he would have done himself, covering every inch of space, filled in among the equipment and over Max's area like a moss that had sprung up. The scent of wet wool filled the room. Neeler was bent over at the shed's far end, opposite the easel, one hand pressed to the metal wall, a burning cigarette in the other. Grant said to him, Good job, Pete, and Neeler almost jumped out of his skin, dropping the cigarette onto the fleece and quickly stooping to pick it up. He'd never looked to Grant so much like a boy, so inessential, as he did now, still half-crouched, a crosseyed cornered look on his face like a streak of mud. He said nothing.

Good going, Grant said. This'll do the job.

In the rusted wall behind Neeler, Grant could see a small hole where Cotter had once backed the truck up too fast with a length of copper pipe in the bed. The pipe had torn through and left a corroded flap that had since fallen off. Neeler had been looking through the hole. Grant said, If you want to fix that I won't stop you.

Neeler closed his mouth and stood straight, a hint of swagger returning to his frame. Hey, all right, he said. Maybe I will, sure.

You might find a little scrap metal in the fire cabinet, or else you could go to town and bring back a sheet. There's a torch in there too. You know how to use a torch?

I think I used one once.

You put the mask on, and then there's a lighter in there.

Neeler nodded, his whole upper body moving with it. Okay, I can get to that maybe.

But something told Grant he wasn't going to do it at all and possibly didn't even know what Grant was talking about. There was a deep meanness and stupidity to the boy which no good will could touch. He doubted Neeler even knew what was in him, no more than a house could know who was living in it or a stream know where it was flowing to. He was like a force of nature, dull and destructive.

That was a heavy load to hang on this dumb motherless boy, Grant knew, but it was hard to shake the impression of malevolence, to believe there was a decent man under there who could do the outfit some good.

There was nothing else to say. Grant touched his hat and nodded at Neeler, leaving him standing on a tiny patch of exposed cement, the only thing he'd left uncovered. He looked back again from the doorway. The boy stood helpless on his little island, wiping his nose with the back of his hand, fleeced in.

7

In a day, when the fleece was dry, the men and Sophia spread themselves out through the shed rolling and tying it up, picking out burrs and bits of skin. For the most part it had turned out better than Grant expected, and with the weather mild and clear in the wake of the rain he let himself be filled up with optimism. Neeler had stacked the empty bags still damp. They had not fully dried and smelled of mold. So Max and Sophia aired them out in the yard, running in circles, holding them over their heads under the bright sun. Cotter hitched the trailer onto the truck and with Grant loaded the bagged wool to bring it to the merchant's in Ashton. They rode with the windows open and the cool wind along the ridge rushed in. Aspens glittered at the roadside like pinwheels. Between the men lingered that strangeness with Max in the barn, but Cotter was unlikely ever to mention it again. Once they were down on the flats Grant fiddled with the radio knob until something came in they could both stand to hear. The music was like an unexpected and not unwelcome passenger, evidence of life elsewhere. It eased Grant, the remedy for an ailment he hadn't noticed he'd got.

The Merchants' Hall in Ashton was a brick warehouse with tall windows set close together on the north side. When they pulled around they were momentarily blinded by the sunlight glancing off its face. Nobody else was here. A wooden chute marked where to back up the trailer. Once they'd done so they began unloading the wool bags through an open steel door. Inside, a fan was moving. Over its roar they greeted the grader, a high narrow man of about sixty Grant could recognize but not name. They all said good morning and Grant shook his hand, and the grader's eyes rested on him a moment longer than was necessary, apprehending and judging him. But the grader said nothing. He stood behind a long wooden table, and behind him stood a dozen wicker baskets, each about the size of Grant's cabin on the *Rose Adams*, into which their wool would be sorted. The grader plunged his hand into the first of the bags and let it linger there. He glared blankly, lost in a private tactile world.

They brought in more bags, stealing glances at the grader's work as they heaved them onto the table. With quick fingers the grader was tugging at the fibers, holding them up to the light. Shortly an assistant arrived, a man of about thirty, shorter and rounder in the face than the grader but nonetheless his very image. His son. Now the work moved faster, the son opening their bags along the seam and, when his father was through, tossing the graded bundles into the bins behind them. Meanwhile the grader made notations with the stub of a pencil on a yellow form.

Their demeanor made Grant uneasy. The son accepted mumbled assessments from the father and flung the bundles with a studied carelessness. For a moment Grant had the notion that he wanted them back, he felt his body tugged toward the bins each time he stepped through the door with a new bag. The bags were heavy and unwieldy and his back was beginning to ache.

Grant and Cotter were finished long before the grader and his son, so they stood inside with the windows behind them and watched the men work. Most of the bundles went into one of two bins close behind the tables. The bins weren't marked but Grant knew that each represented a grade of wool. Outside more trucks began to arrive and Grant could hear men talking to one another just outside the door. After awhile the grader spoke to Grant without looking up.

Your daddy used to raise a fine wool.

Yes, he did, was all Grant could say.

How's he doing? the grader asked. Your daddy. He looked up and met Grant's eyes, and Grant knew he knew that John Person was gone. Panic began to well in the hollows of his body.

Couldn't say, Grant said finally. He peered at the grader's son and found him looking back, and in that moment Grant knew him. Only the last name would come to him. Burt. Their name was Burt. This junior Burt had come back alive from the war. He had a brother who hadn't. Grant held his eyes until Burt turned to his father.

Oh, he's away, is he? the grader had gone on. Now you're the older boy, is that right? You were away yourself awhile.

That's right.

I imagine it's hard coming home to us after seeing the world.

I didn't see much but the inside of a boat.

The grader was finished, the tables cleared of fleece. The young Burt began to fold and stack the empty bags. Grant's eyes lingered on the older man, who stared furiously back, then at last bent over his adding machine and punched in the numbers he'd written. He marked a total on the yellow sheet and handed the carbon to Grant. They'll cut you a check at the office, he said.

Grant looked at the form. Only about a third of what they'd brought had been marked fine, the quality numbers just over sixty. Much of what he used to bring here with his father was far finer, usually in the seventies. The other two thirds was marked half or three-eighths blood, not the typical numbers of a professional outfit. In fact they were worse than last year's: not just disappointing but wrong.

Is something the matter, Mr. Person?

Grant looked up into the grader's eyes but could not comprehend what he was looking at. The man's judgment of him was extraordinary, even absurd. Nevertheless Grant couldn't help feeling it was correct. He grew hot with shame and rage and felt Cotter's hand on his arm.

Mr. Person? the grader asked again.

No, Grant said. Nothing's the matter, Mr. Burt. Burt's son stood frozen now, unsure of what was happening, and the older man himself seemed stunned by the mention of his name, as if suddenly reminded that it was indeed he who had cheated a customer. He hung his head. Grant had it figured now: the bins closest to them were likely reserved for fine wool, the commonest grade received here. Much of his own wool had gone into them. The younger Burt began almost imperceptibly to pale. He hadn't known what his father was doing, nor who Grant was. After another moment Cotter turned and left and Grant followed him out.

Cotter moved the trailer out of the chute and met Grant at the office door on the west side of the building. He took the form from Grant's hand and read it.

He won't do it again, Cotter said. He knows it was a mistake. There's other places to sell wool and he's got a reputation to keep.

Cotter handed back the form. I ain't surprised he done it, he went on, fingering the collar of his shirt where it curled under. The morning sun was throwing the shadow of the hall over and past them, across a gravel lot and up the wall of an apartment house, where it gave way in the middle of a window to a blinding reflection of the sun itself. Cotter said, I figured you was no damn good myself, when you got back. People don't see how complicated a thing is. They think if it was them they'd of done something different. They don't know how weak they are until something happens that's stronger than them.

Cotter held Grant's forearm loosely in his fingers. Grant watched his own fingers creasing the form, the sweat smearing the numbers on it. Cotter said, I ain't saying you always done the right thing, but you never done what that Burt just did. You never cheated an honest man.

For some reason these words evoked Grant's father, a trip Grant took west with him once, over the divide to look at a tractor somebody was selling. They'd been thinking of growing alfalfa on a section of their pastureland, to feed the flock cheaper during lambing. As they topped the mountains and descended into the lushness and warmth of the western slopes, John grew morose and finally pulled over and collapsed onto the wheel.

Grant was still a boy, he didn't understand. What is it? he asked, shaking his father by the shoulder.

Sometimes you want to go back where you came from, his father said through tears. He fished a rag out of the glovebox and wiped his face with it. Then they turned around and drove home, the tractor and alfalfa forgotten.

With Cotter's hand still on his arm, Grant wondered out loud if he would ever see his father again. And Cotter, as if following perfectly this wayward train of thought, said no. Grant's hand fell to his side. He could release the paper he was holding and watch the wind carry it out into the street, and they could get into the truck and leave here. But he didn't do that, it would be crazy. Instead the two of them walked wordlessly into the office to collect their money.

⋅

He woke that night to the sound of scratching above him, something moving around. A vague memory of past dreams crossed his mind and frightened him; he drew breath and threw off the covers. But the memory was gone. The scratching continued, rhythmically: there was a sentience to it. Animals up there. They had an attic he'd forgot about. He lay down and tried to sleep, the pillow clamped over his ear, and in the half-dream that followed, the muffled scrabbling became a man's heavy tread, monotonously pacing as if in anticipation of terrible news.

Morning brought naked daylight and the hotness of summer. The night's noise came back to him. When they were boys he and Max and Robert used to climb up and pretend to guard the valley against the Germans their father had sometimes told them about. Grant couldn't recall if anything was up there now. He could remember no floor, only planks laid loose across the joists. The sound they made when he and his brothers ran across them was like an artillery barrage, or what they imagined one to sound like.

He sat up in his bed feeling the attic's presence like days of unfinished work. The light outside was still new but pressed him to get up, so he did, glancing occasionally at the cracked plaster ceiling.

On the floor next to the bureau Grant had left his bag, the one he traveled with and hadn't touched since he took his pay out of it nearly two years before. When he had first returned it reminded him of what he left behind, and he'd no desire to open it. In time it had become part of the room's landscape and his eyes passed it over without catching.

He dressed, then lifted the bag onto the bed. After a few seconds he sat down beside it and undid the latch. Folded on top was his shirt, the one he'd left home wearing, which had wanted washing and still did. He took it out and laid it aside. Only a few other objects remained. A single black sock whose twin he'd kept his money in. The whalebone box, hexagonal with a carved lid. After a moment's consideration he brought this over to the bureau. It had come from Iceland. A sailor had been peddling his possessions out of a sack on the dock. The man spoke no English but managed to explain with his hands that he was to go to sea and didn't wish to be encumbered by his things. Grant paid him and took the box. Iceland was his mother's country and he'd wanted to bring her something from there.

Now he went back to the bag and removed a wristwatch and Luc's brass compass wrapped in a soft gray cloth. The wristwatch had come out of a cod. It was old and eaten away by salt water and by the chemicals in the fish. Its face was stained and buckled, the glass gone, the hands crooked and corroded into place. The word DEUTSCHLAND was engraved on the back.

The compass had been Luc's grandfather's. Grant wondered where his friend was now. Probably still at sea or back in Belgium. Luc had been too personable for the fishing life: Grant would not have been surprised to learn he had quit. The compass was tarnished by years of neglect, but he could polish it. It seemed to work.

The whaleman's knife, the one he'd got in a card game, still glinted at the bottom of the bag. He reached for it, then thought better. Instead he picked up the bag and brought it to his bureau. He opened a drawer and upturned the bag over it, and the knife tumbled in, to rest in a gap between shirts. Then he shut the drawer and returned the bag to the floor.

Later in the morning he had occasion to go out to the barn, and he took his pannier off the nail where it was hung and added the compass to his camp supplies. There wasn't anyplace within fifty miles of here where he'd need it, but knowing he would have it on hand calmed his nerves, as if now he was ready for anything.

·

After supper, when Max and Sophia went out to the shed, Grant entered her closet and looked up into the darkness. He could make out an opening in the ceiling covered by a board. Standing on his toes he fingered the board aside and began to hoist himself up. But his grip was poor and he came down on his feet. He tried again, jumping this time and hooking his elbows into the attic space. From there it was easy.

The attic was boiling hot, the setting sun outside drowning it in an orange wash. His eyes were drawn to the semicircular vent on the west wall; they fixed upon a distant passing cloud, blazed pink by the oblique light. Only when the cloud left his sight did Grant turn around to see what was here.

Not much. Even the planks were gone, probably taken down and used for something. There were leaves blown in by storms and a raven's nest that looked long unoccupied. The nest had been built in a corner, down between two rafters. He goosestepped over to it, ducking his head away from the ceiling beams, and leaned close to peer at a bright thread running through. Ribbon, the sheen still on it, the kind a girl might put in her hair. He tugged at the free end but the nest had been woven too tightly.

In another corner, the one above his bedroom, was a mound of household debris—bits of cloth and paper, thread, and hair—with a depression in the center. It smelled of rodent. Mice. He lifted this second nest and shoved it out the vent. It quickly fell from sight.

The wind picked up and a meaningless breeze pushed through the empty space. Grant's heart was heavy. He felt bad for throwing away the mouse nest. For the next several weeks, as he tried to sleep, he could hear a new one being built.

◆

It was July of 1950. The Fourth had passed. The only thing that happened in Eleven all year was the rodeo, and it was about to start. Merchants who wouldn't ordinarily have bothered sweeping their own stoops were out painting the clapboards. Roads were oiled and graveled and trucks came rumbling over them full of boxes from Ashton. Unfamiliar pickups and trailers began to appear, and in a trampled pasture outside town tents sprang up, spilling out calf ropers and bulldoggers who were louder than locals and had more money. The bar was always full. This year it was selling beer in screwtop motor oil cans, and the cans made their way out into the street and started piling up in the gutters and flattening under truck tires. Every night there were good-looking girls crying drunk on curbs until somebody came for them and escorted them back to their tents. They had come with their men from California and had been on the circuit more than two months, with at least three more to go. From here they would go to Cheyenne or Pendleton and after that a lot of them would just go home. The riders would continue without them all the way to New York and Boston.

Every year somebody was seriously injured or killed. Grant had seen a local boy get himself landed full on by his quarter horse about a dozen years back, and the boy had stood up like nothing had happened, walked ten feet holding his head with both hands, and fell down dead in the dirt. People got run down by drunks or drove into trees or phone poles. Occasionally somebody got shot, either by accident or in a fight. Typically the county gave badges to a lot of local men and trucked them down to Eleven for the duration of the rodeo, and often these men got involved in the drinking and shooting. The town's own police department, which consisted of one retired cattle rancher and his son, tended to stay at the office and wait for the criminals to come in on their own.

As a matter of habit Grant didn't go to the rodeo, not since he'd seen the boy die. The immodesty of cowboys didn't endear them to him, either, and the events they competed in seemed less like sport than a brutal parody of work. There was a long-standing rivalry between cattlemen and sheepmen that had its origins in territorial disputes. But it endured out of taste. Grant found the cattlemen brutish and arrogant and their games disrespectful to the animal. It was wrong to mock the thing that gave you life. The sheep was not an intelligent beast but in great numbers achieved a kind of elemental dignity, like an air mass. Once he'd seen a flock move across a hillside and mistook it for the shadow of a cloud. He had watched sheep gather where they once found a salt lick years before, even the lambs, who hadn't been alive to see it. A sheepflock seemed to pulse with purpose almost as if it was one creature, a vast and simple mind that understood its relationship to the land and to man, while a herd of cattle was nothing more than a vegetable garden with hooves, a lowing orchard, inefficient and dumb.

But Neeler wanted to go to the rodeo. Since the shearing, the boy had little to do and had grown bored and hostile. Earlier and earlier each night he slicked back his hair and demanded that Cotter drive him to town, and often he stayed there until morning, spending pocketsful of Kittredge's money on drink and getting himself into fights and once into jail. If Cotter refused him his ride Neeler would take a horse and run it to exhaustion on the rangeland. When he got back he would leave it unstabled in the yard. While drunk he jeered at them openly, everyone but Max, who he was afraid of. Max, for his part, never spoke to Neeler at all.

The night before the rodeo began, a thick wind was draining out of the northwest. Dust roiled on their road. From his room Grant watched it eddy and sway in the porchlight, the very air given shape. Its deftness and power were frightening: he was grateful that it was ordinarily invisible. He almost failed to notice the shape moving along the back wall of the equipment shed, hunched over in the dark. A bear? Max and Sophia were in there.

He pulled his boots on and brought a shotgun out into the yard. Hi! he shouted, the word nearly lost over the grinding of the wind! Cautiously he moved closer. The shape was a man's.

He recognized Neeler's posture first: the same stoop Grant had caught him in before, inside the shed. Then, Neeler had been examining the hole in the shed wall. He was doing the same thing now. Not to fix it, to look through it. To watch Sophia being drawn or painted.

Naked of course. Grant had tried to keep himself from thinking about it. He supposed it was only natural for such a notion to cross his mind, but somehow, with Sophia, it seemed wrong. Now Neeler had his eyes on her and Grant wanted to get him. He realized that he'd wanted him for weeks. Everything suddenly seemed to be Neeler's fault, all the ugliness of life the product of his ugliness. Grant shouted and his legs carried him to the shed, the weight of the shotgun asserting itself against his palm.

Neeler stood up with a forced slowness, like a man asked to put down his drink and meet guests. Grant was enraged.

What in the hell do you think you're doing? he shouted, and the wind snatched the words and carried them off. He stood as close as caution allowed.

There was a cigarette in Neeler's mouth which, no longer shielded by the bulk of his head, glowed brightly, releasing a stream of white ash into the air. He said, See for yourself, partner, and pointed at the bright hole.

Grant's right hand twitched and discovered it was holding the shotgun. It was the left that opened wide and struck Neeler in the mouth. The slap was loud even over the wind and knocked the cigarette into the grass. Grant leaned into him now and the boy's fat stunned face filled his vision. You're one move away from gone, you understand me? he said, and Neeler blinked and blinked again.

Maybe you wouldn't be so brave without that shotgun, Neeler croaked. His red lips were split and scabbed and his tongue emerged to wet them.

Grant flung the shotgun into the dirt.

Neeler backed off a bare inch, making room to swing. Grant shifted one leg to steady himself. He could remember every single punch he'd thrown in his life: every schoolhouse brawl and sloppy drunken cuff, every shoving match over whatever stupid slight. In the past he'd regretted each of them. Now they seemed justified, even necessary. Neeler stood three or four inches shorter than Grant but his arms were thick and dense as firewood, and when the fist arrived it had that weight behind it. But it was a bad punch, overcompensating for the difference in height, striking Grant on the cheekbone and glancing off his nose without breaking it. Grant's head shook with the blow's force but he had no trouble righting himself and jabbing at Neeler, whose nose instantly gushed blood. By gripping his neck Grant was able to force him to the corrugated wall and the shed rumbled like an empty truck on a rutted road.

Neeler had already given up, though he was stronger than Grant and could have won. He clutched his face as though it was in danger of coming off.

Tomorrow, Grant said into his ear, you get out.

Neeler said something but his words were lost to the wind. Grant tightened the grip on his neck unnecessarily. His cheek burned from Neeler's blow and a headache flickered to life behind his eyes. He wanted to be in bed.

He'd hit Thornton once. Thornton had hit first but that wasn't the point. Grant had made fun of his laugh—mimicked it actually, still angry over whatever embarrassment had made Thornton laugh in the first place. Guileless Thornton had gone pink as a squalling baby and set upon Grant with his clumsy blows. And Grant had hit him, hard.

How joyful it felt to make contact, how awful the moment just after. He told himself this wasn't like that. He tried to hold on to his righteousness.

A floodlight filled the yard and Max shouted into the night. He was standing under the glare in paint-spattered overalls and an undershirt. Neeler raised up his bloodwet face and Max's eyes fell onto it. Max turned to Grant and back, and Grant released Neeler, letting him slump full against the wall. He was seized by a feeling of unreality and for a moment did not know who he was: his hands sticky with Neeler's blood, the left still stinging from the slap, the headache a black cowl gripping his skull.

Max's lips curled, amused. Which of you's the peeper? he said.

Grant was shocked back into himself. His headache retreated a bare inch. Goddam, he said, who do you think?

I think if I asked, you might both say it was worth looking. He was pleased. Grant noticed his hands, fine and filthy, half in half out of his pockets.

It ain't me. What's got into your head?

Max laughed. The wind had calmed, as if to taste him. Okay, then, he said and turned to Neeler. Get yourself a good look, Pete? You get your fill of her?

Neeler stood, looking at one brother and then the other, trying to figure some advantage. Blood still foamed over his mouth and chin and down into his collar, and he brought up his arm and wiped the blood away with his sleeve.

Now Sophia appeared, dressed in her jeans and a shirt of Max's, and glared at the three of them with her arms crossed. Neeler hung his head and half turned away. When nobody said anything Grant spoke to him.

I want you gone by breakfast.

Max didn't change his expression. He seemed to find Grant's command entertaining.

What happened? Sophia asked.

Grant tried not to look at her. Nothing you want to know.

Max said, Pete got an eyeful of you, through the wall.

Sophia flushed and her eyes caught fire. She looked at Neeler. But it was to Grant that she said, You shouldn't go hitting anybody for me.

He nodded, though it had been for himself, not for her. After that she walked barefoot to the house and went inside.

◆

Grant knew she slept in Max's bed most nights, but for whatever reason they carried on elsewhere, never in the house when Grant was there. Tonight however he could hear them, a rapid exchange too faint to understand but with the quality of argument. This gave way to a silence, and then an audible breathing that quickened into a whine, hers, and he heard them wrestling on the bed, her voice struggling to contain itself, now and then breaking free with a shout that might elsewhere have signaled offense or distress. Of his brother he could hear nothing. It was a message from Max, but what sort of message he didn't know. The deep soundlessness that followed seemed, at this late hour, a conscious compensation for the disturbance. But after an eternity of listening to it Grant realized the silence was only sleep. In time he slept himself, briefly and unrestfully, and then morning had come.

Eyes open, he remained in his attitude of sleep, the sheets bunched around his chin. He heard Max's voice in his head, telling him what he already knew: You love her.

◆

In the kitchen he tried to keep his eyes off her. It might've been his imagination but her movements, seen out of the corner of his eye, seemed to favor him, as if in apology for scolding him the night before. Politeness demanded he acknowledge her but he didn't. He could only nod a directionless greeting and sit down to breakfast.

It was a clear dry cold summer morning. Sophia had the door propped open, gathering the cool in anticipation of the coming heat. Shortly Cotter and Kittredge walked in and sat down. No words were spoken. There were things that ought to be done today but none seemed inclined to do them. The work would be done, though Grant couldn't have said what harm would come to them if they each went his separate way on this day, if time's passing were simply ignored and the whole of future work pushed forward twenty-four hours, never to be caught up on. They ate silently and Grant imagined the rest of them thinking the same thing. Then Sophia sat down across from him and her feet bumped against his where he had them extended beneath the table, and both jerked away.

Kittredge looked up and they all turned to him. He had his hands on the table to steady their trembling.

Say, any of you all seen Petey this morning?

After a silence he went on. I heard him come in last night and then stir real early, I don't know how early, and when I got up he was nowhere atall.

Cotter's eyes were searching their faces. I seen him carrying a bag around daylight, he said.

Yessir, he got himself a kind of a suitcase, and I seen it wasn't in the customary place he keeps it. Kittredge was looking from one to the next of them, his white hands now gripping the table's edge. Grant thought he heard real fear in his voice, and he turned directly to Sophia, who stared openly back at him, her face full of nothing, waiting to hear what he would say.

But Max spoke first. Why don't you ask Grant about that? he said.

Kittredge turned eagerly to Grant. You know where he got to?

Grant set his fork down and leaned back in his chair. I got to be honest with you, he said. I caught him last night spying on the lady here, and me and him got into a fight. He paused, trying to read Kittredge's empty face. Ended up I told him to get out.

He waited. When it appeared no change would come over Kittredge, he went on. I regret the fighting but I ain't sorry for what I said. He wasn't doing nothing around here and wouldn't listen to a damn thing anybody told him. And he ought to've shown Sophia a little respect.

After another moment he added, I didn't really think he would go. And then: I'm sorry, Kittredge.

Kittredge blinked, scanning their faces. He stopped on Sophia. Spying? Spying on you doing what?

She cleared her throat. Sitting for Max's painting. Posing.

For a painting?

Grant said, Kittredge, it was a private thing and he shouldn't have been looking.

Kittredge shook his head. I don't see what harm—

She was naked, Max told him levelly. He was peeping on her while she was naked, that's what Grant got bent out of shape over.

Sophia had no visible reaction but Kittredge blushed deep into his collar. He slid his hands into his lap and looked fiercely down at them.

Well, he said, and it wasn't certain what he meant by it, if the word constituted resignation or forgiveness or a commitment to anger. In any event it was probably the least Kittredge had ever said. Grant looked over at Sophia. It was getting easier to do now. She was still looking at him, glaring maybe, and he started speaking before he had a chance to form the words in his head.

I imagine he's over at the rodeo. I could stand to go to town and do a few things. He turned to Kittredge. I'll ask around and see if I can find him. See if he's coming back.

Kittredge nodded his thanks.

You want to come with me?

No, said Kittredge, I reckon I'm still a mite tired. Maybe I'll just head back into bed. And having said that he left his breakfast uneaten and walked out.

•

By the time he set out on the road he was hungry and the sun had gotten the kind of hot people would be comparing hot days of the future to. He turned on the vents and let the moving air burn the sweat off him, and by staying extra still he almost got comfortable enough to forget about it.

He felt foolish with his impulses and passions behind him now, shrunk to nothing in the heat. To get hit was just what Neeler wanted. The to-do of it. And the girl: the thought of her now made him half sick with shame, he didn't, couldn't, love her and he'd prove it by sheer coldness. He thought of all the thickheaded talk he'd made with her, all of his prideful mouthing in the kitchen when his brother wasn't around, and it made him furious at himself and at her too, because surely she was going back and telling it all to Max. They were lovers after all and lovers had a way of telling each other whatever popped in their heads, however stupid or secret.

The hell with them all.

In Eleven he navigated the sudden traffic and the misparked pickups and pulled over on a patch of ruined grass half a mile past the center of town. Walking back he could hear the sloppy mob hollering behind him at the arena and could smell the roasting meat. He pitied whoever was tending the fire. At the post office he mailed bills and collected more from the box, then took them over to the Sunrise. At the door he hesitated. Then he went in and sat down. Jean didn't say hello but gave him a piece of meatloaf, and he accepted it with thanks. He shuffled through the bills. When he raised his head to look for the newspaper she was still there, her eyes on him. He had a sudden memory of her and shook off a shudder.

How're you doing, Grant? she said, the way a doctor would ask.

Not bad.

You don't look it.

He shrugged. It's hot, he said.

While he ate she hung around wiping down the counter and looking out the window. A couple other men were here, drinking coffee alone at their tables. Finally Jean said, Okay then, and walked off. He found a newspaper on a stool and read the rodeo standings. Damned if he was going to go looking for the boy there, if he happened to come across him, fine, but nothing would make him look on purpose. Kittredge would get over it, possibly thank him in due time. Maybe punching Neeler wasn't so bad an idea after all. Grant squeezed his eyes shut. He was having a hard time keeping hold of his convictions. When Jean was back in the kitchen he paid and collected his mail and left.

The heat drove him to the Eleven bar. Inside it wasn't simply crowded but full. Men inches apart were shouting conversations, their stiff widebrimmed hats knocking together, their hands in constant motion adjusting the hats, raising cans of beer to their lips. They ought to've been bareheaded but the pegrack had come off the wall and a pile of trampled hats lay on the floor underneath. Grant plowed into the mass of riders and ropers and met with a strange resistance around his feet. He looked down to find the floor covered with empty cans, which reluctantly parted as he slogged through as though against flowing water in a fast stream. Some time later he reached the bar, where a seat opened itself for him. When he was settled with his own can and his pile of envelopes he looked down the bar and saw Neeler, staring back at him with a bleary intensity from the far end, his suitcase standing upright on the bartop beside him.

Grant pulled on the can and turned his attention to opening the envelopes one by one, tearing a strip off the stamp end and making a pile of the strips on the bar. Men were stumbling against his back in a constant rhythm and their feet shook the floor. Now that he'd actually found Neeler he didn't know what he was supposed to do with him. Apologize? Bring him home? He couldn't imagine doing these things. As he took a folded paper from an envelope he sensed a motion at the bar's end and looked up to see Neeler's seat occupied by someone else. The suitcase remained on the bar. The cowboy who'd taken the seat bumped the suitcase with his elbow and it toppled into the darkness. In a moment Neeler appeared beside Grant breathing gin and speaking in a fumbling near-whisper. Grant tried to read his lips.

I could put you down right here, he seemed to be saying.

No, Grant told him simply, unfolding the paper.

You're a coward. I could put you right down. Nobody'd stop me neither. These words were audible; Neeler had begun to shout.

Grant concentrated on the paper he'd unfolded. He flattened out the creases against his leg and brought it up into the light from the open door. So focused was he on the appearance of imperturbability that the words took several readings to sink in, and even once he understood their meaning he had to read them again to make sure.

> If you are a relation of John Person, I regret to inform you that he has passed on. He was delivered to me today and has been prepared for burial. This was done at some expense but the alternative would have been immediate burial without your assistance. Please come to retrieve him or instruct me otherwise via correspondence as to the disposal of his remains.
>
> If you are not a relation of John Person I regret the inconvenience.

The letter was signed above a typed name: Lawrence L. Furness, Director of Funeral Services. And below that an address in Lewiston, Idaho.

Grant tried to fold the letter again along its creases, but somehow it eluded his efforts and would not fit back in the envelope. The paper was too large. He closed his eyes. He was not precisely surprised at the news but realized he had harbored some expectation—not hope exactly—of his father's return to the ranch. He couldn't put his finger on exactly what he expected, there was only a vague need anticipating fulfillment. Now the prospect of that fulfillment, whatever it was, was lost. He began to grow afraid.

It was in this state that he felt Neeler's fingers jab his shoulder. He started, nearly losing his balance, only staying on the stool through willful effort. When he looked up, the sight of the stupid boy kindled a horrible fury, much like the previous night's. The fury filled him up. It felt wonderful. He dropped the letter on the bar and clamped his teeth together and might have killed Neeler had not some commotion erupted by the door. A shadow fell across the already dark room and a wave of men staggered toward them, pulling Neeler in its undertow and out of Grant's sight. It was the last Grant would ever see of him.

A horse was standing in the room flinging its head from side to side, lunging forward and retreating, its hatless rider slumped over apparently unconscious on its back. Men were crushing into the corners of the place, upsetting tables and chairs. The horse reared back expelling its passenger, neighing in terror, cans clashing under its hooves.

Grant pressed himself against the bar, stricken with a fear far out of proportion to the danger the animal posed. The horse seemed portentous somehow, the first landmark in this new chaotic world. Grant reached back and grabbed the bundle of papers. He edged along the row of men, Neeler forgotten, aiming for the door and the necessary bearing home of his news. The horse kicked as he passed but Grant dodged, stepped over the fallen rider and slipped out the open door to the street. He hadn't paid for his drink but had not drunk much of it, either.

◆

I'll go, Max said to him. Unspoken but implied was the notion that he would do so alone. Grant had found him up on a ladder replacing a rotted beam in the sheep shed. Now they were in the yard. Max held the letter in his pitchblack hand, squinting against the glare it made in the sun. What's the time? he asked.

Near four.

Max handed him the letter. I'll go clean off and leave.

I'm coming with you.

You got to stay here with Sophia.

Grant let out a mirthless laugh. He felt a weakness in his knees and ankles and shifted his body. She can be on her own, he said. She ain't a child.

Max said, Did you find Neeler?

Didn't look.

He nodded, walking past Grant toward the house. Grant followed. Sophia can come with us, then, Max said.

I don't see . . .

Max stopped on the road and faced him. I wonder what your problem is with her.

I don't much care one way or another, he said carefully.

Max was staring, his chest heaving. Grant could see he was stricken, wracked, and he wondered what form John Person had taken in his brother's heart. Max opened up his mouth and said, Go tell Cotter to look the truck over for us.

The order was issued with the same tone their father would have used, long-suffering and hopeless, as if he knew even as he spoke that it would be carried out wrong or not at all. It was pointless to disobey. He watched his brother go inside, then headed off toward the quarters to find Cotter.

8

They set off at five with bread and jerky and canteens full of water, Max behind the wheel and Grant half leaning out the passenger window. Sophia sat between them wearing one of their mother's dresses. Whatever had made her do this, she seemed to be regretting it now, her knees pressed together and her hands folded over them, her eyes trained straight out on the road. But Grant was moved by the gesture. It was at least clear she intended some kind of respect for their father. And in fact the first words spoken were hers, nearly lost in the noise of the cab. It was the best thing I could find to wear, she said. Formal, I mean.

Max's silence likely meant he wasn't listening, though Sophia seemed to take it as disapproval. She frowned. The dress was handmade, navy blue, sleeveless and cut simply. Their mother had worn it in the weeks after one of the funerals, Grant couldn't remember which. He told Sophia it suited her.

I had to tack up the hem, was all she said in response.

The sun was still high yet low enough to blind them. A visor hung from Max's side of the cab but Grant and Sophia had to keep their eyes half-lidded, as the passenger visor had long ago broken off. The effort of squinting tired Grant and a fresh headache got going right

behind his eyes. When a hill interrupted the glare or they turned
north for a time, the headache only intensified in the light's absence.
For awhile he fell asleep. When he woke, the atmosphere in the truck
had changed. Sophia had loosened her posture, she looked at him
with a benevolence rendered motherly by the dress, and he felt he'd
been talked about while he slept.

What is it? he said, instantly alert. They seemed to have crossed the
divide and were following it north now, the mountains sliding by on
the right and the sun fat and hot on the western horizon.

You looked tired before, she said.

That's what my bones were telling me, looks like.

He looked at her frankly for a moment. Something about the artificial closeness of the truck made this possible, even appropriate. Then
Max turned and said, You want to know who you looked like, sleeping?

Who?

Thornton. You looked a lot like Thornton.

He was hanging on to an unhappy smile as he said it, a guileless
and intimate thing Grant could not specifically recall seeing on Max
before. It was possible that Max didn't know how much this
wounded him, how it sounded like a gunshot. Grant tried to return
the smile. The road pulled them northwest, where their father's body
waited for them.

◆

In the darkness of the cab, while Sophia slept against his shoulder,
Max spoke. They had driven hours in silence since stopping in Montana for food and gas, and now the final stretch of the state forest was
disappearing behind them. Lewiston wasn't far. Already the hills were
populated by logging roads and cabins and the occasional glow of
firelight through windows.

Might be it ain't him, he said.

Fear disfigured the words, rendering them thin and false. But
whether Max feared that their father was dead or that he was alive
was unclear. At any rate the possibility seemed slim to Grant.

Might be, he said.

Can't think of any reason why he'd of been in Lewiston.

No, Grant said, then added, Can't think of where else he would of gone, though.

Home.

When Grant said nothing his brother half turned to him. England. He'd of gone stayed with his sister, what's her name.

Would of written, Grant said.

Margaret. Could be he's with Margaret.

Could be.

Shortly the city came into view, filling its small valley with tiny lights shaken and doubled against the river water. It didn't look like a place that would kill a man. The hour of sleep Grant had gotten earlier had tricked him and he was wide awake now, his mind clear and broad, with the kind of reach it had when he was out searching the range for lost sheep. He was thinking ahead to recovering the body, securing it in the truck, driving it home and burying it. He could feel its hunger for the ground and he wanted to feed it. But he said okay when Max suggested they check into a hotel for the night. It would be hours before Lawrence Furness woke and there was no point in looking for the mortuary until morning.

When Max and Sophia went to bed he left the room and headed off toward the river. He climbed down its muddy bank and found a flat stone to sit on and listened to and watched the dark water. The air was neither hot nor cold, moving about him and over the river with a kind of sentience. The world seemed full of detail beyond the ability of his senses to perceive: a hidden design he was part of. He could climb down into the water and let it carry him off. It felt like the appropriate thing to do. The impulse, not self-destruction but self-abandonment, was so powerful that he inched back on his rock out of fear, holding himself apart from desire. But the effort exhausted him. He fell asleep with his head on his arms, woke just as the sunrise was getting started, and returned to the hotel. In the daytime the hotel looked cheap and uninviting. He went into their room. Max was curled on his side, his sleeping face buried in the pillow. Sophia lay awake. She was sprawled on her back, their mother's dress flat against her body, the skirt folds draped down between her knees outlining the full length of her legs, and her face, polished to glass by the sweat of a nightmare, seemed not to recognize Grant at all. Her eyes followed him to the bedside. He took her burning hand from her belly and held it. The fingers lay limp in his and then her eyes closed and the fingers tightened, crushing Grant's bones together against his skin. His heart gulped blood. Max stirred. Grant released her and turned and went out to the truck to wait.

◆

The mortuary stood on a grassy corner of a residential neighborhood unsullied by dust or noise. It was a one-story structure, windows thickly curtained, with a paved-under archway to keep a person out of the rain between his car and the indoors. Max ignored the archway, parking instead on the far end of a large black lot. The sound of the engine sputtering to a stop rang out across the empty streets, and Grant imagined the civilized inhabitants of these fresh colorful houses waking to their arrival, squinting out at the three of them with pity and disgust.

For a few seconds they sat breathing the damp morning wind that swathed the truck. At last Sophia looked at Grant and gestured toward the door with her sleep-softened face. Their eyes had not met since sunrise. Hers were hidden in plain sight, as if they were everyday things, things you might take or leave.

He opened his door and held it for her. Then he went around to his brother's side. Max was sitting with his eyes closed, hands still on the wheel.

Grant laid his hand on Max's shoulder. The shape of his brother's bones, so different from his own, filled him with sadness. He turned to Sophia standing with her back to them behind the truck, and turned to Max again. Max was watching him.

C'mon, Grant said.

He stepped back to let Max out. The two of them walked toward the mortuary and Sophia followed, hanging back when they rang the bell. The wooden door, ominous in its oversize and impression of age, opened after an interval with no sound to indicate anyone's approach.

Furness admitted them silently. He was tall, plump-faced; his languorous movements betrayed a secret clumsiness overcome by long practice. The parlor was laid with heavy dark carpet. A low table bearing a vase of lilies stood in the center of it and upholstered chairs were placed in groups of two and three throughout, stations for grieving. The place smelled newly minted, a made smell not of death but lifelessness. They stood bewildered, unsure of what to do. When Furness spoke they reacted with a collective start as though the ground had moved suddenly beneath them.

How may I help you? is what he said. His large unlined hands were folded in front of him, his voice smooth as rancid oil.

John Person, Max said.

His only reaction was a slow nod. Grant surmised he had not expected to hear from them, let alone find them at his door.

My letter reached you, he finally said.

Yes, Max answered.

Mr. Person was—

Our father, Grant said. Mine and his. He extended his hand and Furness took it and clasped it and released it. The mortician's hand was hot and dry.

Lawrence Furness.

Grant Person. Max, he said pointing. He didn't introduce Sophia, who stood behind them, her head hung.

I am sorry. Would you like to see him now?

Grant looked at his brother, who stared blinking at Furness as if he didn't understand the question.

Please, Grant said.

Furness left the room through a curtained doorway. They waited. Voices could be heard, there were footsteps and the sound of wood scraping against metal, an involuntary expulsion of held breath.

Grant was reminded of the last funeral he attended, a sea burial. A young man's heart had stopped. The *Rose Adams* had just reached the Banks, to return to land would be catastrophic, no one would be paid. So the man's effects were collected, the pornography removed and distributed among the men, and the body cleaned and dressed and laid out on a plank. The sky was quiet, the clouds a seamless mass. Prayers were said and the men's feet scuffed against the deck. They said goodbye to their crewmate. His body, weighted with sand, struck the water and disappeared.

Sophia had taken a seat against a far wall, a bright smear against the regal dankness of the place. She appeared to want to hide herself. Grant and Max stood very still, waiting where Furness had left them.

Their father's casket came in on a wheeled platform draped with black velvet. It parted the curtains, reflecting the dim lights in undulating confectionery streaks. The velvet caught the curtains and pulled them taut before they broke free and fluttered back into place. The casket was accoutered with brass fittings and was varnished to a stunning depth, like a window onto death itself. There was no way they could pay for it.

The platform came to rest in a kind of alcove faintly illuminated by recessed lights. Furness opened the smaller half of a sectioned lid and left the room the way he came in.

The brothers stood on opposite sides of the low table glaring at the casket, the spectacle of it, each waiting for the other to move. Grant's emotions, uncertain up to now, were coalescing into shame and rage. The mortician's presumption, the worthlessly prettied box: to conceal death in this fake dignity: as if this monstrous thing wouldn't rot away like the tree it was made from, as if the brass wouldn't blacken under the ground and the body decompose. He was thinking he couldn't step forward, that he might have to leave, when Max moved, practically leaping to the casket. He leaned over it, thrusting his head under the open lid while his hands gripped its lip.

Grant tried to read his brother's posture, but it was no use. Max's body knew only the vocabulary of work. It betrayed nothing but concentration, as though he was contemplating the undone gut of a wrecked car. Seconds passed. From behind the curtain came the sound of shoes against a cement floor. Then Max stood upright and strode past Grant, his face naked and old as the inside of a broken rock.

It ain't him, he said passing, and he pushed through the door, splashing the room with daylight for an instant and revealing its dressings as soiled and common.

Sophia trained an alarmed glance at Grant which he didn't return. Not him? Somehow the news was a greater blow than the letter had been. The fatherless self he'd become had seemed a considerable improvement over the coward son he used to be. His head throbbed and he saw Sophia stand up and then sit again, covering her face with her palms.

Grant crossed the room. No point in waiting, and of course he had to see for himself who was in the box.

But it was him. For a moment no, but then the familiar face rose up out of the powdered waxwhite mask that had been put over it, and he saw his father laid out dead, the features relaxed and flattened by gravity and sapped of all opinion, accusation, emotion. You could have said Max was right. The resemblance was purely mechanical. But their father was surely dead, as this body was where he used to be and now he wasn't there.

Grant moved away from the face and curled his fingers under the larger half of the lid and pulled it open. The body was fattened and bent, before or after death he couldn't tell. The suit he wore was indeed his own, Grant recognized it. Why would he have brought it with him, except to be dead in? Unless he thought he would be traveling. Maybe he really meant to go back to England and never made it. Whatever the case it seemed unlikely that he ever intended to come home.

The hands were gnarled and scabbed. Grant reached out without thinking and lifted one off the other, and it wasn't until he'd let go that the feel of it struck him, unyielding, like something cast from a mold, the skin artificial, cold from refrigeration. The gangster of

Grant's dreams came full and real into his mind, taking shape for the first time outside sleep. He jerked away letting the lid fall shut, and the force of it jarred loose the smaller lid, and it too came down with a thunderous clap as though his father had pulled it closed in anger. Grant backed away, his lungs hollering for breath, and as he steadied himself against a chair the curtains parted and Furness appeared, his eyes dark with suspicion and stupidity, like a goat's.

Pardon, the mortician said, is there anything—

What'd he die of? Grant surprised himself at the question, which he'd not until this moment thought to ask.

Furness took a step back. The coroner—it was in a tavern—his heart.

You got something that says so? Grant said, drawing air. And whatever else he had on him. He carried a wallet.

Yes, of course.

When he was gone Grant remembered Sophia. She was standing in front of her chair bent toward him slightly, her hands bunching the fabric of the dress. Tears drowned her eyes and he could see she was nowhere at all, alone very far from home, the only men she knew transformed in an instant by death and lost to her. Her chest rose and fell and her face glowed with terror.

Well is it him or not? she whispered.

It's him, he said, and he knew he could go to her but didn't.

Maybe—, he went on, and realizing he was still out of breath stopped to draw one. Maybe you ought to find Max.

But why—

I don't know why he said what he did but any fool could see who it is. Don't stay here. Go to him. I got to settle things.

She stood rooted to the spot, her tongue moving across her lips. He saw that she wanted to speak, for him to say things back. But he tried to silence her with his eyes.

Please, he said.

This time she heard. When the door shut behind her he turned to Furness coming through the curtain.

You can get him out of that casket and into something I can pay you money for. And you can seal it up, we got a long way to drive today and there's nobody else needs to look at him.

The mortician nodded soberly as if this was his plan all along, and held out to Grant the death certificate and his father's wallet. Grant accepted them without raising his eyes. The wallet was empty of money but it could have been anyone, the coroner or in whomever's presence John Person had fallen, who stole it. Not Furness necessarily. The wallet was surely his father's though, cracked and stained at the edges by sweat, and crammed inside were photos, brittle as the leather, that showed their family: each of them as children and a portrait of John and Asta at their wedding. Grant had never seen these pictures. He tucked them back into the wallet and gave the certificate a cursory glance. It was just a typed paper really, signed illegibly and pointlessly at the bottom.

Furness was waiting. Grant met his gaze and held it and Furness was forced to speak first.

I trust you wish to take your father now.

Yes.

There is the matter of your bill.

I know, Grant said. He had brought with him all the money he had, but now he doubted it would be enough. And there was the trip home, the cost of gas, and food if they wanted to eat. He said, How much?

For a more . . . economical casket? Furness asked. He named a figure. It was not as high as Grant had feared but nonetheless more than he had. He took his own wallet from his pocket and removed all but a few of the bills, then handed them to Furness. The mortician accepted them reluctantly, with an expression of distaste. This was apparently not the way he usually did business. He fumbled, patting his coat, and at last pushed the bills into an inside pocket.

You can bill me for the rest, Grant said. You got the address.

Yes.

How long'll it take to get him in the new box?

Furness crossed his arms. Not long. Twenty minutes.

We'll come back.

Yes. After a moment he added, I'm sorry.

I appreciate that, Grant told him and walked out.

The driver's-side door of the truck stood open. Sophia's head was framed in the cab window. She sat on the passenger side, her white elbow sticking out into the sun. He concentrated on that elbow. It would be cool and rough if he touched it, despite the heat. He stood very still until her eyes appeared in the rearview.

When he got in behind the wheel she said, He wasn't out here, I looked. He probably found a bar.

Daddy died in one, Grant said. A bar.

She stared at him, seeming to search his face for a foothold. He let himself stare back. He followed the topography of her face as if he was preparing to make a map. His fingers in his lap twitched involuntarily. A breeze lifted the hairs on his arm and fondled the sleeves of the dress she wore. It was a nice day. A lot of people would wake happily to it and go to their jobs as on any other. He wanted her and nearly said so. Instead he said, What is going on between you, Sophia? It was the first time he had addressed her by name.

Some seconds later she said, I don't know. She was biting her lip and he could see the tips of her narrow teeth probing the red flesh. I came with him because I hadn't figured him out yet. I thought that once he was home I could figure him out and he would be mine. She blushed.

They looked out at a mother pushing a pram down the sidewalk. The pram had a hood and the baby couldn't be seen. I don't know, she said again, everything I learn just makes it more confusing. Sometimes I think he must be crazy.

He's not crazy, Grant said.

She sighed and her head dropped to her chest. Oh, Grant, she whispered.

This could be the moment, he thought. She would love me now if I took her in my arms. He looked down at his hands on his knees and commanded them to move.

The hands rose to the steering wheel. In a moment he started the truck and pulled out onto the street.

◆

They found him drinking alone in a low-ceilinged tavern near the railroad tracks, illuminated only by the light through a propped-open door. Nobody was tending bar and the two pool tables in the darkness behind him were covered, the cues lined up in a rack on the wall. Grant and Sophia paused on the threshold and then, wordlessly, she stepped back to let him enter by himself.

He sat facing his brother on a wooden stool and waited for him to speak. It might have taken a long time, he expected it to, but Max turned right to him and with an expression drained of pretense or motive said, Didn't bear any resemblance at all. None at all.

Grant said, What are you doing here, Max? It's nine-fifteen in the morning.

When Max didn't answer Grant took the wallet and death certificate out of his pocket and slid them across the bar. Max ignored them for awhile. Then he took the wallet into his hands. He held it and turned it over and over. He looked inside, took out the photos and laid them in a neat row on the bar. Edwin, nine or ten years old, astride a horse. Grant and Max and Thornton together, stiffly posed. Robert standing with their mother dressed in Sunday clothes, somewhere in town. Then the wedding picture, and one, horribly, of Wesley days or perhaps hours from death, laid out in the bassinet, the eyes bulging from the swelling and fever, the skin stretched and shining.

We ain't never had a camera, Max said finally, touching Wesley's image with steady fingers. He picked up the photo and replaced it facedown.

Doc Lafitte took it, I reckon.

Now Max turned Edwin over and then their parents, young and ghostly and framed by a black oval. After a minute he picked up the final picture and folded it under so that only the two of them were visible, Grant eight or nine years old, wearing a pair of angora chaps and a drooping hat, Max clinging to his brother's fringes.

What now, big brother? Max said. At this a door rattled open in the darkness and a figure appeared at the back of the bar and approached. The bartender. He was a tiny man of about eighty with wild white tufts of hair over his ears, a dirty white shirt and a bright red bow tie. He aimed a questioning look at Grant and Grant shook his head no.

We go get him and bring him home, Grant said.

Max was putting the pictures back in the wallet. You think he'd appreciate that, do you? he said, the cut coming back to his voice.

I believe so.

The bartender looked from one to the other. Max laid a bill on the bar.

Okay, he told Grant. You're the boss. He slid off his stool, leaving the wallet and pictures and certificate behind for Grant to collect.

◆

The casket fit lengthwise in the truckbed. They wrapped it in an oiled canvas tarp and anchored it fast through the postholes with rope until it was tight against the side. The box itself was square and varnished, no handles, hardwood, not pine. It didn't look cheap. The wood was smooth and strong with a handsome grain, the sort of thing John Person would have liked to make but lacked the aptitude for. They hadn't seen their father in it so there was no way of knowing he was really there, save prying off the lid. The mortician had helped them lift the casket onto the truck, his jacket off and sweat soaking his white shirt, but now he stood back, dismay bunching his face. He didn't offer to shake their hands. When it was time to go Grant nodded at him and he nodded slowly back. Then they climbed in, Grant behind the wheel, and drove away. It was barely ten.

Later, the sun was high overhead and the air roared into the cab hot enough to burn. Sophia slept, touching neither of them, her head tipped back against the seat, baring the smooth hollow of her neck. Grant kept his eyes on the road and the mountains slipped past on either side.

As if from inside Grant's own head, Max said, This land has ruined us for any other kind of life.

Grant said nothing.

I never really lived in the city, Max went on. I was only ever living not here. Every place I ever been was just not here. All those people and buildings I painted pictures of, it was just not mountains, not grass. There was no life in it.

What about now that you're back? What are you painting now?

I'm not painting anything. I'm just painting notness. He tipped his head back laughing and Sophia stirred for a moment. She opened her blank sleeping eyes and then shut them again, quick, against the brazen world outside the truck.

Notness, Max said quietly. I like that.

Grant said, What I seen of your paintings looks pretty good.

No. Dead as our daddy. Dead as us.

Grant took his eyes off the road to train them on his brother. You been painting her, right? That isn't dead.

For some time Max didn't have an answer to that. Then he said, barely audible over the roar of air, I don't know what that is.

•

Before dark they pulled over for gas. Grant went out behind the station and relieved himself into a junkswept weedpatch. The temperature at last was dropping and the wind beginning to pick up, blowing the stream of piss into an arc, like a tossed rope. When he was finished he felt hungry. He went back to the truck and told them he was going to go find a store. They stayed behind, too tired to move. As he passed the truckbed he gazed along the length of the tarp, imagining he could detect the odor of formaldehyde and dead flesh and face powder in the heat that rose off it.

They were in a little town without much in it, and he moved through its streets making no impression. Soon he came upon a market with a post-office window. The window was boarded over but through the open screen door, scratched raw by a cat, he could see a man working behind a counter. The cat ran out as Grant entered.

The place was lit bright as day, the shelves stocked neatly with boxes and cans and the cooler full of fresh-looking food and cold drinks. He thought of his hands on the casket and approached the counter. The proprietor was bespectacled and fat, wrapped in a white apron. He looked up and smiled hugely.

What can I do for you, son? he said. His voice was cool and clear and for some reason pleased.

You got a sink I can clean myself up at? And then I think I'll get a few things.

Sure I do. Come on back.

The grocer led him down a hallway to a narrow immaculate tiled bathroom with a sink and toilet. Grant washed his hands and after a moment's thought his face and neck and arms as well. When he came out the grocer said, You look like you haven't slept. Everything all right?

The question came as a shock, seeming to arise from a natural and urgent concern. Grant could not seem to answer it.

Look here, the grocer went on, are you on your way to someplace nearby? You are traveling, aren't you?

Yessir.

I can fix you up with a place you can sleep. You look like you just drove a million miles. Are you driving truck, is that it?

No. No thank you, I—

Both of them waited for him to finish.

That's okay, the grocer said. You just go ahead and help yourself. You need anything else let me know.

Grant turned and began to walk down the narrow aisles, drawn to the things on them but unable somehow to touch them. Finally he opened up the cooler door and took out a bottle of milk and a couple of peaches from a basket. When he shut the door he pressed his palm to the cold glass, and then his cheek, and he closed his eyes and all thought vanished from his head. After awhile he brought the food to the counter and took some jerky from a can there and put that next to the fruit, along with his money.

You sure you're ready for the road? the grocer asked him.

Yessir, thank you. But—

What is it?

I can't bring that bottle back to you.

Hell, that's all right, the grocer said laughing. He took a few of the coins Grant had left. That'll do it, he went on. Keep the rest.

Grant swallowed and his vision clouded. He felt the way the grocer looked, heavy yet somehow buoyant. The weight kept pouring into him as he stood there neither thanking the grocer nor taking his change. He knew he must look mad. At last he managed to say thanks and collected the food into his arms. The grocer was saying something to him as he left but Grant didn't answer. He could only pull open the screen door and stumble out into the dying heat.

Outside, the world had undergone some kind of transformation. Everything pulled him with a new gravity. What was left of the sun seemed a wan projection invented by the air. It was clumsy to hold the food to his chest. He realized the grocer must have been offering him a paper sack. Blocks away a dog barked, and the canyon that cupped the town multiplied the sound and drove the dog to more frenzied barking. What was this place called? He couldn't remember seeing a sign. Nothing about it seemed real, the dog or the cat, the bright clean store or the man in it whose kindness was already losing definition, like it was nothing more than printed words on a burning paper.

Now he seemed to have lost his way. Up and down the street nothing could be seen but low houses with flat roofs and silent grass moving in a breeze he couldn't himself feel. The gas station's white glow was not to be found. He set down his things on a hummock of ground near an intersection and stood gazing into the sky where some stars were making themselves visible. He considered what Max had said and felt the sad rightness of it. Both of them had left and come back to find that their home had turned its back on them. And their father would be returning dead. Briefly Grant imagined that the ground would actually reject the casket, forcing it up and out like a wedge of shrapnel from a wounded man. So clear and convincing was this image that for a moment his mind groped for a solution to the problem: maybe they could bury him above the ground in a tomb or in the Indian way, in a tree or scaffold. Then he remembered who and where he was, and he picked up his things, and the route back to the gas station was restored to him.

The last two hours of driving were the longest, with the darkness expanding and the road assuming a frightening sameness, as though it would never end. They were each awake, each aware that a burial shouldn't wait until morning. Grant felt as though his limbs wouldn't respond to the work; his back wouldn't tolerate bending over the grave, his arms and legs could never bear the weight of the shovel or the earth's resistance. But of course work was never far beyond his reach. Sophia would make them coffee and they would just do it. As they drove Grant vainly scanned the sky for the moon. He remembered it was new. They would dig by starlight.

When they got back Grant stopped the truck in the yard. Sophia got out and walked into the house. As they watched, a light went on in the kitchen. She appeared at the sink to fill a pot with water. Seconds passed. It was Max who finally tore himself away and said, Go, and Grant put the truck into gear and pulled it up in front of the equipment shed. He went in and picked out two shovels which he dropped into the truckbed beside the casket. Their clatter cracked the silent black night. In the wake of the noise the silence deepened. Though it was summer Grant could smell woodsmoke: maybe Kittredge was unwell and chilled. They drove into the starveout and Grant backed up against the graveplot gate. He got out and opened the gate and began untangling the ropes from the shrouded casket. Max lingered behind, waiting. Finally Grant pulled off the tarp and heaved the casket out over the lip of the bed. Max moved up to take the opposite end. They set the casket down against the fence and fetched the shovels, then wordlessly chose a spot in the near-invisible ground.

It took them all night. The dirt was loose but rocky. They dug deep until they hit clay, and below it a sandy clumped soil like heavy snow. Below that was rock. They extended and squared the hole and drank the coffee Sophia brought them. By now Cotter had come, roused out of sleep by the sound of digging. He and Sophia stood at a distance as the brothers lifted the casket and brought it to the edge of the grave.

Cotter got the ropes out of the truck. He threaded them under the box and tested them for strength. Sophia had changed into work clothes, her faint outline the shape of Max's when he was a boy. The four of them took hold of the rope ends and together lifted the casket and suspended it over the grave.

If any of them had wished to say something, the time to do so had passed. They lowered the casket and it bumped hard into the open ground. Each rope came out with a sharp tug. Then Cotter took one of the shovels and gave it to Grant, and Max took up the other, and Sophia and Cotter again stood back as the brothers filled the grave. When Max and Grant were finished, the ground was lumped with the displaced earth, and though Grant wanted to tamp it down, to erase its newness, he couldn't bring himself to stand over his father's body.

•

They sat in the kitchen with clean hands and fresh coffee and told Cotter about the trip. It didn't take them long. Ages seemed to have passed in life, but in the telling the journey was lifeless and empty of incident. Sophia, in the silence that followed, looked from one to the other with bright eyes. She said, He didn't have any kind of funeral. Nobody had the chance to pay their respects. The fact truly grieved her. She held her hands out across the table, as if imploring them to reverse it somehow.

The men listened. They turned their eyes to the hands folded in their laps. Grant would put a death notice in the paper but no service would be held. Nobody would come to a service, or if they did it would be out of habit and not respect, because their family was cursed and sheep people besides. He groped for something to say to get them off the subject. At length he turned to Cotter and asked him how Kittredge was getting on.

Cotter looked at Max first, then Grant. He's upstairs sleeping, he said.

At this Max's head came up. A ready, almost eager smirk spread over his face. Grant said, Upstairs?

Sophia hung her head. Grant could see there was something she'd been told.

Instead of answering, Cotter pushed his chair back and stood, motioning for them to follow.

Dawn hadn't touched the yard yet but a starless gray blush betrayed the hilltop. They turned onto the road and walked north. The house light faded behind them and moonlessness took them back in.

I heard him creeping around the quarters late, Cotter said. Two in the morning I'd bet, black out here. I figured he was an animal or something.

Who? Grant asked.

Max, not Cotter, answered. Neeler, he said quietly, and Grant could make out Cotter's nodding head. He was full of questions but decided he'd wait and see what Cotter was going to show him.

But he knew. The smell of woodsmoke intensified. By the time they reached the ruined cabins the smoke was acid in his throat. The cabins had collapsed, the few standing walls punctuated by skewed black windowframes, white smoke hovering above the lot of them, visible against the sky as a ghostly motion of air. The old dry wood had been eager to give itself to fire. Grant walked up and down the row peering into the ravaged interiors where embers still glowed in pockets within.

Once I figured out what he done he was already gone, Cotter was telling them. Or I seen him running anyway. I went and got Kittredge, he's all right, a little burned on his face coming out the door is all.

Sootblack and wrung by heat, a gasoline can lay on its side beneath the last cabin. It looked a hundred years old at least.

How'd he get here?

I reckon horse.

Grant walked back to where they were standing. So what in the hell was he trying to do?

Kill Kittredge, Cotter said simply. He was woke up on account of his shaking or else he mightn't of made it.

There was a fluid pause loaded with significance, like a creek running between two mountains. The clear and quiet middle of something enormous and terrible. Grant had never felt so tired in his life, his legs near to giving way. He sat down hard in the dirt and lowered his head. There had been no sleep for days and not enough to eat. His blood was thin as a gas, whistling through his heart and veins, his body a winter-stripped cottonwood, brittle and hollow and no impediment to the wind and weather. His bed seemed an impossible distance away.

They pulled him up and led him back to the road and into the house. Cotter brought him up the stairs to his room, laid him on the bed and pulled his boots off. Grant hadn't the power to thank them, grateful as he was, not even the power to complete the thought to do so.

•

The dead man didn't frighten him any longer. They were in the yard, spotlit by the porch bulb, surrounded by sheep gently bleating and pressing into them. The sheep were hungry, their wool patchy and thin with gray skin visible underneath. He was trying to explain to the dead man that they had to go out to range, it was long past time, the summer would dry the grass and creek and the flock would waste away.

The dead man smiled. Porchlight pierced his skin. Below its surface Grant could see the blood vessels blackly clotted solid. The dead man's bent white finger said follow and Grant followed, the sheep more urgent around them now, the bleating sharp and irregular like crows' caws.

He was led through the pasture to the starveout gate. There were horses clustered around the fence, colorless and still as if stopped by time itself. They were illuminated by an unseen source, or from within, the light possessing a clinical coldness like the light from an electric sign. As they climbed to the high corner the sheep overtook them. Grant could see they were starving, their hooves rotten and the skin of their legs rubbed down to the briskly glowing bone. Wait, he called out, the sheep— but the dead man walked on, his coat mold- and moth-eaten riding up above his trousers and revealing a deep white fissure in the skin where the salt water had split him.

The dead man passed into the graveplot with the dying sheep all around him. Their sounds were no longer animal but the high reluctant strains of a rusted machine. The noise overpowered the night, so terrible Grant could nearly see it. He ran to the dead man and touched him, shouting, but the dead man pointed to an open grave: the neat squared hole they'd dug for their father, empty of any casket and with no visible bottom. The sheep were diving into it, wasting to nothing as they fell.

9

Grant set out early for the summer range. It wasn't far but he intended to take his time and spend a night camped in the hills. A night out might do him good: Kittredge and Cotter were living in the house now. In truth he didn't much like them there. Kittredge in particular was hard to bear. He mourned Neeler as if he was dead, dragging himself from room to room rendered worthless by grief. Cotter on the other hand remained impassive and practical, yet made it clear by his silence that he disapproved of the arrangements. Max had assumed an air of intense concentration, as if he was very busy doing some kind of work, which he wasn't.

The sound of them recalled the sound of the family, of two or more of the boys fighting in the hours between supper and sleep or a baby waking hungry in the night. His father had been habitual. He got out of bed the moment he woke each morning, and he woke without a clock or whether the sun rose into a clear or storm-darkened sky. He woke, the bedboards groaned underneath him, his feet struck the floor at exactly the same moment, muffled by the frayed rag rug. He took four steps across the room to the closet and slipped a shirt off its hanger, which jangled against the others. Then he pulled on the shirt. He took his pants off their hook, then one foot and then the other thumped the floorboards, and he buckled his belt and slapped the buckle. Grant heard the routine asleep or awake. To the older boys it was an alarm: their father intended to wake them. But their mother made no sound at all when she rose. Larger than their father, she ought to have been heard, but she sat up and dressed by stealth and was posed before the stove when the boys came down, and depending on the year she may or may not have had a baby in the bassinet beside her shielded by the pantry door.

Increasingly his memories were confused, who was alive at a specific time and who wasn't, which boys were considered men and which weren't. Some incidents, a fight or an accident, he recalled differently every time, once with Edwin as a central figure, another time with Max. On occasion he would place a brother into memory at an age he had never reached. He maintained a spurious image of a teenaged Robert swinging across the barn on a hanging rope, bellowing like Tarzan; even less plausibly he could remember Wesley taking his first steps. If one brother did something out of character, but in the character of another, Grant might remember the act performed by the second. Occasionally he even remembered himself doing something Edwin or Max had in fact done.

He suspected it was the nature of memory, not his own nature, that caused the confusion. The truth of a thing only existed as long as the thing itself, and afterward it changed with distance or perspective. His own experience of this very moment, a hot fogged summer morning, belonged only to him; it could not resemble the same moment lived by someone else, Sophia for instance.

She was unhappy here in the house, with the men. Grant feared she would leave them and the intensity of his fear disturbed him. After all, he didn't have her now, and if she left he wouldn't have her then either. But still: the sight of her drawn face turning away from his was too much to bear. For this reason above all others he chose now to visit the herder, putting himself into misery in order to put himself out of it.

He rode west toward the low hills in a light rain. The land was barely visible today, disguised by clouds and mist, its hidden edges arched like muscles. He kept his eyes trained on them as he passed the graveplot and burned quarters. For a long while he rode seeming to come no closer to the hills, then he was in among them, his face beaded with haze, his hat dripping water on his fingers around the saddlehorn. The damp got up under his coat and the clothes pressed coolly against his skin.

He was in no hurry to find the herder. Instead he let his nerves read the map of the terrain they had memorized. They spoke the right directions to the horse, guiding him along the trails, while in his mind's eye Grant probed the gullies and creekbeds and meandered through the breaks for signs of bear.

In awhile he dismounted and pissed and clambered up a sidehill to look around. From a little ways up he could see the first sheep a mile to the south, grazing in a lush depression which graduated into a hill, and now among gray rocks he could make out more of them, still and summerfat and out of danger. There was no sign of Murray and no rain either, only a gray wet heat.

Satisfied, he went back and loosened the horse's saddle and sacking and took out the bits. Then he found a dry outcrop and sat. He shucked off his hat and coat and took in the whole living highland.

Yesterday, in the wake of the sheep dream, he'd set to his father's affairs, bringing the will into town for the lawyer and writing a letter to his aunt in England. He'd sat thinking half an hour without setting a word to paper. In the end he kept to the facts: their father was dead, and if she was ever to come to America she would be welcomed. When he told people in town what had happened they offered their condolence. Jean Tate came around the counter and took him in her arms. Her body, though unchanged, was a foreign thing to him, and unforgiving. Surely this wasn't something in Jean but something in him. He felt stunted, impotent. The Persons were like a shrub cut back too far, he thought. His father's sister had had no children he knew of, there had never been talk of cousins. On his mother's side were brothers and sisters who'd resented her leaving Iceland with an

Englishman and never spoke to her again. Grant didn't even know if they'd been informed of her death. He supposed not. He couldn't imagine himself marrying, couldn't imagine his body giving any woman a child.

After a time his thoughts began to embarrass him. He stood and went back to his horse and tightened up the riggings. In a few minutes he was among the sheep and the dogs ran out to meet him. They knew him now by scent and sight and made little noise, careful not to spook the flock as they led him to Murray's wagon.

The herder was inside making his supper, the elkskin door pushed aside to admit the air. He was holding a potato in one hand and a bent table fork in the other. Without his glasses he looked pitifully insubstantial, something that would wilt in sunlight. Grant leaned his head in and asked him how he was doing.

Murray looked up, and then down again at the potato. Not so bad, he said.

The flock?

A couple of downers a couple of days ago. It ain't catching, if that's what you ask me next.

Grant nodded, unsure of how to say what he'd come to say. Then the herder surprised him by inviting him in for dinner. It was only beans and potatoes, he said, but huckleberries were ripe on the bush and he'd gotten to them before the bears and birds. They could have some for dessert.

All right, Grant said. He went to his horse and took a bottle and some letters out of the pannier. Murray nodded as he received them, in acknowledgment, not thanks.

They ate under the tin canopy of the wagon then sat outside on folding stools to drink. Murray glanced at his letters before sliding them in between the buttons of his shirt.

You come to say something, he said.

Yes.

Grant endured Murray's glare for a moment then told him about the fire. Murray had little reaction. It was none of his concern.

And our daddy turned up, Grant went on. He was in Lewiston, Idaho. I hate to have to tell you he's dead. We brought him back and buried him.

The herder nodded patiently, as if he'd already heard this and was only listening to be polite. He sipped the whiskey from his cup and looked off across the valley to where the dogs were running. Murray's odd cordiality settled over Grant, making him a little uncomfortable. He waited with real apprehension for the response.

Y'boys'll sell, will ye?

He followed Murray's gaze to a nondescript faraway grasspatch. Then the men turned to one another at once. In the herder's eyes was a familiar disappointment. Sell the whole outfit? Grant said. No. No, we'll stay. Nothing'll change.

He looked into his whiskey, reflecting rippled sky. There was some sun now and he felt hot. Murray reached into his shirt and took out the letters. He tore one open along the flap and removed a folded piece of paper. After reading it he handed it to Grant. It was hard to decipher, the shaky hand riddled with crossouts.

> Dear Thomas, I dont have much to say. The girls are growin. The lettuce is all aten by rabbits but we dont miss it to much. A new calf the girls named it Jenny. Send money please we need it
>
> > Sally

This your sister? Grant said. Where is she?

Oregon, Murray said. It's my wife. Them girls are my daughters. You're married?

Murray frowned. That's what I just told ye.

When Grant didn't say anything further he went on. The hell ye won't sell, he spat. Comin' and goin' the way ye done.

Murray drank his drink and leveled a look at Grant frighteningly direct, the look of a creature ignorant of danger. Y'don't even know who ye are, he said, and he took the letter from Grant's hand.

The herder's silence afterward was unembarrassed. He continued to drink, wincing after each sip with a painful satisfaction as if some loose bone was being snapped back into place. Grant thanked the herder for his hospitality. He felt no malice toward Murray, only a desire to get away. He set the whiskey down on the ground and stood, his knees audibly cracking. It'd be dark in an hour or so, he said, he wanted to get somewhere he could bed down. The undersides of the clouds were pinking up and the brightest stars were visible, and Venus and Mars. Behind him the dogs were egging the sheep back toward camp. He could sense the flock clustering nearby, the way you could sense changing weather.

Murray stayed on his stool, the wrinkled letter still in his hand and the ripped envelope trembling in the windshook grass beside him. He was still there when Grant left, and again when he looked back from the far end of the spur where the horse had led him. Then he was in the next canyon with the bottomland spread out far below, and Murray was gone from his sight.

·

He set up camp in a clearing above a creek where he could wake and look down on the water flowing, a hundred feet downslope. In the morning he would pick his way there to wash. He'd bedded here before, as had others before him. A flat patch had been worn around a rock circle that surrounded scattered ash and bone. Dry twigs and thick branches could be found in a mossy deadfall not far from the camp. It was his favorite time of the traveling day, when there's no reason to wander into dark woods and your horse is satisfied and still, and everything you want or need is inside the circle of fireglow. He'd brought a book to read, but instead he lay in his bedroll and tried to picture the woman who had wed herself to Murray and borne his children. Murray must have thought they would keep him, or he them. Maybe he'd once imagined they would tend sheep together, living off berries and game and potatoes planted in loose soil all across their territory.

But Grant could envision only his own mother, daughters she might have had, hard little girls who would seem to have cleaved directly from her with nothing of his father in them at all. They might have saved her life, daughters. Girls are shrewder and more adaptable than boys, he thought. They wouldn't have succumbed to short lives of risk and pain the way his brothers had. They would be here now, strong and supple as greenwood.

Grant believed he'd been her favorite. Maybe not when Edwin was alive, not then. But after. After Edwin she brought him closer than before and gave him jobs to do that didn't really need doing but which kept him near. It was to him she came in the night to tell him he mustn't go to the war. Leave the killing to the killers, she said. She said, If one of you boys must go, God help me let it be your brother, and he didn't know which brother she meant, and didn't care. Tears were in her voice, though not her eyes, and he reached for her from his bed. But she had backed away. Stay, she said.

He did. He kept his mouth shut when to speak would have meant to leave her. But of course he would leave her himself in a few years and never see or speak to her again.

A part of him envied the squalid herder, his solitude, the simplicity of his work. The herder always knew what he was supposed to be doing. His tasks were dictated by the grass and sky and sheep. The flock wanted the same thing always, to eat and be impregnated, to sleep and to lamb. Love and family, the whole reckless world of men—there was nothing there for somebody so attuned to the gorgeous stupidity of nature.

Thornton could have been a herder. He was at ease among sheep, his empathy for them miraculous, his lumbering-head gait a human analog of theirs. Even his dark hair, curled by some providence, beaded rain like a sheep's. When they were children they laughed at this affinity, and so did he. He understood his anomalous nature. To their father he was worthless, a beast that could neither be taught nor eaten. He terrified their mother, who was bound to receive his love and reciprocate without ever comprehending it. But the boys adored him, he was their saint and foil and secret.

Thornton.

•

Grant, he whispered that night outside the bedroom door, Grant, I want to talk to you. Grant could hear him waiting for an answer, his large body brushing the door. He could wait a long time, half the night if necessary. Once Grant had seen Thornton sit three hours in front of a prairie-dog hole. He'd watched him watch the moon span the sky. He got up and opened the door.

What is it, Thorn, he said. From across the hall came the sound of Max turning in bed.

Let me in. I want to talk.

Grant went back to the bed and pulled the covers up. Thornton sat at the far end. He sat there awhile as if he'd forgotten why he came. Grant passed the time gazing out the dark window at the hillside obscuring the stars. The way the stars seemed to rise up out of the hillside like fireflies.

I don't want you to be mad no more. I didn't do nothing wrong, Thornton said, leaning in close, his hand on Grant's ankle. I didn't.

You ain't done nothing wrong, I know.

Why you mad then, Grant?

I ain't mad, Grant said. He sat up and gripped Thornton's arm. No kidding.

Thornton seemed to calm under his touch. He nodded, believing. Daddy said I'm going in the army.

Yeah, you are.

I ain't afraid of it.

I know you're not.

Thornton was eighteen. He carried himself like a man did, his shoulders had the careful set, his hands were gentle and knowing and strong, a father's. Though not their father's. When Thornton was in town people treated him like a child, speaking slow and loud and high, or in the case of women mother-bright, or they offered him little gifts like a piece of candy, or worse, money. If anything he had become an adult sooner than the other boys. Early on he had the look of intense focus, as if upon something only he could see. He looked like the thinker that he was.

You're gonna stay here, right, Grant?

Yes.

You're gonna take care of Mama and Daddy and Max?

I will.

When he had left home they began to get letters. Another soldier wrote them, a boy named Granger with a florid style, the handwriting slanted and schooled, showing Thornton's words and actions as seen from without. Sometimes, even now, when Grant thought about Thornton it was in this boy's voice. They never met him. Thornton sends you his enduring love, a letter might say. Today he ran the obstacle course it was a spectacular success. His dinner tonight was dreadful, the meat was old and tough. He misses riding horses and delighting in the fresh country air. The letters came three times weekly for the duration of Thornton's training, and Max always got to them first and read them alone, often on the post-office steps. Only when he was through did he hand them over to their parents. Grant got them last.

He would have made a good herder, Thornton, alone in the camp wagon thinking his long thoughts. He loved his family but didn't need their company, only their memory, only the happy fact of them. Maybe to Murray solitude was a bitter retreat from other people. But for Thornton it was the full embrace of a natural condition, his truest state of being.

When he shipped out, the letters stopped. In a few weeks he was dead, drowned alone in his cabin.

Grant? he said.

What is it.

You ain't mad at me?

No.

How come you're crying?

I ain't crying. I just want to get some sleep, is all.

You want me to go now?

Yes, Thornton, I want you to go now.

Okay. Good night. He rose from the bed and stood in the dark room breathing. Grant closed his eyes. In awhile Thornton was gone. Grant could hear him trudging down the hall.

Good night, he said.

◆

For all he knew Max still had the letters. He hadn't seen them since the first day he read them. But it was no matter, Grant had what he needed committed to memory, the look of the papers and the writing and the sentences so clear they were almost better than Thornton himself.

The campfire was waning, the wood still piled upright as it had been when lit, as though it didn't yet realize it was only ash and ember. Grant grabbed a branch from the dirt and drove it into the fire. The logs collapsed in a mist of sparks and glowed steady orange. He was hungry already but it was good to sleep hungry, he would wake with a reason to move. He closed his eyes and slept.

In the morning he rebuilt the fire. Then he went down to the creek and threw in a hook with a grasshopper on it. In awhile he caught a brook trout. He gutted and fried it with a few wild onions tossed on top and he boiled coffee and ate a fine, lean breakfast, leaving something to be desired so that he could eat again later with equal satisfaction.

The horse led him up through a timbered stretch of woods and onto a ridge, which he followed south. He could see over the near hills to the flats, and beyond them to mountains a full county away. It was easy to imagine the glaciers moving through, leaving the stones ground smooth, easy to imagine it happening again.

All afternoon he hunted game. When he set up camp two pheasants hung from his riggings. That night he settled down and read his book, an adventure story about exploring the poles. He woke in the morning feeling as good as he had in five years. He rolled up his sougans into the pack covers breathing cold air and exhaling vapor in clouds, and when the sun reached him between the trees he could feel it penetrate right down to marrow.

He took the trails slowly, pausing often to examine a fossil or artifact or to enjoy a good view. For his dinner he ate a bird and some berries he'd found which left a tackiness on his hands. By afternoon he had sweated it off. He avoided the hills the herder was in and circled the ranch, finally coming down upon it from the northeast. The hills were smoother and near treeless with the infrequent outcrop breaking the flesh of grass. He used to come here sometimes with his mother the year after Thornton died. It was as far from home as she would venture on horseback. In Iceland she hadn't traveled much beyond her home valley, and woods made her nervous. So Grant guided her, taught her how to find her way back without a compass by the pattern of hills, to distinguish natural forms and their variations. She liked this land whose characteristic feature was featurelessness. She told him she liked making her thoughts mirror the land. He remembered the way she looked on a horse, post-straight and high in the saddle as if expecting a spill.

They sent an officer from the base to deliver the news. Grant was with her in the yard. They took note of the road dust simultaneously and stopped what they were doing to watch. When the bug face of a jeep appeared on the rise he saw her chest expand with breath. At first he didn't understand, then he did. He went over to her but something kept him back: he stood close without touching, as the jeep stopped and the man got out and came to them.

The officer saluted, then told them. She nodded. Grant looked from one to the other, stupefied, doubting not the truth of the words so much as the uniformed stranger himself, his crackling emotionless voice ringing out over their yard. His face shaven so close he gleamed.

But he just shipped out, Grant said.

His mother's hand shot out to quiet him but didn't quite reach all the way. The thin steady fingers a couple of inches from his shoulder.

There was an accident, the officer said, an explosion. Nobody survived. He blinked, shook his head. I'm sorry.

A pause stretched into seconds as his mother's hand lingered in the air beside him. The sun was wedged between the shed and barn. The officer squinted against it, trying to maintain his composure.

Well, said his mother, you've told us what you came to?

Yes, ma'am.

She swallowed. Thank you, she said simply. The officer handed her a paper. Then he saluted again, got back in the jeep and disappeared into his own still-hanging dust.

Her hand fell but she stayed put, facing but not looking at the road. Grant stepped in front of her, into the path of her eyes. They moved to him reluctantly. That ain't right, he said, he just shipped out. Hell, he didn't even get to the war yet. Mama—

Ssh, she hissed, angry. That was you. It could have been you.

He looked into her face for direction, for what to think about what she had said. The sun lingered behind her and her stray hairs shivered in its light. She seemed insane, and as if to confirm this flung herself at him and wrapped her arms around his shoulders, wordlessly shouting. He stood horrified, Thornton's demise suddenly plausible. She crushed him to her. Over her shoulder he could see Max, emerging from the barn with a rusted hackamore dangling from his hand. He was headed for the starveout and the new colt running there, and then he stopped—stopped in front of the barn and leaned toward them—and took a step and finally ran, his burden jingling with each footfall until he reached them.

And what he did then—at the time it seemed natural to Grant—was to take his mother's shoulders and pluck her, pull her sharply, away from Grant, and turn her around and embrace her. He took her from Grant and held her: and why not? Max was her son, certainly he had figured out what happened, he would give her comfort. Why not?

But as Grant stood watching them he saw the strain in Max's face, saw his arms tighten around her. He was trying to lift her off the ground, almost as if to pour her grief into his open mouth. She cried out and bit his shoulder. Max's narrowed eyes, turning to Grant, appeared to say, She's mine, her sorrow is mine. And shocked at what he thought he saw, Grant turned away from them and went off to find his father.

That was me, Grant thought now as the home buildings came into view. Always going off for something, leaving to other people whatever needed doing. But what choice did he have? His parents, his brothers: they were forever around him, more ardent, quicker to understand, to desire, to act. He lacked Max's aggression, Edwin's skill, Thornton's determination. Their mother's responsibility. His obsessions hadn't the strength or specificity of his father's. His affinity was with the soonest dead: Robert might have made him funny; Wesley, patient. But neither had ever got the chance. What choice did he have but to leave?

So he left, and found no passion, and returned to nothing at all. He wondered what he had been doing when his mother died. September 5. He would have been asea, but where? Engaged in what? He struggled to remember. The years had lost definition in his memory, had flattened into a uniform gray, the color of ocean and sky, the gray of his lies. Probably he'd been eating or sleeping, it didn't matter. No dread sensation came over him. He was overwhelmed by no sudden terrible knowledge.

He had betrayed her by failing to stay, she had betrayed him by failing to live. Only he was left to atone, and so he would stay. He would live.

•

When he got back he found Cotter and Max at work on the barn. It had stood unsteadily for years, always the next thing they'd see to when whatever they were doing was finished. Now they had it stood up straight with heavy beams propped against the lean. Max was inside nailing new supports to the roof joists, while Cotter cut and fit new planks to replace the rotting walls. The horses watched idly from the pasture, the cows grazed in the yard. Grant watered his horse and led him over to the others. Then he went back to the barn.

Cotter nodded hello. Grant said, Long time coming.

These ain't the only hammer and saw, was the reply.

He went to the shed and got the tools then began tearing away the bad planks and measuring the new ones against them. They worked side by side for an hour. The repaired wall quickly took shape. Cotter said, How'd he take it?

Grant fitted a new board into its place. We got paint?

Cotter nodded.

He thinks we're gonna sell, Grant said. And like that, for the first time, the notion did not seem unreasonable. After awhile he added, You know he has a wife?

Two girls.

I had no idea.

He went around to the back where the wood had been baked and warped by years of sun and rain and the paint lay in brittle strips on the ground at its base. He surveyed the whole, wondering if it would be possible to choose planks to replace, or if he would have to choose between taking it all down or doing nothing.

Cotter appeared at the corner and said, So will you?

Will I what?

Sell.

He turned to face Cotter. The older man's eyes were stony, as if the place was already sold and his feet tainted by trespass.

What in hell would I do with myself then, do you think? Move into town? Nothing there for me.

Inside, the hammering stopped. A hawk cried. The rustle of hoppers in the grass seemed to amplify. The answer wasn't enough for Cotter, he stood tapping the hammer sidelong against his thigh, waiting.

No, Grant told him. We ain't selling.

Cotter appeared to consider and at last nodded. I'll go get

Kittredge, he said. He can start painting what we already done. And he disappeared around the corner of the barn.

◆

That night at supper they all seemed improved. Kittredge ate his food. He was shaking less or hiding it better. Sophia had on a dress, it was too hot for pants, she told them. She didn't know how the lot of them could stand it.

You just think about winter, miss, Kittredge said, and they all laughed at the joke.

When they were finished Max went out to the equipment shed. Through the kitchen window, as she washed the dishes, Sophia watched him cross the yard. The other men drank coffee and talked, Kittredge telling some story involving a drunk and a priest. Cotter grunted appreciatively now and then, his eyes on his hands on the table. Grant wanted to go help her—take up the plates and dry them and put them in the cabinet—but he stayed put and watched her work. When she was done she stood with her head hung, seeming to gather herself. Then she went out to the shed. Through the window Grant saw her stepping through the weeds, cautious of the spines against her bare ankles.

He turned back to the table to find Kittredge looking at him. You got eyes for her, he said. It was a kid, but there seemed to be a knife hidden in it somewhere.

Nah, he said.

You got to watch yourself, Kittredge said smiling. I don't know that her and your brother's getting on so good.

It seemed to Grant that Kittredge was looking for information. He wanted to gossip. Grant said, It's nothing. Nobody's getting on so good lately.

Cotter was still looking down at his hands but with greater intent. All were silent until footsteps landed on the stoop and Sophia walked in, her color high and breath heavy. She stopped and composed herself as if for a speech. But instead of talking she looked at each of them, swallowed and went to the stairs. Before she disappeared Grant stole a glance. Her eyes were on him, narrowed in a state of accusation but lacking any specific charge.

We still got some daylight, Cotter said and got up from the table. He nodded at Kittredge. You good to work some more? Above them, the sound of a body falling on a bed.

Course I'm good, Kittredge said loudly. I can go till dark. He stood, stretched his arms out behind his back and left them there with the hands clasped. How 'bout you, Grant? Or are you tired out? He gazed at Grant intently, waiting to be surprised.

I'm okay for it, Grant said, and the three of them went out to work.

·

The rest of that week Sophia stayed in after dinner, or else went out to tend to the animals before going to bed. She didn't follow Max to the shed. Grant lay in his room nights listening to her silence, until Max returned and the two of them spoke. But he couldn't tell what they were saying or even what sort of discussion it was. He couldn't sleep until he heard them. Often he couldn't sleep after that either.

One night he went out to the shed to see what Max was up to. The building was lit up from inside like a private sky, the rusted pinholes in the walls a human starlight. He guided himself across the yard to the door and pushed it open. Behind it a paint can clattered on the cement floor. Max was at work on a painting, his back was visible and his raised arm. The painting was four feet square, a field of cross-hatched streaks with bare white canvas along the edges. It didn't look like much of anything. At any rate Grant's view of it was brief. Max gasped at the intrusion and pulled a tarp down over the canvas as if the painting was some kind of dirty secret. Once the easel was covered he spun on his heels, his glare a mixture of fury and shame. The paint can had been a makeshift alarm. Grant snorted in surprise.

What do you want? Max asked him.

For a moment he had no reply. And then: You know, we barely been saying anything to each other since we came back with Daddy.

Max looked tired. He was holding his paintbrush like a weapon. Reckon we haven't, he said. Then he turned and dunked the bristles into a housepaint can and fixed the brush to the upright handle with a clothespin. He wiped his hands on a rag and came limping toward Grant.

What you working on that's so secret?

Nothing worth asking after, Max said.

For all his childish moping Max didn't look twenty-two but a boyish forty, his hair thinning as their father's had, fans of wrinkles framing his eyes. And his stoop. That's what it was, not a limp. Grant said, You look like an old man.

Our old man?

The old man you're gonna be someday.

Max smiled. Don't count on it.

They went out in the yard together and Max rolled a cigarette. He lit it with difficulty in the viscid air. Clouds had been massing all day, now they were crowded into every available space so that it felt like a rainstorm in every aspect but the rain itself. Grant felt less solid out in it, as if he too had drifted here anticipating release. His brother was an orange dot of ash in the dark that seemed itself to breathe as Max smoked.

She seems broke up over your keeping her out, Grant said.

Max took his time replying, so long that Grant wished he hadn't spoken at all. At last he said, She knew what she was getting into.

Did she?

To this Max said nothing. Grant held out his hand for the makings. The tobacco was fresh and the cigarette tasted good. He said to Max, Is he on your mind?

Sure.

I can't seem to think on him directly, Grant said. I remember Mama easy, and the boys, but even that's all fouled up. I can't get nothing straight in my head.

Max seemed to be turning this over in his own mind, through two or three flares of the cigarette's end. Don't see why you need to, he said.

Grant didn't understand. Was he saying there was no point in remembering, or implying that Grant had long ago left off caring about the family anyhow? It was typical of Max to speak plainly without actually saying anything that made sense. His face was near invisible in the compressed darkness.

You plan to show them paintings to anybody ever? Grant asked. Put 'em in a museum?

A chuckle came from Max's direction. A museum. I don't know about that. Ain't thought one way or another to do something with 'em.

The orange light brightened. You keep a diary? Max asked.

No.

Me neither. But it'd be like that, asking me if I'm gonna put my diary in the newspaper, or was I just gonna let it go moldy in a drawer somewhere. It ain't nobody's business and it ain't something I expect other people are gonna appreciate.

Okay, Grant said.

Like asking me if we ought to leave Daddy in the ground or should we prop him up in the town square.

Grant waited awhile before he said, A good forty miles to the nearest town square.

Max's laugh was sharp and quick, a snapping twig. That's good, he said. You can always change the subject with a joke. That's a valuable thing to know how to do.

I don't like how we got on that subject.

Yeah, well, me neither. He tossed his cigarette into the weeds and stamped it out. Old Petey did a hell of a job, didn't he. I don't see rebuilding those quarters.

No need of it.

Unless you and me get ourselves married and start fathering some babies. What do you think?

I don't know, Grant said. He backed up half a step. He felt cracked open, like Max was rooting around in him for something he'd lost.

Well, Max said suddenly, it's been real nice talking to you but I got to go write in my diary now. He reached out and clapped Grant's shoulder. The fingers were hot through his shirtsleeve. And then he was gone, and Grant stood alone in the yard feeling the coming rain. Standing there it occurred to him that there was someone living in his brother he didn't quite know. A seventh brother, at once enigmatic and familiar, that had taken the place of the one he'd grown up with. Or perhaps he had never known that one, not really.

When at last he turned to go back in the house he saw her, white as a puppet in the kitchen window. He didn't think she could see him. When he came closer to the house she backed away.

·

She was waiting when he came in, facing the doorway with the fingers of one hand curled over the rim of the sink. Her hair was longer than it had been. It hung over both sides of her face and lay against her shoulder like a hand. The light was off but she had lit a candle and put it on the table.

The bulb was too bright, she said. I couldn't stand it. Her voice had a quality of suspended motion, like a spun dime.

We ought to put a shade on it, Grant told her. He sat down to take off his boots.

She leaned back against the counter and faced him. She wore a nightgown with a robe pulled loosely around it and her face was thin and starved for sleep. I don't know what in hell I'm doing here, Grant.

He didn't answer, instead set his boots on the mat by the door, toes to the wall as if a penitent was standing in them.

I used to have friends, girl friends. I don't know if you know what I'm talking about. I had a dozen of them, people I saw every day. You know what I mean?

He said, When you work around sheep you get used to being alone.

How long's that take?

Grant stood and pressed his shoulder to the wall. You knew it was going to be different.

I didn't know Max was going to be different.

Her eyes were right on him. He wasn't sure what she wanted. He said, So what do you want to do about it?

In his head the words had sounded innocent. But on his lips they betrayed him, they implied that he had something in mind. He did have something in mind and she heard it. She took her hands off the counter and a step toward him, and he pushed himself off the wall and stood straight. There was a second then that might have stopped it, had one of them glanced away or spoken or stepped back, but they didn't and the opportunity to stop passed them by. She came into his arms and they kissed. His one hand found her face and the other the gap in her robe, and he stroked her back through the cotton of her gown, pausing at each vertebra and pressing gently into it and into the muscled concavity around it. They shifted their weight and the boards strained underneath them. Her lips and tongue were cool from just-drunk faucet water and he touched her face and her hair and body and she brought her mouth to his ear and whispered, Now.

It'll knock you up.

No it won't. Not tonight.

The men are upstairs—

We'll be quiet.

They were. They barely moved from the spot, falling against the wall in an ecstatic discomfort, making hardly a sound. When it was done she stepped away from him, the nightgown still bunched around her waist, and he saw her nakedness and the high color of her face in the candlelight, and the world tripled in size. He knew nothing about her, he thought as she leaned over the table and blew the candle out. Yet now he had these minutes of her that nobody else did, the hand that held her hair from the flame, the bare foot a ghostly blur against the floor. She said, You must think I'm heartless.

No, he said loudly.

Good.

She leaned into him and kissed him quickly and her fingers touched him where he had loved her. Good night, she said, and he said it back, and she disappeared up the stairs. He had no idea who she was. Possibly neither did she. It would be nearly three weeks before he touched her again.

PART THREE

ICE

10

A hot morning in early August, damp and heavy from a night rain. They had decided to build a chute for shearing as the Mexicans suggested, and to replace a few of the lambing pens which had rotted in the wet. There was no money for this, but a dreamy recklessness had possessed Grant: all that mattered, he thought now, was the betterment of their situation. He sent Max and Kittredge to town early for lumber and hardware and instructed Cotter to fix the fence where a bank had eroded under a post.

He hadn't been alone with her since their first encounter, though that needn't have kept them from meeting. They had all the space in the world to disappear into and wouldn't have been caught. But she had avoided him. Every word they exchanged in those weeks he could recall at will and did, mining them for innuendo. There was none, though: only the words themselves. Do you want coffee? she said. That old mare has a limp. What's today's date? Three times he'd listened to her make love to Max. He had begun to think that what had happened was a piece of mischief, the scratching of a frivolous itch. But if she loved Max, why would she have taken such a risk? But if she didn't love Max, what was she doing in his bed?

On this morning he saw her through his bedroom window, throwing meal to the chickens down in the yard. He yearned for her. Then she turned her face up to his window. The yearning gave way to anger. He pulled on his clothes cursing his body, dashed from the house. He walked straight past her into the barn, looking at her once with his eyes full of cruelty and lust, and shut the barn doors behind him and waited panting in the shallow trough that feet and hooves had cut in the dirt floor.

The animals stirred. Horses nickered and shuffled in expectation of a run. He kicked his feet on the packed dirt. If she didn't come he was giving up for good. Maybe he would leave here altogether. But she came.

He turned to her. She kept a distance, back to the door and head low, but her panicked eyes were on him.

I'm sorry.

I don't understand, he said.

It's hard to explain. None of this is what I expected.

He waited for more but nothing came. To expect a thing and then get it was an inconceivable luxury.

You love him, he said.

I love what I thought he was.

What in the hell's that mean?

I can't explain.

It was true of course, he knew that. Could he have explained his own life, his reasons for doing what he did, to anyone? Still, the explanation was in her somewhere. He wanted and deserved it. He said, You don't get to have what you make up in your head. You get what a person is or you don't get nothing.

Before she could reply he added, All you want's yourself.

He spat this as if it were a sucked venom. It made him feel awful. She was crying openly and he loved her. He took a step toward her and another. He said, I want you.

Yes, she said.

He went to her and held and kissed her, and they went to the mounded hay in the corner and undressed. Her body couldn't have been more different from his own, the uninterrupted paleness of her skin and the plainly described structure of muscles and bones. Like a sketch of herself. Without concern for who might hear, she cried out. In her cry Grant heard the torment of indecision for which he could be no help.

He had one thing that Max didn't: her secret, the secret that was him. What this meant was uncertain. He knew only that he would live here with her or he wouldn't live here.

·

Still it kept on as it was, without relief. From time to time they met. His head filled up with speeches and ultimatums but he hadn't the courage to speak his mind. He believed now that she loved him, believed he had no need for her to say so. Nonetheless he told her he loved her, however much he pleaded with himself not to, and her responses, passionate and sometimes violent but never spoken, left him longing for the covenant of words. It was words that married people and words that pronounced them dead. His desire for them overwhelmed him, caused him to shake and howl, to pound the ground like a primitive. Regularly he took himself off to lonely places to let the emotion spill out of him.

She would long ago have left the ranch if not for him. She told him so. He considered offering to go with her. But he wasn't confident she would say yes, and he feared that in the wake of his offer she would leave without him. And it was here that he wanted her, in this valley, without the foolishness of girls and parties and the distraction of city life to share her with. In the city he would lose her attention and ultimately her love. He would be left alone there with no way back to the life he knew: much the situation she was in herself, right now. If that happened he would have to return to fishing. His only home would be a steel-walled box, or the dreary flophouses of port cities. Or he could go to Iceland and find his mother's family, and they would take him in. He wouldn't have a word of the language, so he would herd sheep, the one thing that didn't require talking. In the harsh endless winter he would wear a lambskin coat he sewed himself with a bone needle.

He would sleep with his dogs and people would think him strange for never taking a wife.

That was how it was. He made these plans, and then, when it seemed like he would never again have her, Sophia would come to him and a life together would seem possible, even likely. Even inevitable. But not for long. That was how it was.

In the fall they let the rams have at the ewes. For the first time he found their rutting comic and horrible. The ewes cried out as the hooves gouged their backs and legs, their eyes filled with elemental terror, and all of sex and birth and life in its redundant splendor seemed a foul joke. When it got cold they pulled up the potatoes and carrots and put them by in the cellar, and this act of faith—faith that they would be here to eat them—seemed tragically proud. He felt the end of everything looming nearby, death and ruin absurdly amplified by the intensity of his love.

He understood that this living couldn't be sustained, that something would happen to change it. In the end it was two things at once.

◆

One morning the first week of November they woke up sick. Grant knew it even in his sleep. He shed his blankets one by one and finally the bedsheet, and woke up afire with the window cracked open and snow blowing in and mounding on the sill. His throat felt like a man's hot hands were pressed to it, his legs were splayed out before him white and dead-looking. Outside the sky was thick with resolve, the snow so heavy that clouds couldn't be seen through it, the flakes huge and clumped together. He tried to raise himself up to see how much had fallen, but when he stirred the hands tightened around his neck and he fell back to the pillow.

Some time later, he didn't know how long, a figure appeared in the door and spoke his name. It was Max.

You got it too, Max croaked.

Grant managed to get up on his elbows. It felt like the thing that had him had died and stiffened, and he would have to drag it along with him forever. He spoke and his voice sounded like somebody else's.

Yep.

You got to get up, Max said. It's heavy out, Murray might need us.

The window had rimed over inside with the moist heat of illness. Snow was falling on the bed. Outside he could see absolutely nothing. Then the shapes of the buildings and grounds rose up out of the white. Already eight inches or more were on the ground.

Sophia got it? Grant said.

I'll get breakfast. Or maybe Cotter's down there already. Max coughed and pain raced across his face. She's in bed still.

When he was gone Grant got himself on his feet and inched across the hallway. She lay tangled in her nightgown, blankeyed and lovely. She frowned when she saw him, as if trying to figure out what he meant.

Max . . . she protested.

He's downstairs.

Go, she said.

What can I get you? His vision blurred and he slumped against the doorframe. You want a hot drink?

Nothing, she said weeping silently. Go, go.

Downstairs he tried to make himself eat the food Cotter had cooked. Kittredge was still in his room, they no longer bothered him with work. He did it when he could. He shook badly almost always, ever since the air turned cold, and his obvious embarrassment moved them to ignore the shaking and to ignore Kittredge, which seemed to make him shake harder still.

Cotter wasn't sick but exhaustion played at the rims of his eyes. He kept glancing at Max and Grant and then out the window. Max pushed his eggs around on the plate with a fork, rubbing his forehead with the other hand.

Cotter said, I think we ought to get out there.

Hard to limber up with this flu, Grant said.

Who brung it?

Max managed a laugh. No more shaking nobody's hand in town. Just nod, he said. Then the telephone rang.

They all turned and looked at it. It rang again. Cotter picked it up. The static was audible from where Grant was sitting and he could hear a woman's voice shouting through it.

Okay, Cotter said. I know the place. He hung up.

Let's go, he said reaching for his coat on the hook.

What! Max said. Grant's flesh was baking with fever, he could smell the sour air coming up off him.

That was Nannie Mott. Dan spotted our ewes piling up in a coulee out by their place. He's up there now.

Max dropped his fork. Can't be ours.

Got our mark on them.

Where's Murray! Where's the goddam dogs! The shouts crumbled into faint coughs.

Hell if I know, Cotter said and shrugged on his coat and plunged out into the weather. Max leapt up cursing. He flung back his chair and made for the door. As he followed, Grant thought of Sophia, her words to him as he watched her suffering. Kittredge would have to take care of her.

◆

They rode through the storm navigating the trails by feel. Here and there was an outcrop overhanging sheltered ground the snow hadn't reached, and the bare brown patch hovered in the air like an omen. Grant followed Cotter with Max close behind. It was not too cold, but a wind rose up now and then and the snow flew straight and heavy against them, and the horses shied. They came to drifts between hills they had to scramble up around and creeks not entirely frozen that the horses broke through, the jagged ice cutting their fetlocks and freezing the wounds. Grant felt like a stone statue moored to the saddle. He'd lost his sense of balance and seemed to stay upright by luck alone. He clamped his knees around the horse's ribs in spite of the ache, and ignored the mucus flowing out of his nose, leaving it to freeze on his scarf and the lining of his coat. This wasn't like his fever in spring. He wasn't hallucinating. Everything appeared brutally real, Cotter's back and the snow and his horse's head, a shuddering plow through the mass of gray light, all of it impressing itself painfully upon him like a brand. He closed his eyes to dispel it but it appeared in reverse, the horses and Cotter and the drifting rocks all bright lights in a blackness. He may even have slept, because when he turned to see if Max was with them it was the dead man riding his horse, his face a vegetable pink in the blizzard like a toxic winter blossom. And then it was Max again, shouting Keep up.

Cotter knew the spot, a blind coulee that admitted water in spring. He led them there easily, navigating the false paths the drifts made as if by second sight. When they arrived a break came in the storm, the snow still heavy but suddenly reluctant to reach the ground, and Grant heard voices from above and saw men on horses peering down at them from the ridge. He knew what had happened. In the night the ewes must have got cold and antsy and went for cover, finding it in the lee of this sidehill. At the start of the storm it would have looked good to them, rocks and trees with no snow behind. The wind would have shifted and the drifts fallen over them. They panicked. One bolted and bumped another and climbed up onto her, and the next climbed on them both, the hooves digging and the snowcaked wool pressing down, and the heat of their bodies melted the snow and ice, and the weight and the water crushed and suffocated. The fickle wind was pulling the snow now like a curtain open-and-closing. He could glimpse through this curtain the piled sheep, dirt gray against the white snow, the hill of them writhing and tumbling and scrabbling against the backs of the dead, so many that the top ones were nearly up out of the coulee, where men were roping them and pulling them to safety.

Cotter crashed ahead through a low section of drift that had blocked off the exit. Of course the ewes wouldn't have made their way out through it, thinking it part of the hill. Max came from behind, startling Grant's horse, and they trailed Cotter side by side through the opening he made in the drift.

There were a lot of half-buried sheep that hadn't yet pushed up onto the pile. These stood bleating in the low part of the coulee, charging forward in confusion and terror a few feet then retreating, frightened by the cries of the dying. Cotter began driving them out through the gap. He pointed to Grant and shouted above the noise. Keep them together!

Grant did what he was told. He was joined by two more men coming off the ridge. One of them was Dan Mott, a cattleman they'd lived next to all their lives but rarely saw except along the fenceline. The other man was his son Tom. The two broke apart and formed a perimeter for the sheep to gather in, and soon their hooves had trampled the area flat. Grant counted as he guided them in. They came to about a hundred. The pileup was bad but it couldn't have killed all the rest of them. When the flow of animals had slowed he called out to Mott, the words gouging his throat like broken glass.

Where's Murray at?

Mott pointed south-southwest. Flock broke up in the snow! he shouted. He went chasing them down, my other boy's with him! Mott's face, blurred by cold, was a stranger's.

Grant thanked him, though by then Mott was looking off over the snowdrift and may not have heard.

◆

He rode where Mott had pointed, toward the lowlands between hills where he knew Murray liked to bed down the sheep in winter. The fever was still running hot under his coat and he begged it not to stop now lest the wind freeze the sweat on his skin. It was getting easier to stay on his horse. The pain in his joints and throat was bad but had been eclipsed by the urgency of the moment. For now he could bear it.

The snow was still heavy but the wind had died, leaving the illusion of safety. There was no trail to follow. Through his fever Grant struggled to remember where the creeks were, and where to cross them. Beneath him the horse heaved, panting, the work beginning to tax. He wiped his face and spat into the snow. He was hungry.

Then for a moment, though he knew where he was and could have got back even if the horse dropped dead where it stood, he began to believe he would perish here. The snow would fall over him and in a few days the coyotes would dig him out. Though Mott knew exactly where he'd gone, though Murray would have to pass this way to meet up with the rest of the flock, death seemed a real possibility. Every direction showed him the same face, thick and cryptic and empty. And then he saw the herder on a hillside, and the Mott boy with him and the flock below, with the horses by the flock and the dogs tied to the wagon, their ropes taut. The dogs were barking wildly.

Grant drew closer and managed a shout. Murray looked up. Like the younger Mott he was holding a long denuded branch and had been driving it over and over into a snowdrift. Now he waved it in the air hollering for Grant to come help him.

He dismounted near Murray's horse where the snow was already tramped flat, and he ran up the hill. Suddenly the ground seemed to give way. He found himself up to his waist in snow. He said, What in the hell—, and the herder lunged toward him.

It's holes! Murray said, his face black against the drift like a hollowed-out walnut, his eyes rough and spent as old coals. The sheep's down in 'em! He thrust another branch at Grant and resumed jabbing at the snow.

Grant remembered. This used to be prospecting territory. Men with picks came thinking they would get rich. His mother had fed a few of them. They wandered the federal land digging holes, thinking there'd be no one to hold them responsible. They were right. The holes had probably looked good to the spooked ewes, and when the drifts blew over they would have been afraid to come out.

He gripped his stick and started poking. There was something comical about the three of them, as if it was treasure they were look-ing for, a buried treasure of childhood. All around him Grant struck rock. He inched forward to the edge of the hole he was in, climbed out, and poked again. In ten minutes he found a sheep, and with the others' help pulled it out. It was dead. He found another dead one, then a live one which Murray carried down the treacherous hillside like it was an infant. The snow was slowing, the hour uncertain. They moved across the hill carving channels through the drifts, and the snow stopped entirely and sheep kept turning up below them, most dead. When Grant thought to look back he saw a cluster of dead sheep lying on their sides next to the living flock, laid out straight and true as felled timber. He turned to Murray in awe of his passion, in the absurd fervor of this search, which surely would produce no further living sheep. He wondered how Murray had let them get away.

When they had discovered five living and sixteen dead altogether, the last ten all dead, Grant again stood straight to look down the hill. He felt the world bow around him, flexing. He could not go on. He sat down in the deep snow and it walled up around him, a silent fortress, and he closed his eyes with relief.

◆

He woke in darkness on Murray's bunk, his feet unshod and wrapped in rags before the roaring cookstove. He couldn't figure out what was going on. When he wiggled his toes a pain raced up through him and he gasped with the force of it. His hands flew to his thighs and he scratched until the skin was ready to give up blood.

There were voices outside. He wanted to see who it was but feared what moving his legs might do to him, so he shouted out hello. His throat ached. The smell of Murray's bunk was all around.

Cotter came in, pulling the elkskin aside to reveal a clear cold starry night. The wagon creaked and tilted under his weight. He sat down on Murray's stool and lit the lampwick with a twig shoved into the stove.

You're gonna lose a couple of toes, on the right, he said. Left might be okay.

Grant looked down at his swathed feet. I didn't feel a thing, he said. After a silence he asked, What happened? How many'd he lose?

About half. Murray's gone.

Gone?

Left the wagon but took the horse and dogs, Cotter said. He shifted on his stool. Ask me, I think he was sleeping drunk and didn't hear the dogs barking.

Was that our horse or his?

Hell, I don't know.

That was that, Grant thought. Murray wouldn't be back.

They stared at the open door of the cookstove, at the deep orange corpses of the burning logs. Cotter said, almost shyly, What do you think about selling now?

Don't know. And later: Who's out there?

Jess Mott. Max went home. For the girl.

For the girl. A reason to go home, Grant's only reason. His fingers remembered her ribs. And then, easy as letting out breath, he pushed her from his mind. I can herd 'em, he said. It seemed not only possible but correct, inevitable.

Cotter met his eyes. He looked down and took to smoothing his dungarees over his knees.

I don't know, he said.

It won't be trouble for me.

About this outfit, I mean, Cotter said. He shook his head. Mott'd buy if you was selling.

After some consideration Grant said, Go work for Mott if that's what you want to do.

I ain't saying that.

Grant looked at him levelly until finally Cotter stood, keeping bent over because he was too tall to stand straight, and pushed the elkskin aside. I'll bring you in something to eat. We'll go back first light.

All right, Grant said and realized the fever was gone, he had starved or frozen it out. The stink of the mattress had stopped bothering him too. He was comfortable so long as he didn't move his feet or swallow or speak. It wasn't bad being here alone, with food coming and nothing at all in his head worth saying, not bad at all.

·

In the morning Cotter tied wool sacks over Grant's feet and led him home slowly on his horse. The day was stunning bright by the time they returned. Above the house woodsmoke massed, unmoved by wind. Cotter and Max helped him through the kitchen, where Kittredge sat sniffling and drinking coffee, and into his bed. Then they left him alone.

On his way out Max stopped in Sophia's room and asked if she needed anything. Grant heard her whisper a reply. After awhile Max came back and set something on her bedside table, a glass of water by the sound of it. Grant heard her lift the water glass and sip from it and put it back. Or was it Max's hand that brought it to her lips?

He appeared in Grant's doorway, watching him with a kind of practical pity.

Anything for you? Max said.

No.

When he was gone, the house empty of sound but for her breathing and the occasional scrape or footstep from Kittredge, he called out quietly to her. Her name came out roughened though he'd meant it tender. Are you all right?

No, came the barely audible answer.

To hell with Kittredge, he thought. With all of them. He said to Sophia, Can you come here? To me. Come on.

For a long time she said nothing. Then, No— My head—

I'll come to you, he said.

Grant, no—

But what she wanted was unimportant. He slid himself off the bed headfirst, supporting his weight on one hand and then the other, and slowly he lowered his legs, mustering his strength to bring each heel gently to the floor. His feet throbbed in unison. Now he began to move backwards toward the door, one hand, one foot, one hand one foot, looking over his shoulder to see where he was going. The motion ignited new pains all over him, in his calves and thighs where he'd clenched the horse and his shoulders and back from hoisting the lifeless ewes out of the snow. He left his room and entered hers. When she saw him she closed her eyes. She said No, Grant, no, but he dragged himself to her side and up onto the bed and pulled her, weightless and hot, into his sweat-damp shaking arms.

Please, Sophia.

You're hurting me, she said barely.

Tell me. That's all I want. Tell me.

She pushed him away, moaning. He thought, I could squeeze it out of her. I could pull the words right out of her mouth. I could.

But when he let go, when he'd lain there for ten minutes listening to her gasp herself to sleep, he got down off the bed and made his way back to his room.

•

Lafitte took off four toes, three from the right foot and one from the left. The rest would heal, he said. He gave Grant a jar of salve and pills for pain and told him that Sophia had got pneumonia. She would recover, though she might easily have died, it was bad enough. For a week he heard her whistling throat, her coughing. When she was out of bed for good she didn't come see him. Max had nursed her and when she was well enough to go outside he let her back into the studio.

Cotter would watch the ewes until Grant could walk. Until then there was Kittredge to keep him company. His trembling was worse than ever, his guilt over Neeler all-consuming without work to occupy him. He came to Grant while he lay in bed, or when he sat drinking nights at the kitchen table. He said he'd let the boy go bad, he ought to have raised him up right in a regular household where they could've lived year-round. Once, Grant suggested to Kittredge that by the time he'd got hold of Neeler, the boy was already who he was going to be, by blood or experience, and there was no reason to worry himself over it. But Kittredge paid no attention. He wanted to be to blame. He'd convinced himself he caused Neeler's mother's cancer as well, maybe it was something he fed her that didn't agree with her, maybe there was something about him personally that rotted a woman out from inside. He talked without end and didn't seem to want Grant to respond.

After a week of it Grant began to think like Kittredge. The flaws of the world seemed to be his own fault. He could feel Kittredge's words weakening his body, arresting the healing in his feet. The voice lived in his dreams, it kept him awake nights. His mind reshaped itself to its cadences; everything he heard sounded like Kittredge. Chairs were tainted by Kittredge's plaintive huddle in them, and Grant could feel his own hands beginning to shake.

At last Lafitte took the stitches out. Walking felt good, though it was hard to keep his balance on the strangely shaped feet. He packed his horse with dried and canned food and two giant sacks of potatoes. Not a lot to eat, but he figured if he kept still most of the time he wouldn't need to eat so much. He brought salt for the sheep and a dog Cotter had gotten from somebody. It was a good dog, reeking and old and cooperative.

When it was time to leave, Max helped him outfit the horse and gave him a stack of paperbacks he'd been hoarding in the shed. Grant had already read them but he'd forgotten most of the plots. He managed to fit the books into an already bulging pannier. When he was ready he let his brother help him into the saddle.

You're going to need to do that by yourself, Max said.

I'll manage.

You ought to know, she told me she's been in your bed.

Grant ignored him. He buttoned up his coat and tied his hat tight around his chin. It was cold and windy and the sky was clear blue.

I ain't going to hold it against her, Max said. I know I was hard to bear after we buried Daddy. He coughed. I ain't got feelings against you for it either.

There was no possible response. Grant took the reins in hand and set out instead with the dog behind him. He didn't look back. All the way out he imagined the two of them killed together by some act of God, a swollen river or rockslide or storm, which he, with his wits about him, unfettered by emotion, alone survived. In the wreckage their bodies would look so slight and pale, almost imaginary.

11

The first week was hard. Snowed in, alone with his thoughts, sometimes he believed he might go mad. It helped to talk to the dog: a good companion, possessed of a certain authority, the dog seemed interested in what Grant had to say. He talked about his travels mostly, things he'd seen, people he had met or observed. From time to time he looked at his compass, the one Luc had given him. It was correct, but knowing the direction was little comfort. Only when the sun shined, when he brought his folding stool outside and sat with his face bared to the light, did he think the work might be possible to endure.

After two weeks he no longer spoke. There seemed nothing much worth saying. The dog kept to itself, rarely demanding any attention. The sun began to feel like an interruption. He came to long for the snow, for those days when the sky and all but the most conspicuous natural features were erased, and his existence became more hypothesis than fact: those days seemed of almost incalculable value. In the world of things there was nothing more precious, he came to believe, than absence.

It was into this state of near-grace that the dead man arrived. He stood on a far hill watching. Grant could barely make him out across the dazzling expanse of snow but he was there nonetheless, unmistakable as a landmark. For days the dead man kept his distance, wandering in the hills or sitting motionless on a boulder, impervious to the wind. After awhile this reticence bothered Grant more than his appearance in the first place. They were already acquainted, after all. One clear morning the dead man appeared shaded by a distant stand of scrub pines, and Grant stood on the buckboard of the wagon and shouted to him to come say his piece or else go away.

You hear me? he cried. A hawk's call distracted him and he looked away. When his eyes returned to the spot, the dead man had gone, effaced by shifting light and shadow.

For a few days there was no sign of him. Grant slept dreamlessly or else forgot his dreams. His waking hours were flat and calm and flawless. He felt as healthy in mind and body as he ever had in his life, though he'd got thinner in the weeks he'd been here and had to gouge a new hole in his belt with a knife. The extra hole pleased him, his rationing plan was working. He ate the food he brought and occasionally part of a deer he'd shot and dried in strips over the stove, and that was enough.

Then the dead man reappeared. Grant woke knowing he was there and took his time going outside. He lit the stove and heated a pot of water for coffee and to wash himself. When he was done he stepped out and looked around. The dead man was closer this time, walking in among the ewes. The ewes took no notice of him; he looked up at Grant over their snow-mounded backs. Grant thought to scold the dog for not barking, but then again the barking wouldn't have told him anything he didn't already know.

What do you want? Grant called out. The dead man was wearing his gangster's jacket and pants. The now-familiar bare cracked skin was rimy and purpled at the cuts from cold. A smile was on his face but somehow not part of it. He looked up when Grant called but he made no reply.

Well, then get out, Grant said. I'm fine here all by myself. After a moment he added, You're making the ewes nervous.

It wasn't true. The dead man stayed. All right then, there was work to do. Grant went back in for his colored glasses and hat and rifle. He came out and circled the flock, scanning the perimeter for coyote sign. Finding none he returned to the wagon and made himself breakfast and ate it. He brought out one of the paperbacks, a mystery story, and read the first couple of pages in the light of the lantern. None of it sank in. For a short while he worked on scraping the deerskin, intending to make something out of it, maybe a vest or part of a cloak. But the work in the close air fatigued him and he went back outside.

The dead man was right in the little bed-down place where the dog slept in daytime. The dog was nowhere in sight. Grant said, I got to move soon, you know. Sheep can't eat the same grass twice.

The dead man turned and looked south to where Grant would be moving. In response Grant went into the wagon and brought out the folding stool and his cup of coffee, near cold now. He gave the stool to the dead man and lowered himself onto the buckboard. The dead man unfolded the stool, planted it in the packed snow and sat.

You want a cup of coffee? Grant said, and remembered his dream, and laughed. He sipped his coffee. It was not blood. Smirking, he raised it to the dead man in a kind of salute. Some time later the dog returned from whatever he was doing and lay in a sunny spot beside the wagon. Steam came up off him.

Grant said, When you live in a house, you can't wait for winter to end. But when you're out in it you wish it'll just go on forever. The ewes are carrying, though. Can't well birth 'em out here, can I?

The dead man nodded but he was looking out past Grant, out north where a dark shape was moving in the snow. The dog stood and shook himself and ran up to meet the rider. Grant watched, drinking his cold coffee right to the bottom. He flung the grit out over the ground. The dog came back and stood by him and waited.

It was Cotter. How's it going? he said to Grant.

Fine.

Getting along on that foot, are you?

Yep.

Okay, Cotter said, his eyes half closed against the light, or maybe in thought.

You gonna get down off that horse? Grant asked.

Cotter dismounted in the fresh snow and took a bottle and some mail out of his pannier. There were a couple of sacks too, feed for the dog and horse. More salt as well. Cotter shouldered the sacks and leaned them up against a wagon wheel, then came around and sat on the empty stool, first studying it as if he didn't understand why it was there.

You look different, he said.

How so?

Them glasses, I reckon. And you're skinny. Cotter raised the bottle and Grant held out his empty cup.

The liquor looked venomous to Grant, so he didn't drink it, only held it up like he was going to. Cotter drank straight from the bottle. He said, Bills due. Max wants to know should he pay 'em.

He can sign the checks. I'm the herder now.

You don't want me to take over for you?

Nope.

Cotter nodded. He pulled an envelope out of the pile and put the rest into his coat. He handed the envelope to Grant. I don't know where he went to, Cotter said. I would of figured he went home to her but I guess not.

It was a letter to Murray from his wife. The flap was smudged with fingerprints, hers or Cotter's he couldn't tell. He set it on the wagon seat beside him and told Cotter he'd take care of it. After that they didn't have much to say. The dog stood up and went off somewhere. To the west clouds were massing with the color and sharp edges of slate. The sun moved slowly toward them, gradually dimming. The sheep began to simmer, their breaths audible. They moved against one another, the icy wool scraping, a sound like a whispered secret. Cotter stood up and Grant stepped down and the dog reappeared, looking from one to the other and sneezing.

Got to move, Grant said.

All right, said Cotter. He looked at the coming weather and back at Grant. His breath hovered around his head, gathering light like a halo.

It seemed like there was something Cotter wanted to say. Instead he turned and went back the way he came.

◆

Grant hooked up the horse and led the ewes south-southeast, where the land was flat and the shrubs stood clear above the snow. It was a seabed here before men were living and there was plenty of salt to the soil. When they'd got to where the grass was thickest between the shrubs, he stopped. Here, away from the hills, the wind had claimed some snow, leaving a patch of nearly bare ground to bed down on. He unhooked the horse and made his rounds with the dog, hoping to catch sight of a pheasant, as he had the taste for meat in him suddenly. But there was nothing to shoot, so he got back in the wagon and ate what he normally did. He made the fire small, trying to conserve wood until he came to the hills again, and fried up a potato and ate it with coffee and jerky. Then he opened up the letter from Murray's wife and read it out loud to the dead man.

Thomas, he read, the girls are good but a goat died today, please send something.

He looked up to see if the dead man was paying attention. I don't know what kind of fool would raise up a family on the goddam plains, do you? he asked.

The dead man was sitting on Grant's bunk. The air, thick and warmed by the fire, was full of sea-smell. Grant remembered his first catch on the *Rose Adams*. He was stationed in the hold where the cod were dumped. In a quirk of the ship's manufacture the fish collected in the shallow end of the hold where the hatch was, and somebody had to stand down in it and rake the cod into the other side. He wore rubber boots too big for him and he slid across the mucus-slicked floor, sometimes falling flat so that the fish closed over him like an oil. For hours the scales abraded his skin where it was exposed. His clothes were heavy with blood and bile and slipped off him from their weight, his trousers hanging low on his hips and his sweater pulling down over his shoulders and hands. He imagined this was what death was like: closeness, heaviness, panic; the light only bright enough to inspire fear, showing the barest outline of the unknown. That was the quality of light in this wagon, with the sun behind the hills and a new moon absent from the sky. The fire was out and cold closed in. He was tired.

Is that what it's like to be dead? he asked. Am I right about that? But the dead man wasn't there, only the mussed bunk with its gnarl of dirty blankets and the stained pillow with the ticking pressed flat.

Grant got under the blankets. He reached beneath the cot and pulled out his pannier, then rummaged in it until he found a pencil and a wrinkled sheet of paper. In the lanternlight he set about composing a letter to Murray's wife.

> Dear Love,
> Im so sorry I was no good to you. Working all alone its easy to forget what it means to be with people. I am leaving here and will be home soon. Tell the girls that I love them. It will be hard to make up for lost time but I have to try.
> Your Thomas

He read the letter over a few times, crossing out and substituting words until they satisfied him. When he was finished he folded the two letters together. He got out of bed and put them in the stove, where they brushed against a grayhot crumb and caught fire. When the letters were burned Grant got back under the blankets. He covered himself up, leaving a space for his nose and mouth to draw air. He wondered what had become of the dead man's killer. Probably he'd been killed by somebody else in revenge.

I won't be the first man to spend his life barely alive, he told himself. Men did it. It was no great feat. He would live—he'd live a few scant miles from the heart of life, on its chill periphery. That suited him after all.

Again he slept uninterrupted by dreams.

◆

February passed and in March he led the ewes back for lambing. With the bitterest cold gone and a chinook wind impending he had begun to miss the company of men. He'd talked to the dead man of course, but there was no satisfaction in it. He wanted to be talked back to. Now he moved toward a destination and could anticipate the work that needed doing, tagging the ewes and readying the shelters. Maybe it was possible to build the flock back up. They could take out a loan. Wool prices could rise. It was possible.

But the sight of the home buildings puzzled him. Their familiarity was somehow foreign, his memory of them unclear: he regarded them as a snake might regard the empty skin it has lived in and left behind. Exposed and graying in the fist of the hills, the buildings looked abandoned. Even the barn, newly repaired and painted, had been dulled by winter.

They must have seen him coming, for the doors stood open at the back of the sheep shed. The ewes shouldered ahead, their bellies swaying, and their hooves on the hard earth made a sound like heavy rain. They poured in seeming to remember, needing little encouragement from the dog. Grant shut the doors behind him and dropped the bar, then he led his horse to the barn, leaving the wagon parked behind the shed where it couldn't be seen from the house. Standing in the trampled grass it looked like it had grown there.

He hayed the horse and brushed him out and the horse rested, breathing loudly with one leg cocked up. It was cold in the barn, but a sheltered cold, one you could get to like. When he was done he stood very still listening to the wind buffet the walls. Then in a temporary calm he heard her behind him. He started and spun, and boiled up in anger and shouted an oath. She shied. She was as white from the winter months as if she'd never spent a day outdoors in her life.

You look sick, he said.

I was. You look crazy.

He tossed the brush in the bucket it came from and busied himself about the barn, rearranging things the way they were before he left. He missed the range and wagon already. Here, there was too much to keep track of.

She said, I want to apologize.

You don't have nothing to be sorry for.

She watched him work. He felt her watching. You won't accept it, she said, is that it?

You got my answer.

He was good to me when I was sick, she went on. Grant felt itchy and hot and began banging the implements into their places. His back was aching. Things changed, she said. It isn't that—

I'm done with you! he screamed at the wall he faced, Get out! He stamped his booted foot and pain shot up from the place the toes had been. Get out!

He waited gasping until he heard the door slide closed behind him, then he fell sobbing to his knees, the months of scabbed and weathered callus cracking in an instant, all the dread of death and madness slashed in this silly fit, all over a girl. He was home.

•

This time there were no hired men to help them. They hadn't the money, nor enough sheep to make it worthwhile. When the first ewes began labor a cold descended, and though the patched barn kept the worst out, it was hard to keep the chill off the newborns. Some of them were so weak they died before their eyes opened. Some of the ewes bled to death. It was not as bad as it could have been but the operation had a sparseness about it, with stretches when nothing was happening and they had to talk about or do something to fill the time. They nursed their fingers split from the freeze and thaw. Grant sat listening to Kittredge. He was used to it. There was no talk of Neeler, obviously Kittredge had forced himself to stop. But the effort seemed to have killed something in him. He spent long minutes nodding in response to nothing, like an old man. After these silences he turned to details of his ailment, how he felt the shaking coming on when he woke or when he was hungry or faced with some task the shaking would keep him from doing. He wondered aloud if it was a bacteria that had got in him that made him sick, or some defect that was there all along. Lafitte had told him to sleep when he was tired and not to tax himself, but a little bit of the bottle helped, Kittredge said, in fact he was drinking a lot more than he used to. He had bought it himself, mind you—it wasn't costing the ranch a nickel. There was no evidence that Kittredge cared about or even noticed the words he was using. Listening to him was like standing in a rainstorm.

It was possible to ignore Sophia. She tended suckling lambs, moved the warming lamps from pen to pen, kept the fire going, and said nothing at all. Max worked alongside Cotter and Grant, leading the ewes in when their time came and ushering the lambs dead or alive into the cold world. Grant thought it must be a shock, living for months in that dark soundless summer, then emerging into winter and light. For some time the lambs would associate the two and maybe for that time they would live only reluctantly.

When it was done they had little more than before. There would not be much money made from spring lambs unless they wanted to cull the flock. Late one night while Sophia slept the men sat around the table waiting for someone to come out and say what they all were thinking.

I want out, Max finally said. His eyes were on his glass but the words were aimed at Grant. Me and her are going to move down to Denver. I can get work and paint besides.

Grant said, So go then.

Max looked up. It'd be nice to have a little spending money.

What you telling me for?

I want out.

Now that he was thinner Grant had found he couldn't hold his liquor too well. Max's figure tilted and smeared.

You want money, let her get it from her daddy, he said, knowing full well she couldn't get her daddy's signature on a birthday card if that was what she wanted.

A rattling on the table. It was Kittredge tightly clutching his empty glass.

You know what I'm saying, Max said. His reasonable tone of voice was a put-on. I want my half. Either you go in with somebody else or we sell and split it. We ain't never been any good at this like Edwin would of been. We never cared about the place. Let's get out.

He was right. There was nothing here for them. The thought of dumping the outfit sent a gush of warm blood out of Grant's heart, and it churned through him making him feel nearly human. And yet. And yet, goddam if he was going to write their ticket to Denver. He said, You do what you want with your half. I ain't buying you out.

He looked up and was pleased to discover that Max was stunned. Well, what had he thought? Did he think Grant was going to say Go, go, brother, take her away to Colorado? Like hell. When Grant opened his mouth he found himself talking a little louder.

You'll just have to find some sucker who'll buy you out. I got your interests to protect up on the spring range and I ain't got time to cut a deal for you. Run an ad in the paper.

There was a silence from which not a single breath was drawn.

Well, hell, said Max.

Hell, nothing. I don't know what you expected.

It ain't like I sneaked off with your girl, Max muttered, his face bent and working. It ain't like it was me who broke my mama.

Max, said Cotter.

Wasn't me who sent my poor idiot brother off to war, it was you. So the least you could do is let me have a piece of the life you wrecked. The way I see it, that wouldn't set nothing right, but it's the least goddam thing you could do.

Cotter's hand had made its way to Max's wrist, pinning the arm to the table. The arm had a fist at the end of it and tried to shake Cotter off. But Cotter held it.

Max, he said.

Some kind of reaction was called for, Grant thought. He was supposed to stand up knocking the chair over behind him. Something.

But Max had said nothing that could be disputed. For a moment he considered giving up. Why not let them go, and begin his new still-born life? He could buy a shack somewhere and squat in it and never think about these people again. But he could neither relinquish this final claim nor muster up the desire to defend it. He sat there.

Max seemed awfully far away. The house groaned, giving up its week of stored warmth from the false spring. Max shook his head.

Look at you, he said. You look like a rock. Two months out in it and you can't even feel nothing.

Max tried getting up but Cotter held him. Cotter! he shouted. Let go of my goddam arm!

Cotter let him go. Max stood, opening and closing his fingers. Then he went to the door and opened it, letting the cold air in. As if to say something he turned on the threshold and faced Grant. But in the end there appeared to be nothing he could say, having exhausted all the unthinkable things, and he went out shutting the door quietly and carefully behind him.

•

Grant expected that once he left for spring range he'd never see Max or Sophia again. They would borrow money from Kittredge, who was certain not to turn them down. Whatever the case they would be gone soon and he could get himself into the hills and forget about them. The prospect warmed him. He spent the next day in preparation, gathering supplies, the dog close behind him, its eyes alert inside rings of white fur.

That afternoon Cotter came to him. He stood watching Grant in silence awhile, his hands in his pockets. At last Grant stopped what he was doing and faced him.

Okay, what is it.

Looks like we'll be here another year then?

Grant sighed. At least through shearing, I reckon. Then I'll think about it.

In that case we're gonna need ice.

Ice, Grant said. Cotter nodded.

It was true that ice would have to be cut and hauled to the house. They did it every year, fifteen miles northeast on the springfed lake this side of Eleven. Usually it was done by now, before the first warm day. Grant said, Nobody did it already?

My back ain't what it was, Cotter said. And Max wouldn't do it by himself.

They were standing behind the sheep shed, by the wagon. The sheep knew it was time and milled at the gate like men, the wanderlust in them. Grant looked at Cotter a long while.

Okay, you're telling me I got to do it with Max.

Ain't nobody else.

He had to laugh. He said, You want us to make nice, do you.

I don't care about that, said Cotter. But I ain't gonna spend the summer eating rotten meat and warm iced tea. Unless you want to go to Ashton and get us an electric freezer.

With what money?

Well, then, Cotter said and stiffened his stance in the weeds.

He wondered if Max had put him up to it. Or if Sophia had put Max up to putting him up. Well, all right—if Max was going to try and talk him into selling, so be it. Let him beg. Grant said, Your back's no good, is it?

I'm old.

He shook his head. All right, let's get it done then. Another day of feed for the ewes, it's hardly worth it, but let's get it done.

Cotter nodded. Okay. I'll tell your brother.

Grant watched as he went, stepping delicate as if to favor his back. He thought about the ice, as much as could be got in a day, shrinking under sawdust behind the barn. Maybe they could get their differences worked out before they put in too much effort. Maybe before they'd finished the drive to Church Lake. He would see. It depended what Max said and how he said it. He would see.

•

They set out in the truck next morning, the ax and saw and tongs clattering in the bed behind them, the day cold, the sky crowded with clouds. Church Lake used to have a church overlooking it, some missionary's folly, that blew down one year and floated off in pieces. You could still find clapboards and planks in the mud when the water was low. People usually got their ice in midwinter, soon as it was thick enough, and in April they fished, lining up on the bank where the spring was and where the browns spawned. For about two weeks you could pull a giant fish out of that water practically with your bare hands.

Max drove. Neither spoke. It wasn't the same silence that was customary between them—a silence of preference—but a prideful silence, a silence of will. The landscape rolled past stunned by cold, the road pocked and rutted, no snow except smooth plats on the low grassed humps. They turned off at a mud track frozen into peaks and troughs and rumbled over it.

There was a beach here where the mud was cut with sand someone had dumped once. Tire tracks led all along it, stopping at the water's edge. Max turned around where the ice looked thickest and backed up. They got out and walked onto the surface, testing with their weight. It became necessary to speak.

Good enough.

Looks it.

Grant let himself grin. You got something you want to say to me?

Max looked up. Sounds like you want something said.

Nope.

Okay then, Max said, and he climbed back into the truck and backed it out onto the surface. Grant listened. The ice was silent. He went to the truck and pulled the ax out of the bed, Max the crowbar, and they walked out in opposite directions. Grant had brought the welding glasses with him to keep the ice from his eyes. He put them on and slung the ax up over his head, then drove it into the ice, gouging out chips that skittered across the bare surface.

It was better without snow. It'd be easy to slide the big chunks to the truck and they could lift them on without much effort.

The ax broke through quickly. He returned to the truck. Twenty yards off Max stood barefaced, gouging a line of holes with repeated drops of the crowbar. He took his time and seemed to enjoy being alone. Grant brought the saw and tongs to his cut and knelt before it. The blade fit snugly. He worked counterclockwise, making as tight a circle as the saw would allow. The cold came right up through the thick glove and he had to sit up every few minutes to rub and clap his hands together. After awhile he had cut a block the weight of a man which dropped into the water and bobbed. Grant sunk the ax into the ice beside it for a foothold. Then he wedged the tongs into the crack and pulled the block onto the surface. The rough underside froze to it. He threw his full weight against the block and broke it free, and it skated toward the truck. He followed along behind, pushing it with his boot until it lay behind the truckbed. Max was already there, smoking a cigarette. Grant went back for the ax and tongs, then they lifted the block onto the truck and shoved it up against the cab wall. Max took the ax and tongs and Grant took the crowbar and they returned to their stations and resumed work.

By midafternoon the truck was nearly full. Grant knew they could go further. The ice would freeze up against itself in the bed and could bear the ride back heaped higher. But he was sick of the work, and it was only for Kittredge and Cotter. It was enough.

He had the tools and was sawing out his last piece, closer to the truck. Max was also nearby throwing the crowbar harder, letting out grunts with every throw. When Grant was nearly finished Max came over and took the tongs back to where he was working. Grant watched. Max had managed to gouge out a small piece with the crowbar alone, and he was hauling it from the hole.

Grant turned back to his sawing. Though his arm and shoulder ached the sawing seemed easier now, and when the block detached and he pried up the edge with the saw, he understood why: half the circle had been cut from thinner ice. Someone had cut here before and the water had refrozen flat over the cuts, but neither as deeply nor as sturdily. He stood. Now he could see the line where the cutting had stopped, a barely perceptible division of dark and light that snaked across the water, running nearer the beach and passing under the truck.

Max lifted his block and humped it to the truckbed. The bed was over the thinner side, where the ice was dark. But it was thick enough, wasn't it, or they wouldn't have parked there in the first place.

Max! he called out.

Max was nearly to the truck. He leaned forward with his block and hoisted it up over the tailgate and dropped it—dropped it hard on the ice pile.

Then he slipped. His feet lost their hold and as his legs slid under the fender he grabbed the tailgate with both gloved hands and the ice split.

First the tires went through, and Max was pinned beneath the bed and its burden of ice. There was no sound on the lake but his groan and the slap of his palms against the tailgate.

That sound: Grant was entranced by it, by Max's labor. By his helplessness. He watched his brother struggle and the saw dropped from his fingers and clanked on the surface. He stood still. Max turned his head, the face flushed and the eyes black with despair.

Then the ice cracked again and the falling truck pushed him down, through the breaking ice and out of sight under the water. The chassis rang out against the surface, the truck tipped farther back and the weight of its load slammed the tailgate open, snapping the latches. The cut ice tumbled into the hole after Max and the truckbed after the ice. A couple of pieces broke free and bobbed up around the edges of the hole and stuck there. Now the surface was solid again, except for the empty tipped-back pickup jutting out of the lake like a gravestone.

A second passed. Grant perceived that he was alone on the ice. Then he ran for the truck.

He crouched on the surface pulling at the cut blocks fused together in the hole. They wouldn't move. He crawled around to peer under the bed, in the lean-to the tipped truck made, and could see an irregular strip of open water no more than six inches wide running along the edge of the thicker ice. Once under the truck he plunged his arm down in the bitter water, feeling back and forth for something he could lay a hand on. But nothing was there. He kept his arm in the water until the cold was too painful, then he got out from under the truck and ran to get the tongs. They were frozen to the surface but at last gave, and Grant stumbled and came down hard on his elbow. He ran back slipping and falling, and he got up and gripped the fused blocks with the tongs but none would budge. He flung off the welding glasses and brought his face down to the surface trying to see through the ice.

Max!

He stood on the floe of cut blocks, pounded it with his boots. He climbed into the truckbed and jumped and kicked in the freezing water that had welled there, and the water ran into his boots and flowed around his feet. The ghost toes cried out. He grew dizzy.

Max!

All along the edge of the lake was no one, not a cabin or horse or truck or tree. He stumbled to the front of the pickup where the fender was hanging four feet above the surface, and he pushed down on it using all his weight and strength. He threw himself onto the hood and felt his heart pressing at its cage.

He jumped down and grabbed the ax and chopped wildly all around the frozen hole. Chips flew and clattered against the truck and slid whispering over the smooth ice. Again he called out his brother's name.

Only then did he run to the beach, to the road, shouting for help to the empty dead land. His waterlogged boots thudded against the frozen gumbo and the pits and troughs twisted his ankles. His elbow throbbed. The sky lit up. It was nearly half an hour before the first driver came upon him, nearly running him down in the glare.

12

It took six men two days to find him: Grant, Cotter, Mott and his boy Jess and a couple of icemen from Ashton. They managed to cut free the jam the blocks had made and somebody pulled out the truck with a winch. But nothing surfaced in the hole that was opened. They'd been cutting near the spring when Max was pushed under; the lake current had likely carried him toward the creek on the opposite side. So the men cut in the direction of the flow, careful not to further weaken the ice. In the daytime hours people from the towns came out and watched them. Pictures were taken for the paper. A horse-faced kid in a big suit came stumping out to get an interview. He came up to Grant and asked him how he felt.

Go talk to the police, Grant told him.

Among the first day's watchers was Sophia. She stood for hours on the beach wrapped in blankets. When he had called home from the sheriff's in Ashton it was Kittredge he gave the news to. He still hadn't spoken to Sophia, not on the telephone nor when Mott showed up with her on the beach. She stood there all day and at nightfall was brought home to sleep. The men worked through the night in the headlights of an idling truck and continued past sunrise.

The police brought them food, which they ate standing.

It was Jess Mott who found him. He had cut a hole and was plunging into it with a hooked pole the icemen had rigged, a broomstick with a clothes hanger wired to the end. The hook caught and Jess shouted. When they came to him there was joy in his face, of being the one. He was nineteen. He reeled in the pole and there was Max's collar snagged on it, and now came his shoulder and his face, the nose pressed flat and frozen in place and the cheeks and forehead scraped and gouged from the irregular belly of the ice.

Grant laughed aloud, recognizing the dead man's face. He took a single step back and crumpled to the surface: it was him all right, fat and colorless as Grant had first found him. The other men pulled the body up and laid it out on its back, and Grant felt a warming as if from memory, thawing him from the heart out to his extremities, and he crouched on the ground before the body and touched its face with his bare burning fingers.

You gonna say something? he said.

He covered the crystalline eyes with his palms and lowered the lids. When he took his hand away its image was left behind, superimposed over the face like a silken glove. Then he was struck in the shoulders and thrown backwards onto the ice and his head cracked against it.

It was Sophia. She knelt at the edge of the hole and grabbed at the body and tried to pull it to her own. But the wet clothes had stuck fast.

The men stared at Sophia and at Grant lying prostrate beside her. Sophia cried out senselessly, tearing at the body with her fingers and thumping its chest. Then she flung herself at Grant, covering his face first with blows and then tears. She pressed herself to him, and the scent of her hair and her hot neck at last tore open the skin that had kept him from grief. He recognized Max's body and ruined face now and wailed for her loss, for his brother gone, for her love.

When later they took up the body, hair remained where his head had lain, frozen to the surface like glacier's tracks on an old stone.

•

Before he would sleep he dug the grave. In the first hours it seemed that the earth had sprouted rocks, like tumors, to thwart him, but then they stopped seeming unfair and he prised them out of the ground the way a sinner would drag the beads across his fingers. He refused help. If the task could occupy him for the rest of his life he believed he would let it: a labor clear and true as a wound. It took all of daylight and much of the night, and afterward he lay in bed until dawn, unable to sleep from the complaint of his muscles and toes and cracked elbow.

But she was asleep, exhausted by anguish. He listened to her breathe.

A few people from town spoke over the casket, later he wouldn't remember who. Rocks and all, the dirt was shoveled into the grave, erasing Grant's work. Then the graveyard, full but for one, was emptied of the living.

Days passed in which he slept when tired, ate when hungry. The sun rose and set. From time to time Grant would look up from where he walked or sat and find himself in a different place from the one he remembered, or in darkness when he thought it was daytime, or alone when he thought other people were around. The only thing that told him time was passing was an inner increase, a stretching and thinning of his skin, a sense that whatever was in him could not be contained. Simple remorse was growing into anger, unease into fear.

He slept and dreamed. It was noon, the sun hot and high, the snow rising into the air as steam, the distant hills shuddering. He was afoot on the flats, his ears attuned to the rustle and strain of the heat-mad grasses. Far away was the figure of a man beside a horse. The man pulled himself onto the horse, first fumbling and falling and at last rolling astride. His body spread across the horse's back, his legs dangling like panniers at its flanks. The horse began to move, stumbling then steadying under the rider's weight.

Grant understood that he was powerless to call back or pursue the rider, yet he struggled to open his throat and lift his feet. Still there was relief in his paralysis. The possibility of action and response fell away and he stood rooted in a world stripped of its moral component, as he imagined a man would stand on a field of battle, ruled only by fear and command.

Then he woke free and tore his bedclothes away in a moonlit night, his hands groping for the bureau drawer where the flensing knife was hid.

He paused before her door, then leaned in. His vision, tinged by blood, held her in a haze of ebbing life. He could see the vein jump in her neck. If he was to climb in bed beside her she might take him in her arms.

Instead he went down the stairs and across the yard to the back gate. There was time enough to walk. Cotter had taken the ewes to range and Grant knew right where he would go: the gentle nearby hills where the grass was thick and the stock lambs could find their footing. The ground released the day's heat and it rose all around him.

The moon was at his back. Soon it was overhead, the noon of night. He wasn't tired. The kinks had worked themselves out in sleep. When he was close the dog ran out to meet him and fell in stride in a companionable way, yet kept a distance, wary of the moonlit knife.

Grant found them bedded down in the low place between hills. He climbed up on a boulder shaded by a spruce tree where he could watch the flock. Cotter was sleeping outdoors on a tarp. The knife was warm in Grant's hand.

The dog whined and Grant put out a hand to quiet him. Below, Cotter turned over.

Dog, came Cotter's voice, roughened by sleep. The dog pricked up its ears.

Go, Grant whispered.

The dog took off running down the hill and around the bedded flock. Sheep on the edges woke and stood and settled themselves in his wake. The dog went to Cotter then circled the camp. Cotter spoke to the dog and the dog looked up to where Grant was sitting. But the tree kept Grant from sight.

Hey! Cotter said.

Grant thought, Lie down. The dog obeyed.

Lie down, he thought, looking at Cotter. But instead Cotter stood up and lit a cigarette and smoked it leaning against the wagon. Then he lay down again. A long time later he seemed to be asleep.

Grant crept down the hill and into the flock until he was surrounded on all sides by sheep. They were stirring, his presence moving through them, and they began to creep away. The dog stood up. Grant showed him his palm, white and empty. The dog lay down.

He reached out and took a handful of wool between his fingers. He straddled the ewe's back and worked the knife down to the flesh at its throat. The animal was calm. He drew breath and plunged in with the knifepoint, then pulled the blade hard through the windpipe and across the large vein. The ewe jerked, air whistled in its throat and his hand was washed with blood. He clamped his knees tight around the ewe and held its head up by the wool. Blood splashed on the ground. The dog heard and smelled it and stood barking. The sheep moved away from him, pressing into one another.

Grant let the ewe drop and lunged at another, catching it by the hock. He got on top of it and jabbed at its throat but the stroke was hasty and failed to penetrate the wool. The ewe screamed out and the others began to bolt and bleat.

A rifle discharged. The dog continued to bark. He stabbed again and the blade sunk.

What in the hell are you doing? Cotter shouted, and Grant swelled with panic and rage, the cowardly ewes crushing away from him, and he ran after them stabbing blindly.

Grant! Grant!

The knife found backs and bellies and rasped against bones. He stumbled, his throat suddenly aching. Dawn was about to break. Blood covered his arms and his knees and the air tasted of it. He sneezed again and again and couldn't stop. Cotter came down on top of him and his ribs cracked against a rock half buried in the ground.

Pain bloomed and spread through him. The dog, invigorated by blood, clamped its old jaws around his ankle. Grant felt sorry for betraying him, a good dog.

Cotter was heavy and his voice was in Grant's ear. Easy, he was saying. Grant could feel the knife lying flat on the ground beneath him. He struggled to reach it but his arms were pinned.

His ribs were killing him. It was hard to breathe. He could hear the flock racing away in all directions.

He'd wanted them all.

•

When he came back, she was gone.

13

Here was an afternoon so clear you could almost see the future. Aspens on the creek a mile away snagged the wind and their leaves turned on and off like electric lights. Hawks lifted and circled and dove. Cars leaving the highway raised dust all across the flats; from his stoop Grant saw the clouds rise and disperse. If he could lose himself, forget the time and place he was in, he might believe they were camp-fires from homesteaders' roofless squats, or even Indian fires. But they were cars. It was a car he was waiting for.

It was too hot for him here. He went in the screen door and busied himself around the place. The floor was swept. Still he did it again, to be sure. He'd put cookies on the table but now he put them away: she might be watching her weight. He got out glasses for cold tea and then put them away, too. Best to wait and see. She might not even want to sit down. He went to the front room and lowered himself into his chair and dozed, his half-dreams punctuated by insect and bird songs. The sound of a car slowing on the highway woke him. He went to the door and watched through the screen.

It was a big black car made for rich men, not good out here for much at all. The windows were shut tight against the heat. He could see the woman's head, the hair shorn close, framed in the wide windshield. She parked it in the weeds and got out.

She wasn't like he pictured: so young, practically a girl. Stout and pretty but for the hair, strong masculine arms. She'd put on a smile as if she knew he was watching, though he was invisible in the shadows. Her steps were wide and fast as if to compensate for the shortness of her legs. For all that, she seemed all right. He opened the screen door before she had a chance to knock.

Mr. Person?

Come on in, he said.

She carried a leather satchel and looked frankly around his house. Grew up in New York, she'd told him on the phone. A city girl. She'd had an uncle who used to play tenor sax when he was young, and the uncle had pen and ink drawings hanging in his apartment, drawings of himself and others playing in jazz clubs, back in the days after the war. He'd told her the artist's name and where he had come from, and when the uncle died and the drawings were left to her, she remembered that Max Person had come from here. An unlikely place. And now she lived nearby, she worked at a museum in the state capital, and she thought she'd try to track Max Person down. Just find out what had become of him.

Now they stood inside the door, blinking as their eyes adjusted to the dim. She let out breath, straightened herself, then looked up at him, expectant.

Well, he said. It's a long drive for you.

All in a day's work.

They sat in the kitchen. He offered her the iced tea and she accepted. She refused an offer of sugar. For a little while she sat quiet, still smiling, as if waiting for him to speak. He cleared his throat. She said, You're all alone out here?

Coming on fifteen years.

Bet it gets a little scary in the winter.

He said, I get by fine. She shifted in her chair and took a sip of the drink. Her eyes went to the window.

Were you married, Mr. Person?

Was. She's dead now.

I'm sorry. She reached out suddenly for her drink and nearly knocked it over. She sipped, then gulped it.

Wasn't your fault, he said, letting her see that he was smiling. Maybe, he said, you want to go out and have a look.

She seemed relieved. Yes, let's do that, she said.

They stood up together. He led her out the back door, around the little pasture where he kept his sheep and goats, and past the chicken coop. They used to have a couple of horses, but it hurt him to ride now and they weren't worth the trouble besides, not to him. Somehow she'd got ahead and he trailed close behind, smelling the town cleanness of her.

The padlock on the barn door was rusted but from time to time he sprayed a solvent in there to keep it smooth. He fished the key out of his pocket. The lock opened easily. For a moment he paused, his hand on the hasp. Then he rolled the door open and switched on the lights.

A while ago he'd sold an old tractor so he could fix things up right. He'd had a solid cement floor poured and was always pleased to note there were still no cracks. The canvases were stood up in bins he'd made out of scrap lumber, the drawings sorted and laid flat in oak drawers. He'd made the drawers too. When he noticed that bugs and mice were getting in, he decided to go down to the state university to see how you were supposed to take care of art. They gave him a few pointers and he came back and did the work.

There were about a thousand paintings and drawings all told. He couldn't believe it when he found them. All those late nights Max must have been in a kind of fever. He had painted and drawn on anything that was lying around—canvas tarps, an old tee shirt, grocery bags, shirt cardboards. These days people'd call it a compulsion. Then again, you don't get good at something by doing it half-cocked. Grant didn't know if Max was any good; that is, if other people would think he was good. Some of the paintings had begun to rot. The man he talked to at State thought he was some kind of crackpot but told him there'd have to be machines controlling the temperature and humidity. Of course there was no money for that.

The girl opened up the drawers first, coming upon the nudes. The subject was Sophia. He'd looked at them enough times to know from across the room exactly which she was looking at. For years he had just picked them up without thinking until his hands began to darken the edges. Then he bought white gloves, which he washed in bleach.

Some of the pictures were too intimate to show the girl, and these he had taken out.

She said, This model.

Yes?

Did you know her? She knew your brother?

She lived out here, he said. Not here, out near Eleven. With us, when we had the ranch. She was from New York too. When Max died she moved away.

The girl nodded, then turned back to the drawings. Soon she had moved on through the landscapes and the few jazz pictures Max had brought from New York, every few minutes sliding one off the pile and holding it up and giving it a long thoughtful look.

Where'd you say he studied? she said.

I don't know that he studied at any school. He knew some painters but I couldn't tell you which ones.

This model. Do you know her name?

He paused. No harm in telling her. But he only said, Used to.

I wonder if she's still alive.

I don't know, he said. I don't know what became of her.

In due time she turned to the paintings. Again there were portraits, mostly of Sophia, some of Max himself reflected in a cracked mirror, his face halved and skewed or staring blankly out of the frame. The painted landscapes varied. A few were realistic. Most were blurred by some intuition, the colors wrong but according to some plan Grant didn't quite grasp. Then there were interiors, mostly the barn criss-crossed by slatted light, and then the light itself without the barn around it, a lattice of color with edges undefined, the occasional band of color leaving the composition and reaching to the edge of the picture. The last ones were the largest, five or six feet to a side, the paint thick and sloppy. They were painted on cloth nailed to boards from the burnt-down quarters or sometimes done directly on the boards themselves. The lines had a fragmentary quality, as if they'd been chipped off of something with a hatchet. At first Grant never gave these paintings much thought, but they had managed to get under his skin. He regarded them as hostile and grew to fear and despise them. Even today he didn't care for them. They seemed to reject the world that had created them. They were too much like Max.

The girl lingered on these the longest, taking each one out and leaning it against the wall, standing back, mumbling to herself. Time passed, maybe half an hour.

It was what he'd done himself when he put the ranch on the market, he looked at and touched each one, trying to figure out what Max had been thinking. He was glad that he discovered the pictures later, when he was getting ready to leave the valley, and not months before that, just after Max drowned. He might have burned the lot of them then.

Before he left, the mail had brought him an apology. He'd never noticed Sophia's handwriting but looking at it he knew it was hers. The return address was written neatly on the upper left corner of the envelope. She was in Chicago, living with her brother and his wife. She had decided to enroll in a college. He began writing to her and eventually he begged her to come back to him. Her response was a long time in coming. I'm sorry, she wrote.

The following year he came upon a woman whose truck had broken down at the side of the road. Her name was Helen, she was a horse trainer. He gave her a ride into town. Six months later they got married. They lived in Ashton and had three children. One was dead of a cancer. The others lived far off, one in Seattle and the other in Eugene. His son had got married and his wife was expecting a daughter, which would make Grant a grandfather at seventy-seven.

The girl had turned and was staring at him, a hungry gaze that reminded him of Sophia, when she looked at him and seemed to see Max there. He'd hated to be looked at like that, hated when Sophia did it, but now he felt a strange, prideful power. He felt his brother coming to life inside him.

How old was he when he made these? she said.

Twenty-three.

Do you have slides?

Slides?

Of these paintings. I want to show them to the curators. I think I'd like to mount an exhibition but other people need to see the paintings.

No, no slides. Take some back if you want.

This seemed to startle her. She looked at the paintings and back at Grant. Yes, all right, she said. I can take some of the small ones. And some drawings. A few of those.

Whatever you want.

I think they're very good, she said. All of them. I think we can mount a very nice show. Not a large one, mind you, we don't have much space.

She turned again to the paintings, arrayed against the back wall in a crooked row. She said, He evolved so quickly. His line, the materials he was using. Almost as if he knew he didn't have much time.

She looked at Grant, her head cocked, inquiring.

That may be so, Grant said.

◆

Fifteen years ago she had been sitting in the kitchen, wearing jeans despite the heat and a loose cotton shirt. Her hat lay on the table next to her glass of water and pills. He sat across from her covered in sweat from haying. It was a day much like this one, hot and clear. He planned to go into town and hoped she would come and have lunch. He'd left the pills and water out for her, she was sometimes forgetful of them. She looked sick, her skin splotched and sallow, but she often looked that way. She was always pale, heat brought the blood to her face. Her face was much like it had been when they met: full and round, the ears and nose small, the eyes set far apart. The impression was one of kindness, and of fearlessness, and she was both kind and fearless. But it had been awhile since her doctor had let her work full-time. She still went daily out to the horse farm to put in a few hours. She loved the horses and missed them when she was at home.

Going back to the garden? he said.

If I feel any better.

I've got errands. You ought to ride along.

Maybe, she said.

He should have looked more closely. He would recall better today what her mouth had been like, her eyes. She moved her trembling fingers through her hair, still blond but now brittle. It made a faint sound, like falling leaves.

Your pills, he said.

She sighed, stood up with her palms flat on the table. I don't know what it is with me. I'd better take a rest. She headed for the stairs.

Helen—

I'll take them later, when I can keep them down.

Would it have made a difference? Now he doubted it, but for years afterward he blamed himself for failing to press the point. At the time he hadn't wanted to make her angry. She was not much over fifty and it was hard to believe in the danger.

He heard her get settled upstairs. After awhile he went to town alone. He ate his lunch then went back home and put on the radio. Though her hat lay on the table, though the pills and water had not been touched, he thought she must have gone out.

Where to? A neighbor's? What for? And she would have worn the hat, it was hot out. He didn't think about that, though. Not until later.

A good twenty minutes passed. He switched off the radio and listened to the house. He went to the sink and looked out over the backyard, the rose hedge she had cultivated, the animals crowded into the shade of their shelter, the trail of a passing plane, needle-sharp at one end and at the other barely distinguishable from sky. His chest tightened and he hung his head and saw the breakfast dishes lying in the sink.

Helen, he whispered. Then he turned to the stairs and began the long walk to where she lay.

◆

Afterward his daughter bought him an air conditioner, as if it was the heat that had killed her. A man delivered it and installed it in the bedroom, then turned it on and went around the house shutting all the windows and doors. Grant watched the man drive off in his van, and when he was out of sight turned off the air conditioner and opened up the house again. The air conditioner was still in the bedroom window, where it shut out the light and air. He slept downstairs on the sofa now.

The girl sat where Helen had sat, her notepad where Helen's pills had lain. She asked him questions about Max's life and he answered the ones he knew the answers to. He didn't know what certain paintings meant or if the images in them were symbols for anything else, or what events in Max's life made him paint the way he did. He told her she could make up a theory if she wanted, it was all right with him. He had a feeling that was what she was planning to do.

The girl coughed and sipped from her glass, but the glass was empty, and she put it down and coughed again.

It's a shame he died so young.

Grant couldn't reply to that. He had a thought he often had, which was that he himself wouldn't have had much of a life at all, had Max lived. He might have longed for her forever. But of course he wouldn't have. He would have had some kind of life, somewhere. It was hard at his age to believe otherwise, despite all that had happened to him.

She was still looking at him, in the wake of what she said. That gaze again, seeking, apprehending. Her eyes darted side to side, taking in the parts of his face. Instead of speaking he reached across the table and took her hand. Gently, barely touching it at all. The girl seemed shocked but did not pull away. Instead her fingers closed around his. He remembered. Then he stood up and she stood up. She picked up the notebook and put it in her satchel. He saw her to the door.

Later on he climbed the steps to the upstairs hallway. He paused at the top to catch his breath. In the rooms he opened drawers and closets and looked into them, finding nothing. At last he reached the bedroom, their bedroom, his and Helen's. He opened the door and walked in. Nothing here had been disturbed. Light leaked in between the curtains over the air conditioner. Photos of their children hung above the bed, their bed. Suddenly tired he lay down on the blankets and closed his eyes. Could it be that she made this bed, fitted and tucked these very sheets? He felt he ought to remember, but he couldn't. It was too long ago.

He remembered why he was here and got up. In the closet, on the floor, were the letters, wrapped with a rubber band and buried in a cardboard box. He slipped one out of the pile at random. The return address was an apartment, she would never be there now. He opened the envelope and looked inside. Folded into the letter was a small black-and-white photograph. It was a tiny portrait of Max and Sophia, both smiling, both impossibly young. A thin beard darkened Max's face. Behind them hung a painted backdrop of a roller coaster alongside the ocean. He unfolded the note.

Grant,

I thought you might want to have this; I found it with some of my old things. It was taken at Coney Island, in New York, when M. and I first met. You can keep it, I have more. I will write you a proper letter soon.

S.

Probably she was alive, he thought. She might not yet be seventy: not old at all, these days.

Maybe he could find her, track her down. But no: she was lost to him now.

He tucked the photo and letter back into the envelope and the envelope into the bundle. He put the letters away and closed the closet door, the bedroom door. Then he went down to the kitchen. Empty glasses, his and the girl's, stood on the table; he washed them, then washed the table and scoured the inside of the sink. For a time he stood listening to the radio: pop songs and bad news. Then he lay down on the sofa to sleep. A long while later he still had not, so he got up and went outside. He could hear the animals moving and saw the backs of the sheep over the hedge.

Some time before, his electric clippers had given out, and rather than buy new ones he'd found an old pair of hand shears and learned how to use them. They were slower and less precise but he liked them better. It was possible to tell from the feel of the cut if it had landed right, from the way the fleece lay on the hand. Now he went to the barn and found the shears. He'd oiled them last season but the rust had crept in, so he scoured them clean and wiped them with a cloth. Then he went out and got the first ewe.

It was quiet in the barn, with light spilling in from the high windows and the smell of hay and rust and mouse. The ewe stood bored and still in front of his stool. He worked the blades into the wool and began to cut, keeping a good level just above the flesh. After a few cuts his hand began to ache, but the ache felt good. The fleece loosened. When he was done he lifted it off and folded it twice and set it down on a spread-out sack. The ewe shook itself.

Thanks, he said to the ewe.

Outside the sky'd begun to purple and the night bugs took flight. He brought the ewe back to its pen and led out the next. In the barn he settled himself and took up the shears. Their sound prophesied, then joined, cricket song. The work was slow. He thought, with pleasure, that it might take half the night.

Acknowledgments

I'd like to thank the following people and institutions for their assistance during the writing and editing of this novel: Lisa Bankoff, Rhian Ellis, Steve Glueckert, Brian Hall, Katy Hope, Bill Kittredge, my uncle James Lennon and parents Eugene and Pauline Lennon, Jack Macrae, Ben Metcalf, Ed Skoog, Robert Turgeon; the Oak (R.I.P.), the Art Museum of Missoula, and the Mann Library at Cornell University, particularly librarian Jim Morris-Knower. Though I read many books and articles while researching *On the Night Plain*, I'd like to single out James Ensminger's excellent *Stockman's Handbook* and *Sheep Husbandry*, and Hughie Call's ranch memoir *Golden Fleece*, which describes some of the dangers (dramatized here) that sheep and their herders are susceptible to in winter. Some, not all, of Max Person's paintings were inspired by those of Henry Meloy, a Montana artist active during the 1930s and 40s. However, Max Person's life is entirely invented. Likewise, the towns of Eleven and Ashton are imaginary, and are not intended to resemble real places. The title is taken from Terry Riley's string quartet "Cadenza on the Night Plain," which, in a recording by the Kronos Quartet, provided a backdrop for my work on the book. I am grateful to the composer for this evocative music.

About the Author

J. ROBERT LENNON is the author of *The Light of Falling Stars* and *The Funnies*. He lives with his wife and sons in Ithaca, New York.

About the Type

This book has been set in Simoncini Garamond, a member of one of the most popular families of typefaces in history. Claude Garamond, a sixteenth-century printer, publisher, and type designer, used the types of Venetian printers from the previous century as his models. The Italian foundry Simoncini created their version of Garamond, designed by Francesco Simoncini and W. Bilz, between 1958 and 1961. Versatile for text and display situations, Simoncini Garamond is more delicate in line and lighter in color than other Garamond versions.

Simoncini Garamond is a registered trademark of Bauer Types, S.A.

Composed by NK Graphics
Printed and bound by RR Donnelley & Sons